NIGHTSWIMMING

A NOVEL

MELANIE ANAGNOS

HIGH FREQUENCY PRESS

Postal mail may be sent to:
High Frequency Press
PO Box 472
Brunswick, ME 04011

This book is a work of fiction. Names, characters, places and
incidents either are the product of the author's imagination or are
used fictitiously, and any resemblance to actual persons, living
or dead, businesses, companies, events or locales is entirely
coincidental. Various names and locations, in and around
Paterson, NJ have been changed for convenience.

ISBN: 978-1-962931-15-1
LCCN: 2025901676

Printed in the United States of America.

PRAISE FOR *NIGHTSWIMMING*

"*Nightswimming* is my favorite kind of crime novel—rich, character-driven crime that drops me right into the action. Melanie Anagnos beautifully conjures a 1970s Paterson, New Jersey that feels so lived in, I practically teleported. This is just the best kind of noir—a crime as complex and relevant today as it ever was, a world where one good man can still make a difference. I cannot wait to dive back into the world of Jamie Palmieri!"

—Halley Sutton, *USA Today* bestselling author of
The Hurricane Blonde

"Contemplative, pacy, and with a setting so vivid you can taste the industrial grit on your tongue. Paterson, New Jersey in the late 1970s is not a place I've ever yearned to visit; by the time I reached the propulsive climax of Anagnos's story, I never wanted to leave."

—Kat Rosenfield, author of the Edgar Award-nominated thriller,
No One Will Miss Her

"*Nightswimming*, set in late seventies Paterson, NJ, once the home of Samuel Colt's factory, the inventor of the "gun that won the West," has all the intrigue, twists, turns, and danger one would hope for in a great crime novel. Anagnos has written a compassionate, emphatic, sweet and sexy protagonist who I not only like but love. Officer Jamie Palmieri, detective in training, may have ended his boxing career after the beloved aunt who raised him dies, but he's never stopped fighting. He's willing to do whatever it takes, even disobeying direct orders and risking his career, to get justice. What starts as him wanting to prove himself and be taken seriously as a detective sets Palmieri off on an investigation and a love story that will warm and break your heart at the same time.

A page turner is an understatement. *Nightswimming* pulls you in and doesn't let you go."

—Patricia TM Dunn, author of the award-winning novel,
Her Father's Daughter

For George, Michael and Chrissie,
and for Paterson

The instruments of darkness tell us truths.
　　　　　　　　—William Shakespeare, *Macbeth*

PREFACE
Paterson, NJ

Paterson is often described as physically static; a time warp rooted by a skyline of once vital mills. Some are brick and some are sandstone and all of them are vacant. Urban revitalization and other missions to lift this once great manufacturing hub, this mighty producer of silk, have been fitful. What has always anchored the city—its beating, iconic heart—are the Great Falls of the Passaic River. The falls are wondrous. They were both muse and motivation sparking Alexander Hamilton's dream to create a national industrial center. The 77-foot plunge of raging water inspired the poetry of William Carlos Williams and the prose of Junot Díaz and served as backdrop for a memorable scene in Season One of *The Sopranos.*

In 2009, the falls were authorized as a national historic park by then President Barack Obama. Yet there is more to the city than the power and natural beauty of the waterfall, and there are other entry points for anyone wanting an introduction to Paterson. Buildings as diverse as the Argus Mill, Public School No. 2, and the Cathedral of St. John are on the National and State Historic Registries.

One building, though not a designated landmark, has exceptionally good bones and a distinctive lineage.

111 Washington Street was initially the site of Peter Colt's residence. The name Colt is all over the city of Paterson; the four-story gun mill directly below the Great Falls; a section of downtown called Colt's Hill. At the dawn of the city's golden age, with the Civil War ended and silk production on the rise, the family was known for textile money and

became the subject of gossipy news reporting. Into the 21st century, the name remains memorable for Samuel Colt and the many guns he invented. Colt revolvers were the legendary sidearms of the Texas Rangers. *The Gun That Won the West.*

In 1869, Paterson's aldermen purchased Peter Colt's home for its first City Hall. When the Great Fire of 1902 devastated the brownstone, a three-story structure replaced it. Designed in the Beaux-Arts style with arched doorways and signature green lanterns on both sides of the entrance, the stately new building at 111 Washington Street then became headquarters for the Paterson Police Department.

ONE

THE TAVERN'S REAR WINDOW WAS A PERFECT BLACK square. With a near empty parking lot as its backing, the mirrored glass gave an angled view inside RJ's Taproom, mostly reflecting a paneled wall lined with photos of the owner-sponsored softball team and the gold-plated plaques from their better seasons. The bottom corner caught a profile of Randall Low sitting on a round-top stool.

Using the freshly wiped bar as a desk, he was tallying the evening receipts, the only task he hadn't hurried since closing. He'd been brisk passing towels over beer spills and crushed pretzels, mindful that Cindy was waiting on him for her ride. She'd helped with the cleanup and the two had settled into a comfortable silence as Foreigner and a few other bands echoed from the jukebox, seemingly on repeat.

Once at the register, he'd wanted it quiet, but Cindy kept pushing quarters into the metal slot. Randall told himself not to get sharp with her and tried to shut out "Hot Blooded." Or maybe it was "Double Vision." He checked his watch, then reviewed the columns of precise numbers he'd penciled into the ledger. The music was more and more jarring to him. He was about to tell her no more when a set of high beams flashed through the window, startling Randall with a brief trail of light. The moment passed in the milliseconds of a camera shutter. Randall knew he was tired and maybe a little too edgy. The glare would've come from a car making an illegal U-turn off the side street. It wasn't unusual.

Still, with the sudden light, there'd been an instinctive reach beneath the cash register, Randall not even thinking he'd already taken his his gun from its hiding spot. Keeping his focus on the again darkened window, he patted his coat pocket, feeling the heft of the snub-nose .38. Then he re-directed his energy into wrapping up for the night. His hand went back to the secret drawer, his fingers running along the chafing wood where the right side had begun catching on the hardware.

The drawer was homemade. If someone had the time and desire and not the key, they could take it apart in less than a minute. Randall was thinking of adding a floor safe, a bit more up-to-date. He'd heard about those in newer bars around Paterson. A place to squirrel away the bigger bills and stacks of fives and tens that often piled up on weekend nights. The decades-old drawer, recessed behind a few specialty shot glasses and souvenir mugs, was solely for his gun. It was good insurance, useful to have in the late hours, especially with the stragglers at last call. Randall hadn't ever used it. He'd never even had to take it out for show. There'd never been any real trouble and so far, it'd stayed hidden until it was time for the parking lot.

Randall told Frank, the day bartender, to stay away from that general area. He said he didn't like his things touched. The random glassware screening the niche was decor he'd put on shelves once he found the right spots. Randall was still new to RJ's and figuring the place out. He and his brother had taken over nine months earlier, planning some minor renovations though keeping the tavern's name, along with Frank, who Randall trusted with the afternoon shift but not the gun.

The three years Randall had been in the service, he'd seen guys drunk or scared or stupid or angry, waving pistols around like they were toys. At bars around Pensacola during his flight training. Later on, at Cubi Point in the Philippines and in Da Nang. *Where* didn't matter. Worse thing, Randall thought, was having someone like Frank grab a gun when he had no idea how to use it, though he wondered how long he could keep the .38 and its hiding place off limits.

It was one thing keeping the drawer hidden during the day, but he couldn't avoid prying it open after closing time in front of the dancers. He often walked them to their cars with the revolver in his coat pocket, so the secret drawer wasn't much of a secret to them. Late night girls like Cindy, who'd begun to look anxious to get home, pacing and hitting her thighs in time to music Randall thought was more Foreigner. He noticed her purse, not on a chair, but pressed awkwardly into her waist.

"I still have to check a few boxes in the basement," he said.

"You won't be too long?"

"I won't be long."

Randall crossed the room and paused.

"Why don't you take a seat?"

"It's hard to sit after I've been in these shoes all night," she said.

"Okay, I shouldn't be more than a few minutes."

As he made his way downstairs, Randall considered potential designs for a floor safe. It'd be a professional upgrade. Jackhammer proof. Distracted and not really thinking of the partially opened cartons and loose bottles packed into the storeroom's ancient shelving, he reached the bottom step and realized he'd left his pad and pencil with the register receipts. Above him, Cindy worked her way back and forth across the pine floors, creating an annoying tapping as she moved to the medley of songs she'd danced to all night. Another reason to keep his review short. He took note of the obvious restocks. For some reason, they'd gone through a lot of Four Roses in the past two weeks. He'd have to remember that.

Randall was feeling the night in his own legs, going back upstairs, then walking past the finally silent jukebox as he tried to close out his mind. Cindy was seated. She'd dragged a stool to the inside of the bar where she was perched and presiding over the cash register. Not pressing any of the buttons, just letting her fingers brush each of the bluish gray circles.

"I'm gonna go to AC soon," Cindy said.

"Yeah? Atlantic City's cold in January."

"I know."

"Whaddya like there? Blackjack? Slots?"

Cindy shrugged, the tiniest movement of her small, rounded shoulders.

"Never been. I think I'll start with the slots. Not too much to really figure out."

Cindy had her jeans on with her mesh blouse resting in her lap, leaving bare her bikini top and its achingly loose knot, flirty and pink. Randall began thinking about Cindy and going into the back with her for a few minutes or so in his office with the leather couch. They'd only been once before. Cindy had a boyfriend and Randall had a wife. He tried not to do that with any of the girls. Once was an okay thing, but he didn't want to have an affair. He didn't want an affair with an eighteen-year-old. He didn't want an affair with an eighteen-year-old with a bad-tempered boyfriend. But then she'd been the one to initiate. Randall knew why. Cindy wanted a nice guy. And Randall usually was a nice guy. The Randall who treated Cindy and the other girls well, walked them to their cars after work, and threw out loud and drunk college boys from the nearby state schools, even the groups who'd been ordering top shelf, that Randall was a nice guy. The Randall who was married but went into his office with a barely eighteen-year-old Cindy, he didn't know how to tell her. That Randall wasn't a nice guy. Not the nice guy she was looking for.

The time he'd been with Cindy, it'd been the same. She'd needed a ride and stayed while he finished for the night, then she'd taken his hand and led him to the couch, positioned him carefully. He'd driven her home after, and she'd talked about how much she liked *Star Wars* for the length of the ride. How much she was looking forward to the next one coming out later in the year.

"They're gonna call it *The Empire Strikes Back*," Cindy had said. "I read that last week."

The new *Star Wars* movie she was looking forward to. The kitten she wanted to adopt and name Chewbacca. They'd had an easy conversation. She acted like he was simply her boss giving her a needed ride home, as if they hadn't spent time together in his office. She remained that way in the weeks since, not seeming to consider that anything might be different.

He could really go for another night like that. Another no-strings-attached night. But leading her into his office, or letting her lead him, that could lead into an affair.

"Almost ready," he said to her.

"Uh huh. You take your time. I'm practicing my gambling here."

"That's not what a slot machine looks like."

"Yeah," she said. "I know. I'm pretending."

Just like with the high beams, it was that sudden. A harsh, rustling sound burst into the tavern, followed by a rush of cold air. Randall was sure he'd locked both doors, sure he'd told Cindy not to touch anything. Surprised as the one leading from the bar's tiny parking lot swung wide.

"Hey," Randall yelled.

TWO

January 15, 1979

TUESDAYS WERE BEST. ADDIE'S MADE THEIR MEATLOAF that day. You couldn't trust it on the weekend and that also meant on a Monday. Never on a Monday. You'd still be getting leftovers, and not the good kind. He could hear that exact sentence in his Aunt Ro's voice, a ringing memory.

Jamie Palmieri ordered the diner's version of a Monte Cristo. It arrived warm and buttery, a thick enough sandwich to get him through a shift that began at noon and ran until eight, sometimes later. He wondered how anyone could know when Addie's made meatloaf or anything else. All he ever saw of the kitchen was an occasional flash when the swing door kicked opened. Mostly that gave him a view of big soapy dish bins and steam from the grill. But it was Monday and he'd remembered his aunt and stayed away from the blue plate special.

He left the exact amount and an extra half-dollar on the counter and slipped on his jacket.

"See you," he said to the new waitress. The tall brunette who never wore the hand-embroidered tag the other girls did. She was quiet too. Especially to be working lunches.

Betty? Joanne? Felicia? He wasn't usually so bad with names.

"Bye-bye," she said, pocketing the coin in her apron.

The diner sat on a pie-shaped corner surrounded by mostly residential streets. All the wood-framed, asbestos-shingled, one-toilet homes. The markers of so many Paterson neighborhoods that circled downtown. Jamie's Datsun 280ZX added a bright red presence. He pulled away from the curb, adjusting the visor even though he was wearing the aviators he'd been given after his graduation from the academy. His these-will-really-make-you-look-like-a-cop sunglasses that'd been a joint gift from a handful of families at a rec center block party. That June, a full sheet cake had been added to the dessert table. "Congratulations Jamie!" beaming up in thick blue script.

He'd kept the glasses immaculate over the past three years, giving him a light-filtered view of the Paterson skyline that stretched ahead. The copper dome of the Passaic County Court House, the familiar spires of St. John's. All the important city buildings. None reached higher than seven stories. Even with a few slow buses on McBride Ave., Jamie made the drive from Addie's to the center of the business district in less than five minutes.

The Police Headquarters on Washington Street was also an important building and would have blended easily in Manhattan. Jamie passed beneath the arched entry, then through the lobby and took the backstairs two at a time, checking his watch when he reached the third floor. There wasn't much beyond the landing, and he was quickly in the squad room heading towards the desk he'd been assigned, a green steel-case model. There might have been cheaper office furniture, but it was hard to envision what that would look like. Jamie had the basic stock for someone who was still working patrol and wouldn't be getting anything like a cherry wood desk, let alone his own office, anytime soon.

"Again?" a voice called out. "We get you on the cover shift again?"

Gary Carlson crossed the floor to Jamie's corner and perched on the closest windowsill.

"What are you doing, fill-ins these days?" Gary asked.

"It's getting me off night shifts," Jamie said.

"So, you got yourself some free time."

Jamie picked up his notes from the previous day but there was no point trying to scan the pages. This was heading to one of Gary's drawn-out conversations itemizing all the off-duty work he'd made his specialty. That was his go-to topic. What was easy. What paid the best. Gary's collection of contacts and opportunities went well beyond Passaic County. Traffic control in suburban church parking lots and other private events and most recently backup security at area concerts.

"It's not bad. Some fights, some kids on acid you might need to drag to the medical tent. Mostly a lot of pot that you have to pretend you don't see otherwise you'd be arresting the whole crowd."

Gary laughed to himself. He looked anxious, fidgeting with a disposable lighter the way he did when it wasn't yet time for a cigarette break.

"Rutgers Athletic Center's not huge, like maybe seven or eight thousand, but you don't want to bust the whole crowd."

Jamie nodded.

"Anyway, it's—you know. It's money. Not bad. It's a drive but if it works out, you can do the summer shows at Giants Stadium."

"Sounds all right," Jamie said.

"It's your kind of music so it's money and not a bad night for you. I'll give'm your number. The guy's name is Kenny. Head of security. Thinks he's *that guy*."

"That guy?"

"He's head of security for the main promoter. When there's a concert anywhere around here that's big, he's in charge."

Jamie scribbled his home number onto the back of card from Pietro Towing. A handful had been floating around the squad room for the past month making for scrap paper in easy reach. They both seemed to hear the boom of Gregg Bachman at the same time, suddenly pausing in a shared understanding. Gary grabbed the card and Jamie swiveled his chair away from the back wall.

"Elizabeth!" the voice echoed from the hallway. "You look fetching today!"

Jamie calculated where Elizabeth was set up at the third-floor reception area and the time it would take Bachman to compliment her starch-collared blouse. The sergeant might stay to watch a blush spread over her wide, powdered cheeks. After that, he might or might not find his way to Jamie's area for a brief appearance. Bachman mostly showed up on the third floor needing someone to locate a file or make copies if the staffing downstairs wasn't sufficient. The past week, there'd been a spate of post-holiday colds keeping too many secretaries at home. Add to that, civilian personnel taking extended lunch hours. Bachman had ventured from his office, hunting for administrative help. Jamie waited for the loud voice to fade, receding into the stairwell, but instead there were footsteps in the direction of his own desk where he hovered, reviewing a report he'd been polishing.

"Palmieri!"

Jamie looked up, into the sergeant's belt buckle, then quickly stood, feeling the inherent authority although Jamie had never been in the armed forces. He'd registered with Selective Service when he turned eighteen but missed the draft, then took criminal justice courses at William Paterson College and eventually entered the Paterson Police Academy. That was enough for him to appreciate the wide variations among his commanding officers. Chummy, formal, imposing. Jamie had easily pegged Bachman.

The sergeant placed a hand on Jamie's shoulder and in one motion began steering him away from the warren of desks and chairs and filing cabinets that cluttered the third floor.

"Let's head down to my office," he said. "There's a case that'll be good for you to get some time on."

Bachman lowered his voice to an unexpected whisper. "You heard about RJ's Taproom."

The full name of the bar only ever called RJ's. The double homicide.

THREE

THE POLICE ORDERED THE DOORS TO RJ'S PADLOCKED late Sunday morning. The evidence team had done their sweep and extracted whatever had ended up on the floor and checked the bathrooms and left roughly three and a half hours after they'd arrived with bagged up casings but no spent bullets. These had been shootings at close range.

Two bodies had been found in a pool of blood. Detective Lieutenant Joseph Miucci told reporters that Randall Low and one of his employees had been killed "with robbery the apparent motive." It was surmised that the killer pulled the door closed as he left, locking it. That part went into the morning papers along with a request for anyone with information to come forward. A phone number was listed along with the explicit promise that all communications would be kept confidential.

There was slightly more in the official reports.

Low's wife awoke on the sofa with the TV a hum of static noise and her husband not yet home. It was almost 3:00 a.m. and she waited until 4:30 and then called Catherine Rose, the tavern's manager, who lived close to RJ's. Mrs. Rose had driven over, finding Low's locked car with a light frost coating the windshield. She used the side entrance and walked gingerly into the bar, then came upon Low lying face down. Frazzled, Mrs. Rose ran into the street, speechless at first but not entirely incoherent.

She began calling for help and Josef Fonesco heard her yelling and led her into his ground floor apartment. The young man poured her orange juice while she dialed the police. Hearing her speak, Mr. Fonesco rushed to prepare a cool washcloth for her forehead, wondering if she would faint.

"Someone's on the floor of the tavern. It's Randall. I think . . . I think it's him. His name is Randall. Randall . . . Oh. I ran out. I didn't check."

It wasn't until the police showed up that they realized two bodies were on the floor. One large pool of blood.

There'd been at least twenty-five patrons in the tavern until 1:30. By Sunday afternoon, several had already been interviewed though, to a man, all denied being a witness. The community's distrust of the police was on an upswing so none of that was a surprise. Squaring off against every charity basketball game and holiday toy drive for the Kilbarchan Home was Hurricane Carter's arrest and prosecution, a process that started in 1966 and spanned over a decade, and the blowup from that had left some people angry with the police. Even without that backdrop, bar shootings in Paterson, like everywhere else, were notoriously difficult. Questioned about RJ's, no one had seen a thing.

The newspaper hadn't been given any of those details so the first article to appear was brief, although it was front-page worthy. Reporters seemed almost hesitant to name the tavern, despite it being well-known beyond its neighborhood. When the former owners sold RJ's to Randall and Craig Low and then opened the Belvidere in Clifton, *The Patch* had done a writeup on their new Italian restaurant and what they called its "cruise ship-style buffet." It included a paragraph on Lisa Moyers who'd retired her old career at RJ's and went with her bosses to the new restaurant. The author of that airy piece clearly had recognized her. "Popular go-go dancer now the prettiest hostess in town."

The initial reporting of the murders was quite different. The tone was somber. RJ's Taproom was named just once and subsequently referred to simply as a local tavern. Perhaps they were shielding Randall from the taint of a certain kind of bar and propping him up as a generic local businessman.

Cindy wasn't named at all. Barely identified. " . . . one of his waitresses had been killed."

FOUR

BACHMAN'S OFFICE HAD THE RIGHT KIND OF DESK, grand and made of expensive wood. Mahogany or cherry. A brass railing wrapped around its front and side. The sergeant acknowledged it with his usual jovial complaint.

"I'm a paper pusher now. Means I get papers from you guys and then I send that somewhere else, or I get papers from somewhere else and send it to you guys."

Jamie sat attentively, as he had the past three years, whenever he was called down to the office. Starting with field training, then his first post covering the Eastside section. Whenever something in his caseload demanded a meeting. Bachman, his loud, abrasive voice, grating over information like sandpaper.

"We haven't reassigned you yet. You're still on . . ."

"Rotating patrol," Jamie said, filling in the answer.

"Right, we talked about having you placed in one of the wards at the end of last year."

"That came up around review time."

Jamie actually liked his patrol that took him through the city. He never knew what part of Paterson he'd be off to until reporting for work. Getting his papers from Elizabeth after clocking in was a roulette wheel of possibility.

"It's not too bad," Jamie said. "I like routing the different areas."

"Yeah, you do get a bit of everything."

That was true. He got stolen cars and suspicious warehouse fires and early evening stakeouts for low level drug sales and increasing spillover whenever detectives needed help with witnesses on their bigger cases. Some of the senior officers he was friendly with from the church's annual motorcycle run threw him extra work when there was an opening he could fill. Jamie's ambitions always clashed with the reality of Bachman and his reputation. The sergeant was known to recommend promotions slowly. Yet Jamie was hopeful, sitting that day to discuss a double homicide.

"We'll go out for a few rounds of interviews but mostly I'll set you up with Gianelli. He's a good guy. You work with him yet?"

"Not Gianelli."

Gianelli was a senior detective who headed a division in Violent Crimes. Jamie couldn't get over hearing the name.

"This isn't his area, really. He does those sexual assaults. Right? That's the word they use for it now. But we're short-staffed, moving investigators around and calling a bunch of patrol in. Mostly, this is a get your feet wet thing for you. 'Cause these cases, I mean. How many times were there guys shot in a bar full of people. You go there for statements and find out a hundred people were all in the bathroom together. I mean, right? But we owe it to Randall to look into this, do it in good order."

"Yes."

"Dot those i's and cross those t's."

This wasn't just a homicide. It was high-profile, front-page news. Morning and evening editions. Even if RJ's wasn't a true cop hangout, the department way too old school for that, both officers and uniformed patrol went there, and they'd known Randall. That meant the case ought to start with promise, hopefully not fizzling into "maybes" and "could haves." As it often happened, crimes that seemed obvious could be maddeningly hard to solve. Jamie recalled all the how-it-really-works advice he'd received in field training.

"That's why we need those extra man hours," Bachman said. "You'll start off with me. Kill two birds. I like to get out and you'll sit in for a talk I lined up with one of the girls. A little refresher for you on how to lead an interview. Then you'll get yourself going on your first homicide case."

Jamie had been doing his own work for almost two years, but it all swung back and forth. Still a patrol officer, when he was thrown on someone else's case, his role was questioning the fringe witnesses. Taking statements from victims in hospital rooms that smelled of stale food, liquid bleach, and poverty. Meeting with informants in jail for unrelated crimes who wanted deals Jamie couldn't give them. Even when assigned the suspects themselves, the charges were so low level, they used their arrest as an opportunity to ask for burgers and fries. Here, Bachman was talking about bringing him on the double homicide. Treating the assignment like Jamie might be further along the mushy path to detective trainee than he'd thought. He knew he ought to dial his energy back, especially since Bachman wasn't all that clear on how much autonomy he'd be given.

"Meet me in the lobby tomorrow at nine," the sergeant said.

Their discussion ended with that command. Jamie told he'd be doing an almost double shift. Leaving at eight that night and coming back in the morning meant he'd have to cancel his plans with Steve. The Eagle's Nest was a few towns away in Hewitt, the rural area where his best friend had moved after high school. The drive was long, and the Eagle's Nest was usually the first of multiple stops. Their routine treks to larger bars and clubs with live music had them chasing after ladies' night most of the time.

Back at his desk, Jamie called Steve with the disappointing news. His friend ignored him and his time crunch.

"C'mon. I swear. Two beers. Just two."

"I got work. Practically a double shift."

Jamie kept his voice down, not that anyone within earshot would have cared if he spent his nights at a bar.

"Like, what? You can't get home by midnight and back to the station in the morning? You need that much sleep?"

Jamie had done that many times, getting home well past one or two and still managing to shower and dress for an early shift. But he wanted to be in top condition for his new assignment, going with Bachman. It wasn't clear who else in the department had been pulled onto the case and would be given their own interviews. He suspected Gary and a few others and that included the patrol units assigned the Fourth Ward. A busy Saturday night at RJ's meant a boatload of interviews.

The important ones, Catherine Rose, Randall's widow, people like that would get detectives. Jamie knew that but mulled over other ways he could get some footing. There wasn't much chance for an edge. What he could do was be as prepared as possible. *Don't ever let anyone work harder than you.* Another shard of advice handed down from Aunt Ro. The interview with Bachman meant he didn't need a night of drinking. He didn't need a situation, like waking to a girl he'd brought home and negotiating his way out of that.

Instead of the Eagle's Nest, he made the five-minute walk from his house to Rails bar, a place where they had stein lifting contests in October and very few women, ever. Jamie got there after stopping home long enough to feed and walk his wirehaired dachshund and then grab his own dinner. Bending to scratch Nugget's ear, he'd whispered his plan to be home early. At Rails, he stuck to Bud on tap. No Jack Daniel's and Coke.

"Taking it easy on a weeknight," Karl said.

The sweater-vested bartender dropped his mug on the bar.

"Pretty much," Jamie answered.

He'd gone there because he lived alone and liked to get out a few times a week, but also to try for that immersive barroom feel, although the tavern was a far cry from RJ's. Jamie hadn't been there often, but he'd been to the Frontier Room, McKeever's, and El Club Mira; the places in and around Paterson that were advertised as "men's lounges."

What Rails offered Jamie was some light conversation if he felt like it, a well-poured draft, and a portable Emerson wedged high on a shelf with the Rangers game on. The glow of that television was all there was to gaze at. Still, the low lighting, the brown cushioned seats, and the rectangular wood bar gave the imprint of a place like RJ's. Jamie watched the regulars break from their drinks every now and then to take in the people across from them or whoever was a few stools down. Jamie imagined what a person might notice and how he might steer an interview and the information he might glean.

His mind was racing ahead, beyond his start in the morning with Bachman. He saw himself in the neighborhood with a partial list of the known witnesses. He knew he'd get the ones who'd left early, his basic responsibility checking off names. What he hoped for was one or more who'd stayed until closing time and hadn't been available in the first round of questioning and potentially the last person to see or speak to Randall.

He considered Rails' Monday night crowd as the conversation with Bachman played in his mind, tamping down some of the excitement and the possibility that he might come up with something useful. Gathering witness statements from a dozen or so people who hadn't seen a thing remained the most probable result.

Behind the counter, Karl had twisted his upper body, trying to catch bits of the hockey game in between serving boilermakers.

"Did you follow that?" Karl asked, pointing to a twelve-inch screen so grainy, it was impossible to track the puck. "What's with Esposito tonight? North Stars are kicking ass."

Before Jamie could answer, the end of the bar began to get loud with a burst of quarreling from the group Jamie saw every time he'd been at Rails. A huddle of wool blend jackets and cropped graying hair, their voices rose with complaints about what it cost to fly to Miami and book a hotel, even if you could get Super Bowl tickets. The Cowboys would be taking on the Steelers in less than a week and anticipation was growing.

"A bunch of guys are going to see Huther."

"Just because he's from Haledon. It's a waste of money!"

"He played for Manchester Regional."

"So, he played for Manchester Regional. I like that Tony Dorsett. I'd like to see his rushing game."

"Cowboys were down the whole first half in the playoffs. That's not no championship playing!"

"Yeah, well they won."

"They almost lost!"

"Yeah, well they came back."

That response was met with a hand pounding on the wooden counter, shaking the Ballentine sign above the ice cooler and Jamie's beer. The heated discussion over football a stark reminder Rails didn't have the energy he was looking for. The dark electricity of a crime scene and the force field that grew around it was hard to replicate.

"Ready for another?" Karl asked.

Jamie waved the offer away. He continued peeling the thick paper coaster and finishing what he meant to be his last beer. As he eased himself from the barstool, Jamie's foot dropped, a heavy deadweight.

His leg buckled with a burning sensation in his toes. Karl caught his eye and slid another Bud across the counter. Jamie stayed to watch the Rangers go into overtime. A few more drafts than he'd intended while his foot recovered. A late walk home in the quiet cold of mid-January.

FIVE

JAMIE GOT TO THE STATION THE NEXT MORNING WITH his stomach a bit sour. At his desk by 8:30, he was sorry he hadn't had much more than black coffee before leaving his house. What he needed was dry toast and he called in a favor. Wayne was less than six months into training and didn't seem to mind running here and there when it was for Jamie. Mostly because he'd taken the time to show Wayne the rounds, but also because he drove a 280ZX that was red. Jamie had done well with his own training and been president of his class at the academy, there was also that.

"You going to Parisi's?" Jamie asked in a flat tone, meaning it wasn't a question. Wayne's head popped up, an awakened mass of dirty blond hair. "I need an order of whole wheat, no butter."

Wayne had been rooting through a rolling cart of labelled baggies sent up from the evidence room. Hearing Jamie, he stood and patted his back pocket, checking for his wallet.

Half an hour later, after his breakfast of toast and some sorting through reports, Jamie let Elizabeth know he'd be gone until his shift officially started at noon, then took the stairs to meet Bachman in the lobby. He planted himself near the flag of New Jersey, the usual waiting spot. It was only a minute or two before the older man appeared, pushing his arms into a thick wool overcoat as he walked briskly, passing Jamie and going straight through the station's double doors. Jamie easily caught up to him on the street and together they threaded their way around a crowd lined up for the Red and Tan.

"I like to get out of here," Bachman said. "That's my little secret."

The sergeant wasn't noticeably straining as he spoke. Jamie figured him to be somewhere in his forties. Still, he adjusted his pace so he wouldn't get ahead of Bachman, slowing himself to what felt like a crawl as they walked shoulder to shoulder.

When Jamie first started with Vince Becker as his field advisor, he'd been warned. "If you ever go anywhere with Bachman, you gotta follow his lead."

Sitting in the cruiser with Becker, this particular tip had been memorable. Up there with the other scraps and pointers Becker fed him. Most of that was the usual things like refreshers on which buttons engage the lights and the sirens and when to use them. Keeping an organizer in the car for file folders, forms, and a clipboard. What his field advisor called "them record-keeping supplies." Becker included a reminder to check and toss "all your dried out pens," along with the helpful material on Bachman.

"He took that spill a few years ago with his Electra Glide. Chewed up his leg. Most days he's okay. But if you're with him where you're gonna be walking awhile you'll see it. He gets tired and eventually he kicks up his right foot with every step."

"Got it." Jamie took in the information. Don't get the sergeant pissed off at him.

"You don't want to show him up," Vince said. "The new recruit. The guy just out of the academy where you ran four-minute sprints."

Remembering his advice, Jamie fell behind Bachman once they got to the garage, making sure the sergeant was first to reach the Dodge Royal Monaco. Sitting in a low corner, its back tire in a pool of melting ice. An unmarked car that had unmarked car written all over it. Anyway, they were both in uniform. They weren't surprising anyone.

Traffic moved slowly through the narrow streets, relics from an earlier century of trolleys and carts. Bachman was still going on about his desk, how he longed to be back on patrol.

"That's the way it always is. You're sitting around at night, maybe following a couple of dipshits, or pulling over idiots with not one but *two* busted taillights and you think, I deserve a little more than this. You know?"

Bachman steered loosely around the deeper potholes, hitting most of the smaller ones, the undercarriage threatening to bottom out. Jamie hoped they'd get through the length of Main Street without losing the muffler.

"The day I decided I had enough, the day I said, that's it, I'm taking the test. I'll never forget it. It was blazing hot. We had a guy outside Jacob's Department Store. A shoplifter. Nothing big, and all of a sudden, he had me on the ground. Just like that. A puny guy but he hit me the right way. It was maybe a minute until my partner, Garrison, got him off me. One of those minutes that feels like three hours, 'cause you're doing everything to make sure he doesn't grab the gun."

"We did practice like that. Combat wrestling on Fridays."

"Yeah? Was it hot as hell and on a concrete sidewalk?"

"Well, not, you know. It was just practice."

A few turns and the former Gentile and Segreto Credit Building was up ahead. The library's Southside Branch. These were the streets where Jamie once rode his bike, navigated intersections and curbs in his first car, and more recently, covered on foot patrol. He didn't bother looking at the metal signs charting their names.

"This is your area, isn't it, paisan? The Italian section."

South Paterson was near Hillcrest where Jamie had grown up and where he still lived. The house they were heading to wasn't in his exact neighborhood and whether this was still the Italian section was up for debate.

"Carlstadt," Bachman said, seeming to anticipate a question. "That's where I'm from."

"Oh."

"Yeah, I could have been sergeant even earlier there. Probably chief of police or close to it by now if I'd wanted a small town, but that wasn't my thing. Plus, the wife and her family are from here. Well, Paterson by way of Macclesfield, England. They came here knowing silk."

"Oh."

"A Jacquard weaver, her father was. Not one of the guys hauling bolts of fabric and that other menial shit."

They passed Grisanti's Packaged Goods, then cut through Gould Ave. A ranch with pale siding the soft color of a creamsicle sat opposite a slushy clearing Jamie knew fairly well, with its baseball field and Little League bleachers. Bachman adjusted the rearview mirror and brushed back his hair before they exited the car.

Lorraine Vasile was waiting with the front door partly open. Bachman handled basic introductions and offered his condolences on the loss of Mr. Low and her "fellow entertainer." They gathered in her living room where Lorraine gave her history at RJ's, a tissue box resting in the fold of her lap. She had worked Saturday night. She had her own car. She lived in the opposite direction of Cindy and had only given her a ride home once.

"It was a lot. After a full night. We were both tired, and then when I dropped her off, I had to turn around and it was almost twenty minutes to get to my house. It was a lot."

"How did Cindy usually get home? Did she have a regular ride?"

Lorraine paused.

"I can't say I really paid attention. You know. I just liked to throw on my jeans and get out of there. I wasn't really looking around to see who did what and with who. You know? I can't say that I cared to know."

"Meaning what?"

"Meaning if Cindy went home with this one or that one, I didn't make it my business."

"Right."

It was Bachman who did all the talking and questioning while Jamie took notes. Using a medium-sized spiral with "RJ's Taproom Book One" neatly scripted on the red-brown cover, he wrote as fast and as clearly as he could. There wasn't much time to steal away from the notepad, but Jamie was curious. He looked up, surprised to catch Lorraine facing him. Not wanting to stare, he turned to the picture window behind her. A rusted swing set with the seats dangling and uneven. The three-step sliding pond almost collapsed under a pile of snow. Plastic bins barely covered.

Bachman, thickish and blurred in Jamie's sightline, leaned forward and took Lorraine's long, tapered fingers into his. A fluid movement and timed, it seemed, to the more sensitive questioning.

"Tell me how long you knew Cindy."

Lorraine sniffed, but didn't pull back her hand to grab a tissue. "Not that long," she said. "She started a few months ago. Fake ID. How old was she really?"

"And Randall Low? Did you know him before he took over?"

"No."

With that, Lorraine turned her head away from both of them and retrieved her hand from Bachman.

"Can you tell us if there was anything unusual that night? Did either Mr. Low or Cindy seem nervous? Act peculiar?"

Lorraine considered her answer. She was, Jamie noticed, very thoughtful. Deliberate in her responses and in the way she had dressed. She'd selected a buttoned blouse for the interview. Beige dress slacks that were loose and heels though she was in her own home. A tasteful, blush-colored manicure. The smell of nail polish had hit Jamie when he'd first walked in. The house was as carefully arranged as she was. A stack of *Reader's Digest* fanned on the cocktail table. Everything dusted and neat.

"I've been trying to think through that whole night. If there was something I saw, something I missed."

"Take your time."

"The night ended like it always did. The place emptied out. Randall walked me to my car when I was ready."

"Were you the last ones out?"

"No, but that was typical. Like I said, I didn't dally once the night was over."

"Do you remember who was in the bar when you left?"

"There were the other girls, Sage and Cindy were still there. A few guys who'd been finishing drinks had been told to leave. They went out before us. Randall liked the customers gone before he walked us out. Because, you know, he'd always want to take his gun."

"Do you remember which ones? The names of the customers that were stragglers that night?"

Lorraine closed her eyes and straightened herself against a throw pillow. Rib cage barely moving. A deep concentration bringing her back to that early Sunday morning.

"There really weren't many. Maybe one or two. Possibly a few more. I don't know which ones."

"And Randall. Randall walked you out."

"Yes. And once we were in the parking lot, Sage yelled goodbye. She must have left less than a minute after we did. Someone picked her up. I heard the car behind us."

"So, you were already in the lot when Sage left."

"We were."

"Where did you typically park?"

"Corner space in the back. That's the area where employees were told to leave their cars."

"It's dark there?"

"It's, I mean, it's not well lit. It's dark, yes. You could say that."

"So, Randall would typically walk you and the other girls to their cars."

"Yes. He escorted us."

"But that night, it was only you. Because Sage followed you out and Cindy was still inside.'"

"Yes."

"And once you were in your car, did you see Randall walk back into the bar?"

Again, Lorraine was thoughtful, not rushing for an answer and running over whatever she could recall.

"I can't say I remember. I probably didn't look in that direction."

"Did you see anything else? Anyone else?"

"No, it was late. The bar was closed."

"How long after you got in your car did you leave?"

"What do you mean?"

"I want to know if you stayed a minute. Brushed your hair. Checked inside your purse, making sure you didn't forget anything." Bachman's voice notched up, a tight intensity, maintaining his eye contact. Lorraine's right hand securely in her lap, curling and uncurling. A gilded detail for

Jamie, who'd been cataloguing all he could in his stealth glances. "If you were there long enough to notice anyone going into the bar, after Randall."

"It was late. I was tired."

"Did you notice anyone in the parking lot, maybe a customer who was waiting for you?"

"Waiting for me?"

"Did that ever happen. A customer wanting to meet up with you?"

"Randall escorted me to my car. That was the whole point."

Lorraine's eyes seemed to change color with her response if that were possible. Jamie thought they might have gone from blue to gray as they narrowed, along with her back stiffening. Anxious for the next question, Jamie ran his thumb along the barrel of his pen while a pause lingered dangerously, Lorraine holding back on giving Bachman a full-on glare. He'd been unrelenting, bearing down on her. Maybe it was a necessary question for Bachman to ask. The possibility she was there in the pitch-black parking lot, possibly with someone else, both of them invisible to whoever ran into, then out of RJ's.

"You said he carried a gun in the parking lot."

"He did. I knew he kept it in his coat pocket."

For the entire interview, heat blasted in watery spurts from the radiators. The one behind Jamie hissed the loudest and needed to be bled. Jamie wondered who might do that. He looked cautiously at her hands again and the gold ring he hadn't expected, then back at the side table littered with family photos. A few of Lorraine with her hair lighter. The largest frame, a wood inlay, held a photo of her with her three young children smooshing their faces into her neck and against her cheeks.

"Well," Bachman said, standing and stretching and letting Jamie know they were finished. Once the three of them were at the front door, Bachman said a short goodbye while staying toe-to-toe with

Lorraine, forcing her to redden and turn away and making Jamie wonder if that was part of the sergeant's hardcore messaging, drilling in the importance of his questions.

"You get all that?" Bachman asked when they were outside on the landing. A pair of thin bayberry bushes instead of guardrails edged the stairs, their branches coated in ice.

"I wrote it all down."

Bachman took his time on the steps and over the pavement. They were both seated and their car doors slammed shut before he continued. "Shame, she didn't really know anything."

"Frustrating. She was there so late. Maybe just missed the whole thing by minutes."

"Minutes count. Proves what I've been saying. Nothing happened until everyone was gone." Bachman slapped Jamie's forearm. "Anyway, that's how you do it. I know they tell you this shit in the academy but it's different when you go in the field. In a homicide, every answer is important."

"Right."

"You make sure you take down the answers. Don't get sidetracked with what you're gonna ask next. Get your answers down. Go slow and don't let them mess with you. With what they want to tell you instead of what you're asking."

"Right," Jamie said.

"You're the cop. I know you're out three years, but this is a homicide. *Double* homicide."

Their breath was visible. Bachman hadn't even started the car.

"Helluva thing," Bachman said, a puff of white vapor shadowing his words. "Helluva thing."

It was, Jamie thought.

"You ought to go look at the crime lab. Get yourself down there.

The photos, the reports. You need to know what that stuff looks like. For real." Bachman turned to him. "You're on the case. Not the lead, but what the hell, get a look at all of it."

"I will," Jamie answered.

The key rested in the ignition as Bachman faced Lorraine's house, seeming stiff and distracted. There was so much that needed to be done, so much that Jamie needed to learn. Answering "I will" hadn't been a great show of his abilities. He worried that Bachman, looking far off in the other direction, might be having doubts about keeping him on the case.

"That'll be it for the day so you may as well go look at the real live detective stuff. That's probably the most you're gonna learn on this."

The engine finally turned over. Cold air blew from the vents and Jamie used the back of his hand, waiting to feel heat mix in. He was thinking ahead again. His mind circled on the list he'd be given of people to interview. A few knew Randall and the dancer who was killed with him. The hint of bravado in Jamie crept back, hopeful he might have a shot at finding something and proving to the sergeant he could handle himself.

"The witnesses are gonna be for shit on this," Bachman said. "I'm just telling you."

SIX

THERE WAS STATE-OF-THE-ART EQUIPMENT AT STEELE'S
Gym and Sports Club and a drive out Route 46 in rush hour traffic
in order for Jamie to reach it. In the end he went to the Y in Clifton
and lifted free weights and bench pressed and did without the rowing
machine and every Nautilus imaginable. After an hour of strength and
conditioning, he joined a small group to shadow spar and practiced
throwing combinations with a few teenagers who recognized him from
his days at Lou Costello's. He finished just as the tightening in his lower
leg started in, grabbing a clean towel and passing through the gym doors.

"You still jumping rope?"

Jamie recognized the voice, then saw the weathered face of Gene
Edmonds, a guy from the neighborhood who'd divorced and moved to
Botany Village, the section of Clifton where RJ's old owners had opened
the Belvidere. Gene wore a fitted suede sports jacket and boots with
Cuban heels and Jamie vaguely recalled the details of his marital troubles.
Another woman. Maybe several.

"Gene," he said. "How's everyone?"

They were stopped in the hallway beneath a poster for the Passaic-
Clifton swim team and its smiling dolphin mascot, which allowed for a
minute or two of conversation.

"Pretty good. Gloria remarried. I guess you heard that. She's in
South Carolina with the kids."

"I did hear that she sold the house. About a year ago?"

"Last March. Right before Easter."

Jamie bent to rub his left calf. It tended to spasm after he did squats.

"What are you lifting now?"

"Same as when I was in serious training."

"And you're a cop."

"I am. I am. Three years now."

The sounds of grunts and weights dropped too suddenly shifted their attention. Jamie hoped to be done with the conversation, but his former neighbor didn't move.

"Gotta stay with the basics," Gene said, waving a thumb at the padded floor and collection of barbells visible through the open double doors.

"I usually jump at home. I do the weights here, or you know, over at Steele's. I tend to go there when I can."

It was coming. Jamie waited for the awkward silence. The expectation for him to fill it and explain in detail why he wasn't boxing anymore. To his relief, Gene squinted as he scrutinized the wall clock, then offered a handshake.

"Great to see you here," Gene said. "I know it's not Steele's but still, not a bad workout."

"Yeah, not bad. Good to see you too."

Gene raised his hand, a wide-palm salute before turning towards the Y's main entrance. Jamie felt fortunate. Gene didn't hang around too long and hadn't followed him to the locker room, asking about the Golden Gloves career he'd given up on. If pressed, Jamie usually said it was an ACL tear. He didn't get into the fact that the injury wasn't a full tear and that it'd come within a few weeks of his aunt's diagnosis.

Showered and changed and relieved, Jamie returned to the familiar blocks he'd driven through with Bachman. Passing the street that led to Lorraine's ranch, he kept going, all the way to the Totowa border where he'd been living since he was nine. The Cape Cod he shared with Nugget.

He'd been told it took time when someone died to get over it. *"That and a few nights out, tying one on."* He didn't think about his aunt daily, but he was pretty sure he still hadn't gotten over her loss and wasn't sure it was within him to do it. Five years was a long time, but it felt short to Jamie. Little things would call her up. The reminder of his boxing career. His aunt had been the one to sign him up at Lou Costello's when, in her opinion, he and his energy were getting too big to contain in what was barely a two bedroom. The house itself spoke volumes about her. As he got older, he was struck with the audacity she'd had to buy it. For her to imagine something would ever come from sheer willpower. Doing without bottles of soda as a teenager, unlike the other girls at Continental Can who splurged their nickels during breaks. What should have been her pin money, she saved and cobbled enough together to open her passbook account. Then she trained herself to walk in a smooth rhythm and lost her New Jersey Italian way of speaking. Getting a job at Meyer Brothers in hosiery was her start. She moved on as head floor person at the Florence Shop, their top saleswoman.

She wasn't someone easily erased. Not by a new couch and TV stand. Not by the new furniture in the bedroom he'd gutted and taken over. Not by scraping off the pineapple wallpaper in the breakfast cove and repainting the whole room moss green. All the remodeling her suggestion. More like a command.

"Make it into a place a man lives in. Get rid of all my frills and doilies."

Not that Aunt Ro had any frills or doilies. She wasn't that kind of an aunt. But Jamie got the point. *"Don't live in the past."*

With all that, she'd pop up sometimes. A mild sense of her presence as he was running the laundry or when he was shaving. Often, he'd get her voice telling him the thing to do if he were floundering on a decision.

Jamie shifted his focus to Nugget waiting next to his bowl.

"Give me a minute," he told the dog who followed him as he went to change. Jamie carefully laid out his shirt and pants on the bed, inspecting the dark blue fabric for stains and arranging the pants so the pleat in the front was crisp. He always used wooden hangers for his uniform.

His thoughts turned to the first round of interviews he'd done that afternoon. RJ's regulars. Men who worked in the area and often came back on Saturday nights. Dotting i's and crossing t's so that Bachman could load up the file with statements. *Did you see anything? No? Okay, thanks.* It felt that he was biding time, in a way that was demonstrated for him by the lengthy interview with Lorraine that yielded not one lead. Bachman liked efficient files. No fat, he'd told Jamie. Cases start with a 72-hour blitz. The trail's only hot for so long. Jamie itched to find whatever it was that would keep the case fully active. To be the one.

Having his before-dinner beer, Jamie fished around the kitchen counter and sorted through a few days' mail, still holding the PSE&G bill when the phone rang. Kenny from Arco Concerts.

"You available Friday night?"

Jamie couldn't think of any reason not to try it. He'd set himself up for summer work at Giants Stadium.

"Great, great. Get there by five o'clock. There'll be good parking near the back entrance and we'll get you settled. I'll have your name on the security list. Go to the big metal doors by the ramp, you'll see where they are. When you walk in, they'll check your paperwork and give you a T-shirt. I'll meet up with you and figure out your section."

"Okay. See you at five."

"Yeah, five. I'll see you around then." Kenny paused, "Do you carry a gun usually?"

"I don't usually say," Jamie answered.

"Not a problem."

The call ended and Jamie returned to his mail and flicked on the TV for the white noise, background sounds of the news. President Carter denied that his budget director had been given a job as payoff for loans that went to the family peanut warehouse. Popping open another Miller's, Jamie learned there'd be more snow on Thursday. Nugget licked and nudged his just-emptied bowl.

SEVEN

JAMIE HAD A BATCH OF FILES SURROUNDING HIM THAT
he'd decided to arrange by witness type. These were not all witnesses he
had interviewed or would be interviewing, necessarily. He'd been folded
into the ad hoc team that was the RJ's investigation and tasked with
corralling everything from the full reports to half-page statements that
were floating around. The first of his files, marked "Tavern Workers" had
Lorraine's report along with folders for four other dancers, Catherine
Rose, and the day bartender. The people who the team had tracked
down by canvassing the neighborhood, and who were willing to talk,
were in the thinnest file marked "Area Residents and Other Possible
Witnesses." There was a nice, chunky file for patrons who had been at
the bar the night of the shooting and an altogether separate file with
specific names coughed up by the dancers. The "Longtime Customers"
file. That file had the name Gil Christian.

That was the most telling information Lorraine had come up with.
She hadn't worked with Cindy long and Lorraine said they hadn't spoken
much, although she made a point of saying Cindy had a genuine smile.
Though she'd eyed Jamie often, that had been one of the few times in
the interview she'd spoken to him directly, her voice tightening as she
tried to keep control.

Where Lorraine had really opened up was remembering Randall.
He and his brother had been keeping the place the same as much as
they could. Lorraine described customers expecting the french fries and
burgers they'd always been served and how everyone liked RJ's themed
parties. From Lorraine's description, they were getting the upstairs set

for a Country and Western Night, with haystacks already delivered and stored on the second floor. In all, Randall and Craig were trying to keep it "a real nice place to work" and Randall was "a real nice guy." Then she'd added her information on his friend.

"Gil didn't come in all the time, but he'd stop by, mostly on weeknights. He wasn't there Saturday. I didn't see him. But he knew Randall personally, you could tell. Whenever he was in, they'd sit and chat. He's a person you could talk to."

Jamie had been sitting next to Bachman, writing his notes. Maybe that was why he'd been given the interview. A decent name. Someone who might be informative. Maybe Bachman wasn't as put off by Jamie's inexperience as he'd thought.

Christian & Christian, LLC was on a side street in Haledon, not far from the town's main road. A squat, single story building finished in tan brick that was easy to get to and had its own parking lot. The law firm's name shone in bold silver letters on the front. Jamie waited for Gil in the reception area, avoiding the low, mid-century loveseats.

Gil came out just when Jamie was thinking it might be better if he sat, since standing meant hovering near the receptionist and her pristine collection of miniature cacti. A fair-haired man, with soft shoulders and the beginning of a beer gut, although Jamie would eventually learn Jameson was his drink of choice, Gil was noticeably not wearing a suit or tie. Everything about his demeanor was casual. His gray flannel slacks and loafers. The Oxford shirt that ought to have been ironed.

"Sorry, I was waiting for my dad to clear his papers out of the conference room. I hope this didn't cause too much of a delay."

Gil turned to the receptionist desk. "Did we offer Mr. Palmieri a beverage?"

Pressing the receiver between her ear and her shoulder, she made a mix of hand gestures, conveying both a response to Gil and a miming of the phrase, *"I'm on the phone."*

"I'm fine. Really," Jamie answered for her.

It was one of those law offices that was in a modernish building yet decorated with all the traditional trappings. The framed Certificates of Admission to the state and federal bars displayed alongside the blurry photography taken by the firm's junior partner, Gil's older brother. Sandy dunes. Salt marshes. Plastic buckets brimming with hard-shelled crabs. Brightly colored Victorian homes, one with a flag mounted high on its cupola. Photographs of Cape May that would have been easily recognized by Jamie if he'd ever been.

They sat across from each other. Jamie with a fresh notebook out, still reaching for his pen when Gil began speaking.

"It's so terrible. We've known Randall a long time. His family's a client. Did you know that's how they found the bar? It might have been my dad or someone from our block. The old owners, Richard and Jerome, R and J, had been wanting to sell for a while."

"The block?"

"West Paterson. That's where my family's from. The Lows lived close by."

"So, you knew Randall well?"

"I did."

Jamie considered his next question, stopping to review his list.

"Is this repetitive?" Gil asked.

"Repetitive?"

"Am I giving the same information as my brother? He was set to meet with a detective. The RJ's purchase. That was his closing, his file. You know, he was the lawyer on it. I'd have to check with him about an interview. We didn't really discuss it."

"This is about your time at the bar. Anything you might have observed when you were there."

"Oh, I see. Okay. Okay."

"Right. Were you there regularly?"

"RJ's. Okay. I'd never been before the Lows purchased RJ's. Like I said, the law firm helped put the deal together. It wasn't until after the closing that I went to visit Randall, get a drink on the house."

With that, Gil paused and lifted his coffee mug. A sad smile as he put it back on the coaster.

"The place was different than what I'd expected, to be honest. A decent place. People were very nice. Not the rough crowd you'd think. I began to go, you might say, more frequently. I wasn't there Saturday, I didn't know that . . ."

A silence stretched out and Jamie thought he'd caught Gil in a moment, trying to come up with an answer. But as he rubbed his cheekbones, Jamie realized the man was collecting himself. The affable demeanor he'd had when talking about the business end faded. A pivot that interested Jamie.

"You knew them both."

"Yes. I knew them both."

"When did you first meet Cindy?"

Gil's hand rose, examining his left eyelid.

"I guess, I guess it was a few months ago. I noticed her around last Labor Day. Maybe it was then, around then."

"And did you talk to her right away?"

"I don't remember talking to her that night. Maybe I did. But eventually we would talk. She'd stop by on her breaks. We'd talk a little. She was like that. Friendly. A good kid."

"You ever give her a ride home? Spend time with her outside of the bar?"

"Never a ride home. I always left before closing, but I mean, I wouldn't have left with her. If that's what you're asking. I wouldn't have."

"Why not?"

"I just don't do that. And I wasn't talking to her for that reason. I was talking to her because I like talking to people when I'm in a bar. That's where I spend a lot of my time. I guess you should know that. I spend a lot of my time in bars and a lot of that time is drinking more than talking and there are times I don't remember much the next day. So, you should know that about me as a witness. If I am a witness."

Gil paused his dialogue with a brief cough.

"Am I? Am I some kind of witness?"

Jamie took in the room. A pair of diplomas dated 1939 and 1967, both from Cornell Law School, were mounted on the wall directly across from him. One for Jonathan T. Christian and one for Jonathan R. Christian. Spaced perfectly in between them was a signed print featuring a stone tower that looked grand and academic and Ivy League.

"I don't know yet," Jamie answered. "I'm here to find out if you know anything. Anything that's useful."

Gil rubbed at his neck, like he wanted to be useful. Like he wanted a drink although it wasn't even ten in the morning. But maybe the time wasn't a big concern for Gil.

"This is what I know about Cindy. She said she was eighteen when I met her, but she had a party around Christmas for her eighteenth birthday and she was real excited for that. Invited me but I told her I wasn't really her crowd. That's what a good kid she was, she'd mention a party and then invite me so I wouldn't feel left out. She had a shitty boyfriend. She was off a week around October because she had bruises, that's what I heard, and Randall told her to stay home until she was better."

"Who told you that? Randall?"

"I think it was Randall. I wish I could remember."

"Was her shitty boyfriend jealous?"

"I don't know. I never met him. She didn't talk about him much, though she did tell me she was planning to leave him. That was late October. Maybe it was November. Said she met someone who was going to help her. There'd been their big fight and the neighbors called the police. I guess that was the breaking point. Then nothing happened. As far as I know. She didn't mention it again. Her boyfriend bought her a coat for her birthday with fox trim. Gave it to her early because it was starting to get cold and she was wearing that. No more plans to move out."

Jamie was writing as fast as he could. Gil was lobbing information before Jamie could think of what his next question ought to be. He hoped Gil, who was again sipping from his mug, might be taking a long break so Jamie could catch up with his notes.

"You sure about that? She just turned eighteen?"

"She said it was her birthday. She got the coat."

"Sounds like it was a Christmas present. The timing."

"Her birthday was Christmas. The twenty-fifth."

There was probably a note on that in her file somewhere, Jamie realized. Her recent birthday. Her age. No one bothered to dwell on that, perhaps not wanting to make the Lows look bad. That unseemly information about underage girls quietly tucked away in a folder and meant to be ignored.

"You have a name? The guy that was going to help her leave her boyfriend?"

Gil raised his hands in the classic I-don't-know gesture.

"Did everyone in the bar know that stuff or did she just talk to you?"

"No idea. But I am an easy person to talk to. It's my gift. Cindy wasn't the only one to tell me her life story. I've heard a bunch of them. They say that bartenders are the ones with the ear, but really, I'm the one that gets the stories. Sitting by myself, nursing a drink. The seat next to me isn't empty for long. I'm the good-listener guy."

"Did you like Cindy?"

"She was a great girl. Pretty girl. Enjoyable to be around. But I told you, I hadn't looked for anything with the girls at RJ's."

"She go off with anyone? Ever?"

"I don't really think that she did."

"What else?"

"What else what?"

"What else about Cindy?"

Gil inhaled and exhaled twice. He talked in long spurts. He needed his breath.

"Her mother's been married a bunch of times. She lives up in Sparta. Her last name is Sutter. Not sure what her first name is. I guess you already know that. I should make a note for myself. I've been meaning to give her a call."

"Was there anything particular about her family that she told you?"

"Like I said, the mother was married a bunch of times and I think that's why Cindy left the house and moved in with her boyfriend. That wasn't much of a topic for her. She liked to talk about last names. Cindy was into last names. Hers wasn't Sutter but whatever it was, she wanted to change it legally. She used different ones on and off. She asked me if I liked Monroe, Mansfield, Harlow. Names like that. Theatrical. Mansfield seemed like her favorite, the one she was leaning to."

"Kaczorek," Jamie said.

"What?"

Jamie was supposed to ask questions. Not offer information. But what difference did it make to share that small fragment.

"Cindy Kaczorek."

"That was it. Her last name," Gil said softly, checking his watch. "I have more time, but I told my dad I'd get him the conference room back by ten."

"Do you have anything else?"

"Not about Cindy," Gil answered. "But we haven't even discussed Randall. I thought he was why you came to see me."

"Right." Jamie was writing and listening. "Give me a minute here and we can schedule the follow-up."

EIGHT

FRIDAY NIGHT WAS COLD AND ROUTE 80 WAS WET WITH slush. The Datsun handled the slick road like the low framed car that it was. But even slowing to sixty, only managing sixty-five when there was a clear patch of road, Jamie got to the Arena by five. It looked like a big, truncated tent, with trapezoidal sides on the far ends. The design was meant to allow noise to resonate, creating a deafening sound, as Jamie would soon experience for himself.

Inside, Jamie found a table that fit Kenny's description. A girl with round glasses and excessively curly hair asked him to repeat his last name and handed him a T-shirt. He checked the size and handed it back to her.

"Extra large," he said.

That required her to get up and pick through a cardboard box.

A man wearing a black polo shirt with the words "Arco" on the back and "Phil" stitched across the left side of his chest circled Jamie while he waited for his T-shirt.

"I know you," he said. "Costello's, right? Over on Gould. You went there. I saw you in some preliminary bouts a few years ago. You train at Lou Costello's, right?"

"That was a few years ago."

"I knew I knew you." The man let a broad grin spread across his face. His reddish beard opened to reveal his great white teeth and then a full-on laugh before he bent forward and wrapped Jamie into a bear hug. "Whoa, Golden Gloves! What's up?"

Jamie was never comfortable with "what's up" and that sort of talk. Especially talk about Golden Gloves, coming up twice in less than a week. He jutted his chin forward, a response that was Jamie's way of saying *"I honestly don't know how to be around people like you."* People he didn't know who grabbed him, getting close enough to reveal how much pot they'd smoked and how many drinks they'd had.

"Did you eat?" Phil asked. He was an in-the-moment fast friend. "No," he went on, "you just got here. C'mon. Let's go to hospitality before they're all stoned out of their minds."

It was the silent understanding amongst the off-duty cops. Gary warned him. Hospitality was notorious. Really anyone who was backstage. They supplied the bands with drugs and girls who'd been nominally hired to serve tacos and sloppy joes cafeteria-style. Jamie had been instructed not to eat the desserts. Gary said he'd seen chocolate chip cookies that were bright green from the Hawaiian weed baked into them.

Jamie walked along with Phil, who was mumbling about fire exits, until they arrived at the bustling kitchen in a far corner of the Arena. He didn't smell the pot he'd expected to waft over. It was cayenne and other sharp spices mixed with fried onions.

"I'm gonna grab us a few beers," Phil said.

"Just a soft drink for me," Jamie answered. "Whatever you have."

Phil turned, his mouth and its wiry facial hair screwed into a smile. "Yeah, sure."

Jamie had meant it though. It didn't matter. As it turned out, Phil wouldn't be back. Jamie saw him down the hall with a group he thought might be roadies, a plume of smoke above them. Jamie was left standing on a buffet line with the same china plate Addie's Diner had been using for years, not sure what to do with himself.

"You have to get closer."

The voice speaking to him was soft, not yelling although they were several feet away from each other.

"I can't reach you all the way back there."

Jamie moved forward obediently.

"That's better."

The voice belonged to a girl wearing a tank top even though it was January. Jamie guessed that was because of the hot plates and makeshift kitchen she was working in. She scooped shredded beef steaming with peppers and onions onto his plate and used tongs to place a corn muffin on the side. Her face was small and delicate. Elfin and pretty.

He hadn't been looking at the plate and when she released her side after serving him, it felt suddenly heavy with food. Jamie eyed the baked-good suspiciously and she misread that.

"All right," she said. "Here's another. But don't tell anyone I gave you extra. I know we're gonna run out. Everyone knows we're gonna run out. They didn't let me bake enough. They didn't listen to me."

When she turned to find the shaker of black pepper he'd asked for, it gave him time to consider her honey blonde hair twisted and held up by a tortoiseshell clip, revealing the curve of her neck. A light sweat he found appealing.

Abruptly, she was facing him, a tin of McCormick's in her hand. He'd been busy watching her, not anticipating her movements, and spending too much time preoccupied with her shoulders. One had a finely-drawn tattoo.

"That looks like a symbol," Jamie said, hoping he sounded interested in the inked shape, as if that might explain his hard stare in her exact direction. It was unfamiliar. A half circle arch with two lines on either side and a full line underneath.

"It is a symbol," she answered. "I'm a Libra."

Jamie took the pepper in his free hand and sprinkled it evenly on the shredded beef, then placed the tin next to the chafing dish.

"Oh?"

"It can either be the setting sun or scales. I always think it's scales. Balance, you know. Evenness. That's what it means. What Libras are known for." She cupped a hand, weighing an invisible object as a way to demonstrate.

"So, no one has to ask you, 'what's your sign'?"

She picked up the pepper and slid the red plastic top over the shaker holes slowly before looking up. "No, I still get that. You'd be amazed."

Jamie nodded.

"You're a Scorpio," she said.

His eyes flicked wide. "How did you know that?"

"You just are. I'm surprised you even know your sign. You don't seem the type. You're too sensible to go for horoscopes, I think." She nodded, a little glow about her. "I get that impression."

Jamie was wearing the security crew T-shirt, but his aura was entirely different. His clean-shaven face. His well-groomed hair. Thick, dark hair, brushed back neatly.

Her arms wrapped around her. Hugging herself in a way. Body language he couldn't read. But there was a glint in her eye as she met his. Challenging him to keep going.

"I read my horoscope," Jamie said. "It's like the third or fourth thing I look for in the paper. After the sports. The box scores. The really sensible stuff."

"Ah, so what was your horoscope today? Mine said to be more thoughtful of family members."

"Really? That's good advice. Helpful."

She nodded some more.

"So?"

"So?" Jamie echoed back.

"So. You check yours in the paper every day, huh? You haven't told me today's."

In a response that was shocking to him, Jamie answered her.

"Mine told me I'd meet a pretty girl with wavy blonde hair and really great eyes, and she was going to serve me homemade chili."

She was all quick beats. No longer hugging herself, her hands rested on her hips. Fully free of serving spoons and spices and plates. Just there.

"That is so much better than 'what's your sign'."

Jamie's friends said he had a good game. Lines that got results. Favorites he used often when he went bar hopping with Steve. But this was different His ears felt warm and he imagined them openly burning. He wondered where he could possibly sit and eat his chili after what he'd just said. Having dinner standing in a stairwell what he thought to be his best option. Throw his plate in a garbage instead of returning it to one of the gray utility bins where he knew he was supposed to place it. He'd have left the area where he and the girl stood on opposite sides of the chafing dish as soon as he heard himself speak, but his feet weren't moving. Between curiosity and embarrassment, curiosity was winning. Keeping him fixed.

"Did your horoscope say what time you're picking me up next Saturday?"

Jamie thought ahead to the schedule he might have.

"I usually work an early shift on weekends. So six-thirty? Is that good?"

"Your shift?"

She studied him closer.

"You're a cop," she said.

"Yeah. Is that okay?"

She held his gaze while he waited. Unsettled with how hopeful he found himself.

"Six-thirty's perfect."

While she began serving an Arco lighting technician who'd wandered in, Jamie found a seat near the back where he managed to have dinner somewhat anonymously. Then he met up with Kenny for the beginning of the concert, essentially the sound system playing the second half of a Dire Straits album. There was no live warm up for the headline act, a New Wave trio no one had ever heard of, not even the regular security, even though the band had drawn a full house.

Jamie spent the rest of the night policing the aisles, staying late and waiting as fans spilled out of the arena, grabbing the ones who'd drank too much, smoked too much, or dropped too much acid and heaving them onto chartered buses. Then he drove home with Missy Hollum's address and phone number in neat script on a piece of cardboard folded and tucked in the top pocket of his shirt. He thought about Homestead's Hearth and Inn, the restaurant he'd like to bring her to. How much he enjoyed her voice. Equally throaty and soft. Mostly, he thought of what he imagined she looked like naked.

NINE

THE DRESS WAS A NO-NONSENSE DARK BROWN, WITH pale mauve flowers and thick green stems.

"What is this?" Jamie asked Brenner, one of the day shift officers. Paterson wasn't a first name station or a last name station. How they all addressed each other was utterly random. Like so many officers and detectives, Ray Brenner had always been Brenner.

"It's your size."

"Yeah. It's pretty ugly, too."

"Well, you know. Finding nice looking dresses in a size eighteen is a bit of a stretch."

"I guess no one will even see it under my coat," Jamie said. "Where is the coat? Where's the rest of my outfit?"

"Not sure. That's what was sitting on the desk when I got here."

Jamie held up the dress. It felt thin and he was sure he'd be cold and he wondered for the first time how women fared wearing nothing but pantyhose to cover their legs in the dead of winter.

"We're not going out until next week, so you have time to get the rest of your stuff together. I think the guys left the dress on your desk to bust you. Welcome you to undercover."

Jamie rolled the dress into a ball and put it into the file drawer. Once finished with the cheap chiffon, he noticed what it'd been covering. A typed report sat on his desk with a note routing it to him. He read the paperwork carefully. Three times.

"I'm going to the courthouse for about a half hour," he said.

Brenner waved. Gary stayed hunched over his typewriter as usual.

It was a ten-minute walk to Hamilton Street, but Jamie stretched his legs and quickened his pace as a cold wind pushed him forward. Rick Andres had said to find him on the third floor, outside Judge Matteo's courtroom. The detective was exactly where he'd said he would be, waiting in a straddle position on one of the polished benches. He wore a gray suit and tie that confirmed a court appearance. Andres hadn't looked up but seemed to know that Jamie was approaching and rose to greet him.

"Thanks for coming by," he said, grabbing Jamie's hand and pressing his bicep with his other. "Looks like I'll be stuck here all day."

"It would help if they let you know when you'll actually testify," Jamie said.

"Yeah, that would be efficient. They've been in chambers reviewing evidence for almost an hour. That's why I sent a message to you. Figured we could get some work done."

Jamie brought out the report that'd been left for him by Andres. Financial information about the tavern. Reading it over had Jamie even more unsure why the detective was called on the RJ's case. Within the Violent Crimes Division, Andres and his partner's specialty was sexual assaults and that had been specifically ruled out.

"It looks straightforward," Jamie said, fishing around for the right interpretation.

"Sure does. Still, it's something to look at. Who the hell knows. Can't imagine that Craig Low shot his brother. Or had him shot. It's not likely. But it's an avenue. That life insurance policy for two hundred thousand. Bought it September last year. What's that? Four months ago?"

"Has he filed a claim?" Jamie asked.

Even if it wasn't proof of a crime, at the very least it would have been an ill-chosen move. Cashing in when his brother had just been murdered.

"The brother, Craig, needs to give us all the financials. Voluntarily, I hope. You already went to see their attorney, so I figured I'd flip this part to you."

As they spoke, a heavy wooden door opened and a tall, thick man with a brimming moustache and a suit that almost matched Andres' emerged. His partner, Marc Gianelli.

"They told us to take off and have lunch," he said.

Andres nodded.

"I hate this shit. She has to sit there waiting. Like the last thing she wants to do is get up there and tell her story and now she can't even get it over with. That bastard and his fucking delays," Gianelli said. "You know it's a tactic. He's trying to get to her."

"Colleen's with her parents," Andres said. "I think she's okay right now."

Gianelli shifted his full body, ignoring Jamie, ignoring the report Andres was holding. Ignoring everything, his eyes pierced the courtroom door, tearing into the defendant on the other side.

Andres turned to Jamie. "C'mon. I'll walk back with you."

The two of them began down the hallway, passing more doors, more benches. The cool, marble corridors had been designed decades earlier for the equity courts and area businessmen working out complex arrangements involving money—not for the defendants in orange jumpsuits and handcuffs who currently took up most of the space. Jamie's thoughts were on the life insurance and another trip to Gil's law firm, but also the heaviness he'd seen on Gianelli's face. Andres held it differently. He was silent. But it was there for both of them. Their cases were their cases.

As they were almost at the stairs, a steady pace picked up behind them. Without looking, Andres slowed for his partner. They were a tight unit, Jamie noticed, and didn't need to say a lot to each other.

TEN

WHAT GIANELLI AND ANDRES NEEDED FROM JAMIE WAS background information on Craig Low that they could work off of. That was the core of Jamie's briefing from Gianelli when they were back at the station.

"When you talk to that lawyer friend of his, see if he had a girlfriend. Or maybe he gambles. Is he known to go to the corner deli and place bets?"

Gianelli stopped and pulled a wrapped toothpick from an inner pocket.

"Girlfriends and gambling problems. Those are the guys that find themselves suddenly needing cash."

Gianelli shook his head.

"It ain't just an insurance policy. Gotta have the motive to go with it."

Jamie returned to his desk and the aged, electric typewriter. With his new work, his desk, the squad room, all of it became a little more promising. Detective trainee was beginning to take shape. No longer so far off. He was getting the grunt work done with before his better cases.

Given that Jamie would be working in the Fourth Ward with Brenner that day, running a minor stakeout from their cruiser, his imagination ran to trailing Craig Low. Jamie was almost embarrassed by his excitement at the prospect of following someone who might have done more than the petty crimes he was used to. Practice for when he'd get the undercover car and regular partner. A move up from his reality.

"Whole lot better than out on the street," Brenner said, patting the dashboard.

Brenner was a patrol officer with a lack of ambition matched with the limits of his abilities.

"It's warmer," Jamie said.

"Warmer's good. I'll take it."

Jamie drove to the deli at 19th and Market that had a reputation for selling nickel bags. As they rounded the corner, Brenner pointed to a blue two-family with a fair amount of space at its curb.

"Here," he said. "Turn around so we're facing Market and park over here."

Jamie maneuvered the car, catching a full view of a house he'd never seen before but seemed to know. This was exactly the Paterson where Jamie's father and Aunt Ro and their three younger brothers lived growing up. Chain link fencing surrounded much of the yard and yellowed blinds covered every window.

Neighbors would still know everything that went on in a house like that. The families and the places they lived were too confined. Stacked on top of each other. You couldn't turn down the volume on the screaming. The slammed doors. The thrown furniture. Jamie didn't know why he thought of those scenes every time his extended family came to mind. He was glad that wasn't often. All of them were long gone, including his father. Scattered around and landing in different places—Maryland and Mississippi and Oklahoma and who knew where else. Only his aunt had stayed in Paterson.

He shook off the thought. Together with Brenner, he watched a small group mill around the broken sidewalk beneath an RC Cola sign that had once been a crisp white and red. Typical waiting-on-the-corner boys who'd recently begun shaving and decided to stop to see what happened and found themselves with thin, uneven patches of beard.

The tiny store was a relic. To its left was a closed-for-business locksmith with a one-page note taped inside the front window thanking shoppers for their loyalty. A few doors away, a latched metal grate covered a TV repair service. Maybe that also wasn't ever going to open again. Each of those shuttered entries was a friendly offer to all on the street. Plenty of space here to go sell drugs.

"They're not coming outta there with smoked kielbasa," Brenner said.

Jamie had a clear view through the plate glass. The adult behind the counter didn't reach for cartons of cigarettes. None of the teens picked up packs of wintergreen gum or bottles of generic aspirin or grabbed Gatorade from the standalone refrigerator. They were handed small packets. The kind with white powder.

"That's new. I thought he sold pot."

"Yeah," Brenner said. "Entrepreneurs there."

"You want to go in?" Jamie asked.

"You wait here. There's probably one or two that'll try to run."

Brenner was right. Once they were out of the car, their uniforms on full display, the group separated. Jamie's options appeared in a flash. One was tall and skinny, his face hidden by an overgrown shag of brown hair. Behind him, the teen was blond and heavier. Neither wore a winter coat. Brenner wasn't going after either of them, and Jamie had to make a try for both. The blond was moving slower behind his friend and what Jamie saw was he'd be easier to get later. Jamie sprinted, seizing the shirt of his first choice, a surprisingly fast runner. Pushing him to the side of a building and twisting him, Jamie had his handcuffs already swung open.

Then Jamie ran towards Oak Street, cornering the blond who couldn't make it half a block and stopped, wheezing in surrender. Eventually Brenner emerged from the deli with a fourteen-year-old and called for a backup car.

That day increased Jamie's arrest record and raised his numbers for the month. He liked the adrenaline high of the chase, but what he liked most was making the calculation in the split second he had, deciding where to put his energy. It felt like a progression. He could see himself making the right calls when he had to. Trailing someone like Craig Low and looking for something more complicated than drug deals in a deli. Gambling. What Gianelli referred to as "girls on the side".

ELEVEN

THE LATE-NIGHT TELEVISION ADS RAN AS A BLUR. A squeegee mop. Polyester and cotton blend shirts sold in packs of six. Cheap electronics at S&W on Canal Street. He wasn't even sure what show he was watching, his eyes blinking as he poured himself two fingers of Johnnie Walker Black, waiting for the house to finish settling. Background sounds of his wife and the older of his three kids upstairs still hummed. They might not even know he'd gone to the basement.

His usual manner was thudding down the stairs, but he'd stepped lightly, aware of his movements. Taking care with each of the thirteen steps to the partially finished room he'd made up with paneling over the home's pipes and wiring and a square of indoor/outdoor carpet under his desk and swivel chair. His office where no one was allowed, though just in case, current issues of Penthouse and Hustler were in a bin near the rolltop, so they'd be easily found. The prizes for his thirteen-year-old son. No need to worry about drawers rifled through once the kid had his hands on those. Even with the new lock, he imagined the inevitable breach if he hadn't thought ahead.

He slowly inched open the file drawer where he'd hid the plastic twist-tie bag. The bills he'd taken from the deposit pouch had been counted and bundled. Mostly ones and fives. A few tens. Not many twenties. Apartment keys he'd grabbed in the hurry of threats and pleas and the pocketbook flung in a frightened rage. And then gunshots. All of it so fast. He'd had to improvise and put together a credible crime scene.

He'd taken the cash. The cops had noticed that missing so that was in place, giving them robbery as the obvious motive. But it wasn't what he'd been looking for.

TWELVE

JAMIE'S NEXT SHIFT HAD HIM ON ANOTHER SURVEIL-
lance. By 10:00 a.m., he'd left his patrol car in the lot and taken the
Monaco he'd driven with Bachman. At noon, he was two hours in and
there hadn't been much. Sitting and waiting on a quiet street for activity
froman aluminum-sided house that looked like all the others surrounding it, although this one was reported to have a sizable marijuana
and cocaine operation inside. Drugs meant there'd also be illegal guns and
the rounds of ammunition to go with their cache of automatic rifles and
assorted pistols.

"The warrant's coming from ATF. Jot down what you see, and we'll
get it in an affidavit for them."

That's what Jamie had been told when given the assignment. His
notes included the mailman's activities, dropping off what looked to be
mostly flyers held together with a rubber band. Then he'd observed two
women in biker jackets and low-rise jeans leaving the home within fifteen
minutes of each other, both with dark brown hair, one he knew to be a
paid informant.

When he got back to the station, Bachman was waiting for him.

"Go to interrogation. Something interesting for you."

"For me?"

"Yeah, get over there. Go take a look," Bachman said.

Jamie hurried down a flight of stairs, past a series of storerooms to
a suite with an observation area where he joined Andres. On the other
side of a two-way mirror, Gianelli sat across from a suspect, ignoring
him and sorting through a thin pile of records. The man was handcuffed

to a chair and the chair was bolted to the floor. He shifted occasionally as curls of smoke began to fill the windowless room, finally forced to turn his head. It would be almost five minutes before the court reporter stubbed his cigarette against a Styrofoam cup, then stood and worked his machine from its case. At roughly the same time, Gianelli set aside all but one document, motioning that he wanted to get started.

"Let me get this right. This is the first time you ever had a gun in your hand? That's what you're telling me? This was the first time."

"Yeah, it was the first time."

"Convenient. You go into a liquor store on Grand to get your practice in?"

"What do you want me to tell you? I went into the liquor store. Cops already on the street by the time I got out. They can tell you everything. What do you want me to tell you?"

Jamie turned to Andres.

"What's going on with this? Anyone shot?"

Andres shook his head.

"Guy went into Carnavale's with a gun this morning. The minute it opened. So, we know he's pretty stupid, since there wasn't going to be a whole lot of cash."

"So, why's he so interesting?"

"The favorite theory for RJ's, it was a robbery. Idea is, the guy was upstairs, hiding out and waiting until the close to sneak up on Randall, making sure he was first with his gun. That's the theory that most people like."

"That's what I understood."

"So, they figure if the RJ's guy had been looking to hit a bar, he's got a preference. We find a guy robbing a liquor store. Makes that interesting."

Jamie nodded, although not actually seeing a direct line between the two.

"Anyone doing a robbery with a gun these days is interesting. Especially a liquor store. Bar. Anything that points to RJ's."

The man in the bolted chair puffed his cheeks and let out a long, silent whistle. He had the edge Jamie saw all the time around Eastside Park.

"They think he ties into RJ's?"

"He's nervous with a gun. It went off when Domenic, Sr. was emptying the cash register. Sprayed glass and fancy liqueurs all over the wife. Nice lady, trying to keep calm behind the counter, then she's covered in crème de menthe. This one says he wasn't aiming at her, it just happened. Stupid. Adding a year to his jail time for that."

"Nervous with a gun," Jamie said.

"Yeah, but he's not the guy. He didn't do RJ's," Andres said, answering Jamie's unasked questions.

"How do you know?"

"He's not the type to wait quietly upstairs while the bar closed."

Dropping his voice, Andres added, "Anyway, RJ's shooter isn't gonna risk botched robbery number two, you know?"

"Hiding somewhere?"

"RJ's was a shit show. The whole thing went way off the rails. Shooter's probably far away by now, praying he don't get caught. If he is around, which I personally doubt, anything he does that gets him arrested—littering, a parking ticket, especially another robbery with a gun—ups his chances of getting tied into two murders. Points to him not doing anything for a long, long time."

"So why, I mean . . ."

"Listen, some of the higher ups want a splashy arrest. They can get that way. The press is on them. Also, Low's family. Keep that to yourself, but don't forget it."

In the still-smoky room, Gianelli slid a card across the table to the suspect, asking him to read it as clearly as he could. The man's raspy voice went over each word, acknowledging he'd signed the form knowingly waiving his Miranda rights.

"You sure about this?" Gianelli asked.

"Yeah, I signed it. I ain't got nothing to hide. Your guys were there."

Gianelli looked up at Andres. They seemed to make eye contact even though one of them was looking at a blank mirror.

"I need a minute outside," Gianelli said.

The two detectives conferred in the booth, with Jamie tucked near the door.

"This is bullshit. Such bullshit. I don't care what he signed. I'm telling him he needs a lawyer."

"Your call," Andres said.

"Get one of the assistant DAs over here. Someone needs to deal with this."

Jamie didn't even have to ask. He knew exactly where that was going. They'd been told. Warned with this point repeated throughout the department. Be real careful when you get someone waiving their Miranda rights. Even if they're sober. Even if they say they know what they're doing and sign a written waiver in front of a busload of priests. No coercing. Not suspects. Not witnesses. The Hurricane Carter case loomed in that way. Even for a small liquor store robbery. Jamie couldn't imagine who'd be stupid enough to pull out one of those cards for anything touching the RJ's murders.

Gianelli tapped Jamie's elbow on his way to the exit.

"C'mon," he said. "We're done with this."

"You're officially checking him off the list?" Andres asked.

"Pretty much," Gianelli said. "Couple of the guys upstairs got real excited when they heard liquor store and gun in the same sentence. You know that."

The splashy arrest.

Jamie stayed curious but didn't ask who had given the man with the frayed mohawk and homemade neck tattoo a waiver form to sign. Maybe Andres already told him as much as he could.

THIRTEEN

DEBRA HAD BEEN JAMIE'S LAST GIRLFRIEND. THE DATING-for-two-years girlfriend who'd begun to expect a ring about a year into the relationship. They'd met at college. She was one of the few young women taking criminal justice classes. She had chestnut brown hair she kept back in a headband. She looked nice in a sweater. They had coffee after class one day. She began to stay over once or twice a week. Jamie couldn't think of a reason to break up with her, but he couldn't think of a reason to buy an engagement ring. In the end, it was Debra who broke up with him, angry that he'd made her be the one to do it.

"You just can't make any decision. Any! You just don't know what you want," she'd said on a Saturday night when they were supposed to go bowling but she'd opened up a resentment that'd been festering for some time.

"Good thing I can make a decision," she'd said. "At least *I* know what *I* want."

They didn't go bowling that night. Debra didn't stay over.

He'd thought of calling her a few times when he was lonely and once when he'd genuinely missed her. But he never did. That's what ran through Jamie's mind as he sat in the dining alcove, the cardboard with Missy's number in his hand. The excitement of seeing her.

Missy lived in Haledon with a few friends.

"I'm in C," she'd said. "You'll see doorbells on the left side of the foyer. The exterior door isn't locked."

"I'll pick you up at six-thirty," Jamie said, confirming that for the second time in their brief phone call.

She'd wanted to know where they were going and what she should wear.

"We're going to Homestead's," he'd told her.

Jamie thought of the thin dress he'd been given for his undercover shift catching the muggers who worked the bus stops downtown. How wintry and bleak it was once the sun disappeared by five, as it always did in January. Even the well-shoveled sidewalks could have a glaze of dark ice. Heels were no match for that at all. He hoped she'd wear something so she wouldn't be too cold and at the same time hoped he could see her pretty shoulders again.

Her apartment was down the street from Ace's Rod and Gun where Jamie had been taken to buy his Detective Special while still in the academy. Like all the others on Belmont Ave., hers was above retail space. On top of Kline's Redwing Shoes. He found the letter "C" taped over a yellowed button, licking his upper lip and shuffling for a moment before he pressed it.

Missy wore white boots that went up to her knees and a dress that wasn't too short but left a space where Jamie saw her legs as she sat in the passenger seat. Her hair was down, a barrette holding a few strands back on the left side. Tiny pearl earrings. A cluster of three in gold-colored metal. The car still warm.

"How long've you been in Haledon?" he asked. The basic filler Jamie used on firsts. First dates. First time talking to a girl at a bar. The question eased out of him.

"I've been here a little while," Missy answered.

Stopped at a light, he caught himself looking at the edge of her dress.

Homestead's was classic. Dark and intimate, beginning with a cavernous entryway lined with burgundy benches for anyone not choosing to sit at the bar while waiting for their table. Jamie had his hand on Missy's back as they moved towards the hostess stand lit by a brass lamp positioned near a large appointment book, giving them a better vantage point to see inside the restaurant. A cart set discretely to the side with silverware roll-ups in cloth napkins. The formal waitstaff in black uniforms, white shirts and bowties. Missy's straightening spine told Jamie she'd never been inside.

It was the perfect date night restaurant. Candles in the center of tables barely illuminating the booths they passed. The acoustics were excellent. No buzz of other conversations. Only the occasional fork hitting a dish too hard, a busboy rattling a bin of china and glassware.

Their waitress introduced herself. Fran. When Missy ordered a Chablis, she was carded. She wasn't embarrassed at all, and reached into her purse for a tan folding wallet. She handed over her driver's license.

"You're twenty-one?" Fran asked.

"People always think I'm young. Sometimes, when I'm out during the day, I'll get asked if I'm cutting school."

The older woman turned to Jamie.

"It's standard. We ask all the girls." She shrugged. "Policy."

After Fran left for the bar area, Missy said to Jamie in almost an apology, "I do look young."

She had silky, shampoo-commercial hair that sat at her shoulders. Eyes that melted into her ready smile. He liked her posture. Poised in the booth. But standing five-foot four, weighing maybe ninety-five pounds, Jamie understood why she'd been asked for proof. And he found out her age, she'd turned twenty-one in the fall.

"So, your birthday was in October," Jamie said.

"I told you I'm a Libra."

Jamie squirmed.

"I don't really read horoscopes," he said.

"I knew that," Missy said. "You're too sensible."

Conversation was fine when they got their drinks. A Jack and Coke for Jamie and a Chablis for Missy—who took small, careful sips so she wouldn't smudge her shimmering rose gloss.

Missy set aside the oversized menu and faced Jamie.

"You're a cop. I mean, I know that. So, I'm just saying . . . I want you to know . . . in case . . . "

She was so spirited. Even with her brow furrowed and her mouth tightly pressed into a flat line, Jamie enjoyed that.

"I'm not a party girl."

She brought her hand to her face, briefly checking her lips with her fingertips. "Meeting at the concert, I was working and everything, but I'm not about that."

He waited for her face to relax so they could get to the pleasant small talk that made up a date.

"I'm not."

"I know you're not a party girl. I never thought that."

"Right. I thought we should clear that up."

"Okay, good. Then I won't ask you for pot or uppers or downers," Jamie said. "Or sideways, I won't ask you for anything sideways."

Missy raised the menu, a move to cover her cheeks and slight dimples and the smirk she meant to hide.

"Nothing sideways," he said.

He wanted her to have a steak, but she ordered chicken croquettes.

"I like the way they browned this," Missy said, inspecting the round of chicken patty on her plate. "I watch how they work the saucepan whenever I'm in the kitchen. Fast. The real chefs work it fast."

"And you're an assistant? An assistant chef?"

She'd worked at a restaurant in Jacksonville. Skipping mostly over her time in Florida and how she got there and who she'd gone there with, she shared a minimal history.

"I was a waitress, but I helped with some prep work. I like that better than hostessing. What I'm doing now."

She left an opening for Jamie to ask what she did exactly, but he wanted her to eat and she'd just taken her first bite. Instead, he drank the rest of his Jack and Coke.

"They use butter *and* oil. I can tell. Butter for flavor and olive oil because that doesn't burn."

"Both," Jamie said.

"That's why I liked being with the chefs. There was always something to learn."

"I bet they don't mind having you back there."

"They tell me I'm curious."

Jamie reached for the pepper a second time, grinding more black flecks onto his plate.

"I remember you like pepper."

He tried a bite of his steak, satisfied with the amount of spice on it. "I think that my aunt was a very basic cook. I got used to adding pepper. A lot."

Missy let her fingers rest on the stem of her glass. It had been some time since she'd lifted her fork.

When Fran came back, she was offering their dessert menus.

"Thank you, no," Missy said.

Jamie ordered a banana pudding square that was topped with "schlag," their famous Bavarian whipped cream and meant to serve two. He wanted to force feed her, get her to have more than her delicate bites. Keenly aware of how cold it was. How tapered her arms were. The dress she wore, all flounce, puff and charm. Not nearly warm enough, he thought.

"Don't you like whipped cream?"

"It's very heavy."

She was, of course, right about that. He pushed the plate aside and suggested they go to the bar for Sambuca. Most of the leather stools were empty by then. At that hour, no one was waiting for a table to open. One lone couple who looked to be in their late forties were rooted in the corner, falling into each other, and sipping from the same Martini glass.

"I think, maybe not," Missy said.

While she was gone, off to the restroom far in the back, Fran came a final time to ask if Jamie needed anything else, then left an open billfold on the starched white linen and dropped two mints on top of the check. Jamie stared at the cleared table and the telltale markers of a night that was ending, knowing there'd be no second half. Missy wasn't a party girl. At least, she wasn't going to be one on their first date.

He didn't ask Missy back to his house or make another offer for after-dinner drinks in hopes they'd wind up there. He waited until they were out of his car to kiss her goodnight.

Within the tiled entry, the smell of stale cigarettes gave way to Missy's perfume as Jamie gathered her close. A rush of florals and sandalwood deepened when he nuzzled into her hair. Missy ran a finger over her lips, wiping away the last of the gloss. Her eyes slowly closed as her mouth opened and her arms reached higher, wrapping around his neck. A kiss that went on, longer than he'd expected. Giving him that die-a-little-inside feeling when it ended.

Missy drew back, framed by the foyer's glass and metal door, her chin tilting down, shy and inviting.

"Goodnight," she said, then turned and disappeared.

FOURTEEN

GIL'S APARTMENT WAS ON THE WEST PATERSON SIDE OF Garret Mountain. South Paterson, where Jamie interviewed Lorraine, was a section of the city. West Paterson was actually another town. It wasn't a part of Paterson and it wasn't even particularly west of it, though it was closer to Route 80. That made it suburban. Woodsy in parts with a rustic feel.

Jamie followed a winding road going up about two and a half miles, the complex nestled in an area cleared of the rugged, basaltic rock the Garret Mountain reserve was known for and that bordered all the local trails. The drive there, even in the winter, was green and shady. There were many thick pines and conifers making up for the maples' stripped branches. The parking lot full of newer cars like Jamie's offered a commanding view of lower Manhattan. The World Trade Center stood out immediately. He parked next to a Corvette secured within a custom cover. Jamie shuddered briefly with a thought. *This is how a guy lives. This is how you move out of the neighborhood and on with your life.*

"Any trouble finding me?" Gil asked.

"Not at all. Pretty easy ride over."

"That's right. You guys do your target practice near here."

"On the other side of Rifle Camp Road," Jamie said. "A little farther down."

"Right. I hear it driving when I'm close to the base. You know, when the weather gets better."

Gil was a bit unkempt, more so than their last visit. Khaki pants. What might have been the same shirt he'd worn when they met the previous week in the same it-needed-to-be-ironed condition.

Once inside the apartment Jamie was offered coffee, but it seemed more a pleasantry. They were walking to the living area, which looked hastily cleaned. No glasses on the table, but round brown rings. An empty ashtray coated with a fine gray dust.

"I'd have met you at the office," Jamie said.

"It's hard to get space," Gil said. "The conference room. It gets used a lot."

He took a sip of whatever he had in a mug and Jamie found himself wishing it was coffee although he suspected it wasn't.

"They're having a big closing at the end of the week."

Jamie didn't pick up on what Gil was getting at.

"I wasn't planning to go in until later today anyway."

"Oh."

"I'm not a lawyer," Gil said finally. "I don't have my own office."

"Oh."

"Look, I didn't mean to mislead you. I work at the firm and I'm Gil. Gil Christian. The firm name, Christian *and* Christian, that's my father and brother."

A gaping hole hung in the air. The mystery of Gil. How Gil got to be Gil. The curiosity he elicited with that tease of information.

"You want my story?"

He took a long sip, then began looking around, scouring the gaps in the cushions until he located the remote. He tapped on a few buttons and the screen brightened without sound.

"Like to have this on in the background."

Even with the TV on mute, there were comforting sounds in the apartment. The clock that ticked nosily from the kitchen. The fast movement of toddlers who lived upstairs.

"Here's the version I give out in bars whenever it comes up, which isn't often because like I said, I'm the one everyone likes to talk to. But when it does come up, it goes like this."

Gil inhaled.

Jamie stared at him blankly, his notepad in hand but his pen sitting in his shirt pocket. The TV screen was a series of hospital settings. It had to be a soap opera.

"Ready?" Gil asked.

When Jamie didn't answer, Gil continued.

"Went to the same New England school as my father and brother, and no, it wasn't Harvard. You ever hear of Bowdoin? Bowdoin, it's in Maine. I got into their fraternity and wasn't really feeling it. But it was what I was supposed to do. Then one Friday night, I'm a pledge, and they gather us into the basement and they have this pit they made with chairs on their sides and there's this big snake in the center and one of the guys has a rabbit he's holding."

Gil winced. He didn't like thinking about this, in the same way he hadn't liked thinking about Cindy. Only the second time he'd sat with Gil, and it was a look Jamie had seen.

"And you know what? I saw that and I turned around. Didn't think twice. I just left. Went back to my dorm and my roommate, the one my dad said was a loser because he smoked pot all day and listened to Jackson Browne and Laura Nyro and had no interest in fraternities and looking at my side of the room, with the beer pilsner on my desk and a wool pennant or that month's centerfold pasted over my bed, I knew who the loser was. Packed my bags, or should I say bag. Borrowed Ben's car keys. I never told him I was driving to Mexico, but you know, Ben was the guy who'd have given me the keys anyway."

"You drove from New England to Mexico?"

"Not in one night. I stopped. Slept in the backseat. Once in a really shit motel. The car was better."

"So, you're Gil Christian, but not the Christian written on the side of the building."

"Pretty much."

Gil nodded to Jamie who'd flipped open his book.

"I work for the firm, doing whatever. Some days it's delivering papers to the courthouse or dredging archives from the basement, but I do real work too. I'm pretty competent when I'm sober and they're not rocket scientists. It's a lot of house closings, wills that are standard. Just change the names on the documents."

Jamie took out his pen.

"I did the Low file. A lot of it, anyway. Put together the key man insurance package with a broker the firm uses."

Gil paused. "You sure I can't get you something."

"No, I'm fine."

Jamie's high school friends had mostly migrated to places like Hewitt and other towns around Greenwood Lake, their homes filled with furniture like Jamie's. Living room and bedroom sets bought at discount stores. Jamie looked around for hopeful signs of how a guy lived in an apartment complex that had tennis courts, but suspected Gil wasn't the best example. From deep within the kitchen, a Felix the Cat clock clicked its pendulum tail.

"That was my dad's idea. The insurance."

"How much?"

"Policy was for one hundred fifty thousand, I think. Maybe two hundred thousand. That range was pretty much the recommendation."

"Has Craig filed for it yet? Do you know?"

Gil laughed. Again, his sad laugh. "Cindy, shit. She was such a great girl. This really sucks."

Jamie knew he wasn't going to reach over and pat Gil's shoulder or do anything other than sit there. And Gil was good at getting back to what he needed to do.

"Craig's whatever. We all have our shit. He probably messed with the girls. Maybe Cindy. Who knows? He wasn't in the bar much. He has younger kids. Randall is . . . Randall was the more responsible one."

Gil waited for Jamie to finish writing, alert to the rhythm of the questions and answers.

"But getting his brother killed or doing it himself? No," Gil said. "Absolutely not."

It was the first time Jamie felt the case take any sort of shape. Gil's assurance. A probably hungover, and now drinking at one in the afternoon, legal assistant telling him with certainty to rule out a suspect. A certainty that felt right to Jamie. Something he could encase in a report.

FIFTEEN

"WHATCHA GOT?"

Bachman was all bright smiles. His voice as shiny as the look on his face.

Jamie sat as upright as possible and presented a file with neatly typed notes and some photocopies from the forensic lab he'd been asked to pass along.

"It's not much yet," he said. "But I'm developing some leads."

He cringed at the word "leads". He thought of *Barney Miller*. He sounded like a cop on a show like *Barney Miller*.

"Leads?" Bachman said. "Like real witnesses?"

"Well," Jamie said. "No one was in the bar at the time of the shooting. I think that's clear from Lorraine. She and Sage were the last to leave, other than the victims."

"Right. Right."

"We're working on the brother and the insurance policy. It's a side theory. Not sure if there's enough to change this from a straight robbery. Like it pretty much looked like from the start."

"When will you know?"

"Gianelli and Andres have him scheduled for a meeting. It's not clear if that'll mean anything. Even if he has the policy, is that enough of a motive?"

"And you're the expert?"

Jamie swallowed.

Bachman was shuffling papers absently, the way a person did while calculating his thoughts. Jamie stayed silent. Ashamed. He wanted nothing but accolades and if not accolades, at least a pat on the back. The attaboys that came with doing his job right.

"It's a shit case. No witnesses. There aren't going to be any." Bachman seemed to be apologizing in his way. Dialing back on the insult.

"I'll put the insurance reference in the report. Lieutenant will have a talk with the prosecutor running this. Tell him about the brother. See what they think. If they'll sign off on letting it go. Depending on what you find."

He flipped open a binder on his desk then closed it. One of the big books maintained for larger inquiries.

"DAs are used to cases that don't go well. Not the happy ending we all want."

Jamie thought that might be the sentence Bachman would seize on, to tie up all their briefings and what he ought to get used to.

"Listen," the sergeant said. "That's not what we tell the family. Not what we tell the press. We tell them there's hope. Right? Even a case like this, we always tell them that there's hope."

The extra coda. Bachman was throwing in the faith-based message Miucci often shared. For Miucci, it was a deep truth. There were cases that should have been solved that weren't, just as there were cases that should never have been solved that were. For Bachman, the words were what to say about a case that wasn't going anywhere but still needed the busy work done. A reminder to Jamie that even Gil was busy work. Bachman probably knew he'd have nothing. He hadn't even been on the list of people there the night of the murder. At least Jamie was doing his own witness interviews. Interacting with the two detectives assigned to lead the case. Looking at forensic files. He had that.

Bachman stood, seeming to use Jamie leaving as an excuse to stretch. Then he rounded his desk and grasped Jamie as he walked to the door, pulling him back. It was full and meaty, and Jamie jerked instinctively before the sergeant loosened his hold to a good old boys' grip.

"They're solid detectives, Gianelli and Andres," he said. "But don't let them get you caught up in their hero stuff. Their noble work."

An unexpected piece of advice for Jamie to carry forward.

"They lay it on a little too thick for me," Bachman said.

SIXTEEN

WHAT WERE THE EXACT RULES? HOW LONG WAS JAMIE supposed to wait until he called Missy again? Since Debra, he'd only seen a few girls for real dates. Fix ups put together by Steve and the other guys who had girlfriends and wives with cousins and sisters and young women they worked with. Beyond those blind dates, there'd been a legal secretary who liked to have early dinners the same time he did at Addie's. He took her to a movie and brought her back to his house and then never called her and she stopped showing up at the diner, which was a relief to him. Then there were the women he met at the Eagle's Nest and the Greenwood Lake bars, but those weren't dates at all.

After their dinner, he'd wanted to call Missy the next day but thankfully had stopped himself. Jamie sat with Nugget on the couch, stroking his ears and thinking the dog could use a bath. He smelled of tar. Just as Jamie rose to clear the last pot from the kitchen sink and make room for Nugget, the phone rang. His heart moved with the thought it was Missy.

At home, Jamie liked to answer the phone on the third ring. In the office, it was more of a game. A challenge if he was far from his desk. But at home, it was different. He never rushed to pick up a personal call.

"Hello," he said.

"This is Sandy."

The voice was unclear, like she was standing away from the receiver. He pictured a middle-aged woman in a house dress. A neighbor he'd met and immediately forgotten.

"Sandy?"

"Sandy. Sandy Santasiera."

Santasiera. He noticed she whispered each "S" in her name. Now he saw a woman, younger and thinner. Dark-haired. Her name was intriguing. A fog of the past few weeks formed around the girls he'd chatted up on campus and at Steele's. Nothing really came into focus. He couldn't recall having met anyone, not specifically. Jamie usually didn't give out his home number, but it wasn't unlisted.

"Do I know you, Sandy?"

"You don't know me, but like, aren't you looking for me?"

Aren't you looking for me? That blew off the fog.

"Listen, what is this?"

"I told you, it's Sandy. Someone told me the cops want to talk to me. Wanting information. Everything's confidential, isn't it? My name."

Sandy took a deep breath and it sounded like her fingernail scraped against the phone.

"This is between us," she said. "No one else."

In the background, a sudden movement sounded like the wind machine they used in movies. A man's voice yelled, "Get the fuck off the phone. Hang it up!" Sandy's voice was thinning, nowhere near the receiver. "Wait, just wait. Stop grabbing!" Then a dial tone.

SEVENTEEN

ANDRES AND GIANELLI HAD ARRANGED TO MEET JAMIE in a second-floor office for a discussion on Randall Low's brother. As always, both detectives were in sharp, well-tailored suits. Gianelli's was charcoal gray and Andres wore a blue pinstripe. Before they started the briefing, Linda, a part-timer on the civilian staff, stopped at the open door, asking if they were taking calls. Then she reminded the detectives she'd be off for rest of the week, listing the days. "Wednesday, Thursday *and* Friday."

"What days does she actually work?" Andres asked once she'd left.

Gianelli eyed the wooden door and elbowed it closed.

"Look at you," Gianelli began. "All wet behind the ears and getting time on a homicide."

"C'mon," Andres said, grabbing Jamie's shoulder in that familiar cop-mentor gesture. He guided Jamie towards a report on the desk.

"You're getting a refresher on bullets today."

Jamie thought he knew enough about bullets from the academy. Mostly, all the ways to quickly replace cartridges if, hopefully never, he found himself in a protracted gunfight.

"This'll be an advanced lesson, so to speak. Once the labs decipher where the bullets came from, looked at the little fingerprints, you gotta know what to do with the information," Andres said, rubbing his forehead. "In this case, not so helpful. The cartridges were .38 special. You ever heard of that?"

"Everyone's heard of that," Jamie said.

"Report says the gun's probably a Smith & Wesson 36. Everyone's heard of that, too. The Chiefs Special everyone uses. Have fun tracking that one down without a serial number."

"Should I look at Craig Low anyway? See what guns are registered to him?" Jamie asked.

"We'll see. You find anything decent on him?"

"I spoke to the law office that put the insurance package together. The administrator, he was pretty sure Craig wouldn't be involved. Seemed sure of that," Jamie said.

"Yeah, well. You think you know people. I mean look at that clown. Literally, that clown in Chicago, Gacy," Gianelli said. "What's his full name?"

"John Wayne," Andres answered. "John Wayne Gacy."

"Yeah, I can't with that shit. I just can't."

The two detectives worked so closely together, it was hard to tell whose office Jamie was standing in. Almost all the framed photos had them both. Bowling trophies held high. On a boat, the sun in their eyes, one holding on to a Bigmouth bass, the other with the rod in his hands. Some beefsteak with everyone in suits and flowered leis around their necks.

"The key man insurance, it's a big policy," Andres said. "That's why we're talking to him now."

"Didn't they just have the funeral?" Jamie asked.

"This is a homicide. We're not that polite," Gianelli answered. "He was supposed to be visiting us. A meeting here and his family lawyer with him. Low key. Not like he was getting arrested."

"Oh," Jamie said, after the briefest pause.

"Yeah. But then we got a phone call. Location changed."

All three were standing, Andres taking the lead out of the office.

The detectives had one of the nicer cars in the department. They weren't all that high up on the list. Not yet lieutenants. Somehow, they had a fully-decked Monte Carlo. Jamie pushed back the front seat and planted himself behind Gianelli, who explained the specifics as they drove.

"See. This is what everyone gets wrong. Low isn't under arrest. He's just being questioned. This whole—he needs a big-time lawyer, an expensive lawyer like Virgilio—that's not how it works." He swiveled so he could face Jamie. "We don't even have to Miranda a guy like that when we bring him in," he said. "Not required."

"He must think he needs a lawyer," Jamie said, wanting to make clear the point was understood.

"Yeah, well. Yeah, he does think that."

Craig Low had lawyered up. And not with the firm of Christian & Christian. He'd hired Pat Virgilio, a former Passaic County assistant prosecutor turned expensive defense lawyer. He did white collar crimes. He represented reputed gang members who worked the Newark docks. He took healthy retainers. He wore a rose gold pinky ring, the initial "P" encrusted in diamonds.

Virgilio's office was quite different from the functional building where Jamie had met Gil Christian. This law office had the full upper floor of the glass and steel two-story set on a wide commercial lot. Lots of leafy plants and other modern details. What most struck Jamie when he entered the conference room was the pasty Craig Low. But then, he was standing next to his lawyer, a man still tanned from a Christmas vacation in the Bahamas. The recent trip was mentioned over handshakes with Andres and Gianelli, along with other details. Jamie was introduced as "our extra guy, in case we need backup." Hearty chuckles with that.

After the introductions, all the brightness leveled off. A secretary appeared with a pitcher of water on a tray along with an ice bucket and glasses, and a tight skirt that none of the men commented on. Only Craig Low seemed to give her a second look. Andres began the questions.

"We are sorry, Mr. Low. It's a terrible loss. Please understand this is just a necessary part of the investigation. An ugly business. We're sorry it has to be this way."

"Mr. Low completely understands," Virgilio answered. "We've reviewed why he needs to have this discussion. Obviously. He knows this is part of the process. A necessary part, as you say."

"Right," Craig said.

"Let's start with who your brother knew that he might have had trouble with," Andres said. "Pretty girls working for you. Did he ever have an issue with any of their husbands or boyfriends?"

Craig shook his head. "The whole bar thing fell in our lap. One of our neighbors, our lawyer . . . " He coughed into his hand. "Our business lawyer knew our family. My dad owned a pub years ago. Not a bar like RJ's, more of a regular pub in the Fourth Ward, down by President Street. Packaged goods. That was supposed to be the family business, what Randall and I were going to take over, but the Cork and Keg closed down when the neighborhood turned, and we went on. I worked in concrete pouring. Randall was in auto salvage, then went to Allied. Jon Christian, the older one, he knew the owners of RJ's. They were looking to get out. He thought he could put together something where we were back in the family business."

Both Jamie and Gianelli took notes.

"So, the girls, that was just part of the business. Not what attracted us to RJ's at all," Craig said.

"Neither of you ever had any involvement or relationships?"

"Relationships?"

"With any of the girls."

"I didn't bartend. That was Randall and Frank. I was barely there."

"And your brother? He wasn't friendly with the girls?"

"We owned it less than a year. We were still figuring out how much Schlitz to order every week, how to keep the lines for the keg clean. Two of the regular girls who'd been at RJ's for years left and went to work at the Belvidere with the old owners, so we had to figure that out too, how to hire new ones." Craig pushed back his hair with his right hand. "That was a nightmare. Ads in the paper. I got calls at the house and let me tell you, that wasn't a pleasant evening with my wife the night those came in."

Everyone but Jamie was laughing.

"I'd guess not," Andres said.

"Our wives were on us like hawks. Even if that was our interest, we'd have had to been like super spies to do anything and get away with it."

"Did Randall owe anyone money?"

"No."

"Play the horses?"

"No."

"Have bad habits?"

"No."

Gianelli broke in. "Tell me about the insurance," he said.

"The key man policy?" Craig asked.

Virgilio interrupted. "I have some papers my client is willing to turn over. They're technically covered by attorney-client privilege, but he's willing to partially waive that."

Craig sipped his water.

"You see that?" Gianelli said to Andres when they were back in the car.

"The guy's right-handed."

"Not that it proves much. Just doesn't rule him out entirely."

"Left-hand shooters are so much better," Andres agreed. "Easier to pick those guys out in a crowd."

"What'd you think?" Andres asked Jamie.

"Me?"

"Yeah, you. What'd you think?"

"I saw him tapping his leg," Jamie said. "Saw that under the table. But other than that, I didn't really notice much."

"Tapping his leg. That's good. That's good," Andres said, stopping the conversation while he negotiated the merge onto the highway, accelerating behind a much-dented station wagon.

"Did you notice he was doing that the minute he sat down? Not when we started in with talk about the policy. Usually means he's a nervous guy all around."

"Oh."

"What'd you think of his answers?"

Jamie tried to put together an overall impression. They'd been given the letters from Craig's lawyers at Christian & Christian, begging him to sign the insurance documents. Constant reminders. What Virgilio called cover-your-ass letters. Jamie paired that with what he noticed about Craig seated at the conference table.

"I thought he was believable. I mean, I believed him."

"Me, too," Andres said. "I think he's not our guy."

Gianelli piped in. "You believed everything?"

"Well maybe not the 'I was barely there' part. That, you know, was probably bullshit," Andres said.

"Yeah," Gianelli said. "I saw him looking at the secretary." He reached into his inside pocket and pulled out a toothpick, slowly peeling the wrapper. "Too bad he's not left-handed. Could cross him clean off the list."

"The cover-your-ass letters from his lawyers pretty much get him off the list."

"See," Gianelli said. "That's where I differ. This whole thing, the setup. Maybe that was a ruse. Maybe he was dragging his feet to make it look like he wasn't interested, not interested in the insurance. You can throw the policy in with a girl or two behind their wives' back. Too early to rule either of those out. Maybe one's still a good angle."

"Maybe anything," Andres said.

His partner was answering before Andres finished his brief sentence.

"Damn right, maybe anything."

EIGHTEEN

JAMIE COULDN'T REALLY SAY WHY HE HADN'T GONE TO Andres and Gianelli about the phone call from Sandy. He was sure it was real. He felt that. But he was just as sure he hadn't handled it correctly. Had he done something wrong that witnesses were calling him? Revealed too much during interviews instead of staying silent and asking questions? She called him specifically, which also raised the issue of keeping the communication confidential. Just between them. She'd hung up before clarifying that point.

His actions after the call weren't much better. He hadn't noted the exact time nor written down the exact words when they were fresh in his mind. He wasn't even sure he'd heard her name correctly and had no idea how to spell it. Since the call, he'd placed a pen and pad next to the bowl with ripening bananas on the kitchen counter. The spot closest to the phone. Even if he was flushed with nerves and excitement, as he had been with the first call, he'd be reminded. Go slow. Observe. Make sure to take care of all the information properly. He told himself if it was legitimate, he'd get another one and figure out what to do then.

He was also waiting on a different phone call. He'd left a message for Missy with a young woman he assumed was a roommate. A young woman who hadn't been friendly. She hadn't said, "Oh, hi! This is Carol or Joan or whoever," when he'd called. Instead, she'd made him feel anonymous and unimportant in the life of Missy and her apartment. But they'd had a nice time together. He enjoyed her company. He was in the zone. Not in a monogamous relationship with her. Not even close to that. But not really interested in scouting the girls coming out of their exercise classes, maneuvering for phone numbers. After his workout, he left Steele's straight away instead of stopping for the water or Gatorade he often sipped slowly at a table.

Jamie took Route 46 through Clifton, passing the exit for Allwood Road, then passing the exit for Gil's apartment complex with its pool and tennis courts and the sleek layouts with modern kitchens and sliding windows, not casements with pulleys.

He thought about an apartment like that. How buying new furniture and scraping off wallpaper hadn't transformed his living space the way he'd wanted. Girls he took back to his house saw him as instant marriage material, as if he'd been waiting for them so he could plant a swing set in the rear yard. That's how the house presented him.

He'd driven a little aimlessly, eventually stopping at the mall and parking in a space next to Ben's Toyland. Jamie felt restless and distracted and lingered in the food court with a slice of pizza and large Coke, not sure what to do with himself. He wasn't ready to drive home or in the mood to see Steve, much less his other friends from high school who still were single and had a house together off Skyline Drive and went out every night of the week. The friends who were married and invited him to barbecues in the summer were packed in for the winter with their wives and kids all under the age of five and family obligations. He dumped his paper plate and cup into the trash and walked past the toy store and the record store and the sporting goods store and the store that had both *Animal House* posters and plastic bonsai trees in their front window, unsure how to lose the feeling he was waiting for Missy's call.

The loudspeaker calling for a manager in the jewelry department interrupted his thoughts and he caught a glimpse of himself standing in the vestibule of Macy's with a few vending machines and not many options for the night. An elderly woman with a kerchief tight around her unkept hair was heaving a pair of shopping bags with distinct black and white stripes as she shuffled to the exit doors. She was the exact woman his undercover work was designed to protect. Though the mall was in the suburbs, he still felt an obligation to guide her to the bus stop, which was a decent walk across the parking lot and her likely destination. He'd have to identify himself as a police officer. She'd never trust him otherwise.

NINETEEN

"I KNEW IT. THE SECOND I GOT INTO THE DRIVEWAY this morning. Like a fucking ice rink. I knew it."

Gary had gathered extra tactical equipment and was securing his radio into its holster.

"Route 80," he said. "You don't even have to tell me, Liz. It's out on Route 80. Am I right?"

"You are so right. Route 80 about a mile past the turnoff for that electric supply warehouse," Elizabeth answered.

"Black ice." Gary shook his head. "That is the worst." As he grabbed his field jacket, he pointed to Jamie. "Warren's delayed coming in. He called a few minutes ago. You'll have to ride with me."

The late morning was shiny with sun and melting snow that was mostly slush, but there were frozen patches Jamie had to watch for as he drove along a stretch of highway that'd been all ice an hour earlier. The patrol car radio clicked and made static noises. Gary picked up the handheld and responded with their location.

"You ever have a fatality?" Gary asked.

"Once," Jamie answered. "Just the one time."

"Sucks, you know. It really does."

Jamie hoped the ambulance would be there when they arrived. That always made things easier. Or so he'd been told. A Ford LTD had hopped the divider, crossed into oncoming traffic, and found a resting spot wedged into the right guardrail. The two cars that had spun out trying to avoid the Ford crashed into each other and were blocking the fast lane with tires and fenders and other debris scattered wide.

"See if you can start directing those cars backing up," Jamie said.

Gary pulled cones and some flares from the trunk and went with Jamie to a part of the highway where they might clear a full lane and get some of the rush hour traffic moving. Jamie negotiated his way onto the road. Hard packed snow had been plowed to the sides, taking up much of the blacktop. He'd forgotten to bring gloves.

As he'd hoped, the ambulance got to the scene before them. No one was dead, but the Ford's driver was unconscious and remained so the entire time. Jamie busied himself measuring tire marks and photographing the busted guardrail. He conferred with the tow truck driver from Pietro's, then went back to his thoughts on black ice and the difference that one or two degrees in temperature might have made in melting the surface. The man in his nice pants and starched shirt, slumped over the wheel of the gray Ford would never have lost control of his car. The girl with the macrame belt and broken arm, blood running through her strawberry blonde hair, wouldn't have crashed her Corolla into a white panel van trying to avoid a head-on collision with the Ford as it careened across the highway. None of it would have happened. He'd carry the weight of the accident scene and its randomness for the day.

The rest of the morning was typing up the report and looking over his schedule for that week's undercover shift, once again pretending to be a grandmother at a bus stop near Meyer Brothers to catch drug users pushing women who really were in their seventies onto sidewalks. Stolen purses filled with ancient Social Security cards encased in plastic shields and balls of tissues and wallets with family photographs and coins and a few singles. Rarely anything larger than a five-dollar bill. There were always envelopes stuffed with coupons.

"These guys don't take a break in the winter?"

"Nope. When you gotta get high, you gotta get high. Even in February," Gary answered.

"Just asking."

Missy returned his call that night. Jamie had finished with dinner. The dishes were cleaned and the house airing from a trout he'd fried. Both the kitchen window and back door were open. Even huddled in the other room with Nugget pressed to his side, it was cold. Very cold. He considered downing a few shots though it was rare he drank anything stronger than beer at home, because having a Jack and Coke or some Wild Turkey would mean drinking alone. He was already living alone. Drinking alone wasn't something he'd tack onto that. Technically, it was "lite" beer and two or three some nights was fine. That wasn't drinking. He was on his second Miller's when the phone rang. He stood and grabbed the receiver. In his heart, he knew it was Missy. Not Sandy. Not Steve wanting to go out. Not anyone else.

"Hello."

"Hi. It's Missy."

"Hey."

"You called a few days ago. I wanted to call you back earlier. It's hard sometimes. To get the apartment empty so I can talk."

"Right."

"I wanted to say this in person. But maybe on the phone is better. I really don't know."

Jamie didn't answer, letting the girl on the other end of the line take form. Her soft hair and barrette. Her tiny hands. All of her coming into focus.

"I really liked dinner with you. I really did."

A gust of frigid air blew from the kitchen.

"It's just, I have a lot of roommates. They're not my real friends, but the people I live with. I can't . . . ," she said. "I can't risk getting you in any trouble. It wouldn't be me. I just have all these roommates."

"Missy?"

"And you're a cop. I really can't see you right now."

"Missy?"

"I have to go."

Jamie thought he heard sniffling. But maybe he just wished that. He put the phone into its cradle, shut the window and double locked the door.

The TV screen was a vista of prairie grass. Whatever show he'd been watching had ended and been replaced with something else already mid-episode. Jamie eased himself into the cushions, back with Nugget and onto his third beer.

TWENTY

HE'D HEARD HER WHOLE STORY.

Cindy's boyfriend, Brad Rogan. They began seeing each other when she was a waitress at Hiram's, up in Sparta. Her hometown. Pretty in her red and white uniform. He'd bothered her for her phone number and she'd said no the first night. But then he kept coming back and eventually she gave in. She'd already dropped out of high school and was looking for a way to move out of her mother's house that was basically a trailer.

Brad was the one who suggested RJ's. There were new owners. They were desperate for dancers and she could flash them a fake ID. They'd never know and if they knew, they'd never care. They were worrying about new business things like transferring the liquor license, appearing before state boards, keeping the bartender who covered day shifts and wouldn't rob them blind. A pretty blonde who'd bring in all the college boys, the fact she may or may not be eighteen wouldn't be a huge concern.

Brad liked the money Cindy was making but he was jealous of the guys that gave her big tips. He rarely sat in when she was working, the owners didn't like it and told him so.

"It makes her nervous," they'd said to him. "Not a good feeling for anyone, you know?"

They were nice enough, though. Always gave him drinks on the house if he showed up at the end of the night to drive her home.

That was the story from Cindy.

What were the odds? What were the fucking odds that Brad would be in jail on January 14th? He'd actually been there since the 11th. Got drunk on a Thursday night and started his weekend early. What were the odds?

It was just his luck that Brad was locked up that night. Brad, that piece of shit.

TWENTY-ONE

ALBERTO'S WAS A LUNCHEONETTE, ONCE KNOWN AS THE "Bonton" until it changed hands. That was the name Gil had used when telling Jamie to meet him there.

"Can you meet me at the Bonton around one?" Gil had asked.

"One o'clock? You mean for lunch?"

"Perfect time. I feel like having an empanada."

Alberto was Italian, originally from Palermo, but Jamie learned over small talk waiting for Gil that he'd stayed with some relatives in Argentina for a while. That explained the fried pockets of dough on the grill behind the counter.

When Alberto moved to the register Jamie began to pivot on the fake leather stool, too big to make a complete turn. Tired of looking at the grill while he waited for Gil, Jamie inventoried the shelves. Alberto's carried the usual things: aspirin, packaged goods, rolling papers, and Spaldeen High-Bounces. But there were also tweezers, cheap mascara, table fans and, as it was the week leading up to Valentine's Day, heart-shaped cardboard boxes with assorted chocolates. The kind that Jamie began to buy for his aunt when he was ten and discovered he could make money collecting glass bottles in the neighborhood and cashing them in for pennies.

"They smell great, huh?"

Gil had clapped Jamie on the back and in one motion, occupied the stool next to him. In the short time he'd been sitting, Jamie gathered Alberto had more of a takeout business. He watched as the dark man with thick black hair cut into a shrub-like bulb wrapped empanada after empanada, then pressed the warm wax paper into the hands of men who came in streams. Gil mentioned it was lightening up and Jamie imagined the lunch crowd rush peaked at 12:30.

The Bonton's window offered a solid view of RJ's, sitting catty-cornered on a stretch of Madison Ave. The door was no longer padlocked. The rugs would have been professionally cleaned. Jamie wondered about the business reopening. With enough alcohol and enough go-go dancers, there was a crowd willing to forget it'd been a crime scene weeks earlier.

"What'd you think?" Gil asked. Jamie was on his third empanada.

"It reminds me of a pierogi, except the outside's flaky." Jamie chewed thoughtfully. "Like pie dough."

"You know, I've never had a pierogi."

"Really?"

Gil waived Alberto over, asking for a Dr. Pepper. "In a bottle if you have one of those cold."

"I'll take a look."

Gil turned when Alberto had left and whispered to Jamie, "I have some names for you."

"Names?"

He slid a folded sheet of yellow-lined paper to Jamie, scattering a few crumbs as it moved.

"You know, people around here don't always like to talk to cops."

"True," Jamie said. "I'm finding that out."

"Yes," Gil said. "But me, like I told you, I have that talent. People tell me shit. I mean, not that I want to be cruel. I don't mind listening to people. But it's never been helpful in any real sense."

Gil picked at his pants, noticing he'd pushed some crust onto his lap.

"Helpful," Jamie repeated absently.

"Helpful," Gil said. "Until now. There's something to be gained, don't you think? People want to open up to me and I can poke around in their stories. Get them to topics I find interesting."

"What topics do you find interesting?"

"Cindy," Gil said. "I always found Cindy to be interesting."

She was just a girl who'd been in the wrong place at the wrong time. Found herself in the middle of a botched robbery. Gil's voice made Jamie acutely aware of the file that'd been put together for her. It was unreasonably thin and in that moment it felt wrong. Her personal information might have been only half a page with Cindy's full name, her mother's name, and the most recent address for each of them. Another page devoted to her boyfriend who'd been in jail the night of her murder. Bachman said talking to him had been a complete waste.

What the hell was he going to know about any of this?

Bachman's ears had reddened, giving a clipped description to Jamie.

The sergeant was testy to work with. He was all smiles and back slaps at the blessing of the bikes that began the riding season every May. Lot of laughs those times. Not so much at the station. It could have been the case itself. Jamie was having trouble getting his hands around what he should be doing. It would have been a throwaway, another tough one to unravel except that Randall was more than a tavern owner. He and his brother had roots in town. They'd taken over sponsoring the softball team. The Lows paid for the uniforms and had thrown beer parties every weekend the previous spring. Practice was due to start in a month following the training schedule of the major league teams, and that'd keep the name RJ's afloat. The local newspaper. The community. They expected answers. They expected the crime to be solved, no matter how unlikely everyone in the department seemed to think that would be.

Bachman had Jamie on what was a loose working group. A few other patrols who spent most of their time on foot and who'd been sent to canvas the neighborhood for witnesses, it being known there wouldn't be any useful ones. Those days they'd taken borrowed used cars so they wouldn't stick out, to no benefit. Andres and Gianelli nominally in charge of the finer details. Ballistics. Forensics. Strategy. Sparing enough time to be thorough with Jamie when he needed them while itching to work on their own cases. Crimes with the potential for actual convictions. The material collected for RJ's was enough to feed to the news stories. Leads were being investigated. The whole insurance policy angle got covered. That wasn't enough for Gil, who'd gone poking around.

"So?" Jamie asked. "What is all this stuff? How'd you get it?"

"I talked to the guys that I know live in the neighborhood. Got them to share what they'd been hearing?"

"And?"

"I got you some names. Someone who works late security at the plant across the street said he heard a car door slam. That sounds like the most promising lead. What I was told, he thought it was around the time of the shooting and mentioned it to someone else. There was this other person who was coming home late. Real late. Saw a guy in the parking lot when the outside lights were already turned off. That's the best I could get."

Jamie hesitated. The information was more than anyone in the department had come up with so far. He needed a response to Gil that didn't include that fact.

"I'm not the lead detective. I'm not really in charge."

Gil took a long sip of his Dr. Pepper, the way he took in his Jameson. One of his comforts. He reached over and laid his hand on the folded paper he'd offered to Jamie, still resting near the paper plate with its crumbled balls of wax paper and oil stains.

"You're smart. Fancy titles don't impress me."

"I don't know if I can make this really go anywhere, but thanks. I'll do right with whatever you have for me."

"Not too much yet. Gotta be patient. This stuff percolates through the neighborhood, you know. There's a buzz around. You tuck in your files for the day, go home. But what happened at RJ's, it's still breathing here."

Jamie hoped the witness statements were real. Not fluff coming out at the chemical plant. The barber shop. Wherever people talked. Locals so close to it and wanting to seem knowing. He'd been warned about those kinds of witnesses, just like the ones who say they'd been in the bathroom the whole night.

Alberto's. The Bonton. Whatever the luncheonette's name. It wasn't the most comfortable place to sit and have a private conversation, even though there were barely any customers at half past the hour, when Gil and Jamie were finished with empanadas and going over Gil's legwork. Alberto was at the register ringing up the remnants of the lunch crowd. A trucker or two passing through. Addie's would have been better. Grilled cheese and bacon instead of empanadas. Jamie knew why Gil wanted to meet on Madison.

He walked by RJ's, circling the block on his way to his car. Against a stuccoed wall gritty with dirt was the silhouette of a woman. She'd been alive in neon on nights the bar was open, advertising the real girls inside. Sandwiches and burgers and cold beer and rolled up dollar bills might happen again. Maybe soon. Along with dust motes of memory. Whatever Randall and Cindy had lived through in their final moments. Had the robbery lasted five minutes? Ten? Jamie wished he knew.

TWENTY-TWO

BEFORE TAKING OVER THE TAVERN, RANDALL LOW HAD been a color mixer at Allied Textile. The newspaper also noted he'd been a naval flight officer who served two tours of duty in the Vietnam War, a member of both St. Paul's Episcopal Church and the Paterson Orange Lodge. Having been gunned down in the tavern he'd purchased with Craig nine months earlier, he left behind his brother and also a wife and their son. Both his parents were still alive. There were aunts and uncles, nieces and nephews.

Jamie looked at the partial obituary tagged onto the bottom of an article entitled "Search for Witnesses in Bar Owner Killing." It ran in the same news section that reported "Robert Keaton, age 74 born in Paterson and most recently living in Virginia had died." In another headline further down the page, "Alan Hermann aged 76." The clipping from the paper detailing the specifics of the crime victim's life found its way into police files. It didn't seem like enough.

In spite of his work on the RJ's homicides and the increase in his responsibilities, Jamie was still on rotating patrol. That designation meant he hadn't been assigned an actual partner for some time. Billy Sanchez, who he'd worked with quite a bit, had been transferred to the Sheriff's Department and Jamie noticed in his place, they'd been pairing him lately with one of the guys he'd been told about in the academy. A guy with a next door neighbor who was a lieutenant or even higher. A guy who couldn't scramble over a six-foot wall even in his prime, which was several years past. Never able to run a mile in even close to seven minutes. Henry Falcione had been passed around from partner to partner and it seemed like it was Jamie's turn. The upside was that Henry was quite happy to stay at the station while Jamie worked the homicide case, not questioning the time that Jamie was taking. There'd been no need for Jamie to explain a fairly convoluted assignment he'd just received.

Earlier that day, Bachman had called Jamie down to his office, muttered a few words and sent him to interview Cindy's mother as part of a follow up. There'd been a statement in one of the files from a dancer named Tina Shalant about underaged girls, a fact that was obvious from the information on Cindy in the file. Because someone had made a fuss, openly questioning the practice, the paperwork needed some beefing up to at least give the appearance the department was looking into the rumors. Not that there was anything to be done.

It was known that the prior owners had been sloppy and began turning a blind eye once they were on their way out anyway. Girls seventeen, maybe younger had been working for them. Randall and Craig agreed to be watchful when they applied for their liquor license. They didn't have enough connections to stay clear of the Paterson Excise Board, who'd crackdown on irregularities and shut businesses down for a night or two. Then they found out how tough it was to run the tavern and keep customers in their seats.

No one wanted to give Craig Low a hard time if he'd slipped up or been taken in with a particularly good fake ID, not at that point. But there'd been no official inquiries on the allegations and the files needed to be perfected and that triggered second interviews, including the one with Mrs. Sutter.

"It's bullshit," Bachman said. "Go get a statement from her and make it look good. Rod Gaines did the first interview and he's lazy. Miucci will be pissed if that's the only one. It really doesn't matter, just get it done."

On his way to the thick paneled door that Jamie had been seeing a lot of, the sergeant barked a final instruction.

"Listen to me, Palmieri. Don't get into it with her. It'll look like harassment."

Gil had told Jamie there'd been a small memorial for Cindy that he'd attended, with Lorraine the only person he recognized at Gorley's Funeral Home. He'd paid for the arrangements after he went to see Cindy's mother to offer his condolences and asked when services would be held. She hadn't needed to say that a few dollars would be appreciated. Unlike Randall, Cindy hadn't been mentioned in the papers. The information from Gil and the pitiful interview notes from Gaines gave Jamie his starting points.

For more preparation, Jamie read the interviews from the Carmine family, who'd painted a flattering picture of themselves, selling RJ's to the Lows because of Richard's daughter. She'd turned eleven and the kids were talking in school. Personally, Richard had been reluctant to sell. The place was a goldmine, according to his statements. "You know what I got for a roast beef sandwich at lunch? And from guys working down the street at the auto body shops. Not the owners. The guys rotating tires. I kind of hated taking their money."

It wasn't all that illuminating. Jamie doubted getting an additional statement from Cindy's mother on the underage dancing would be, either. He set the paperwork on the side credenza as he put on his coat and made his exit known to Henry.

"I'm going out for one of the follow-up interviews," Jamie said.

The man nodded, barely raising his eyes above the paper's morning edition he'd taken off Jamie's desk, folded poorly to the comics.

"Be back in about an hour or so."

"Sure thing," Henry said. "I'll be here unless there's a call."

Jamie checked his notes for Cindy's mother's address. That was the most useful information from the interview with Marlene Sutter that'd already taken place. Jamie's would add to the file and make Cindy's case notes thicker with pages showing effort. Someone was looking to see who had killed her.

The drive out Route 80 had the landscape changing quickly. There were blackened snowbanks bordering the highway as there'd been in Paterson, but further west gave way to scenic rest stops and rows of pines and growing suburbs just off the exits. He continued onto Route 15 North, passing the Picatinny Arsenal and Tomahawk Lake.

Marlene lived in Sparta, towards the Delaware Water Gap where Jamie went hiking in the summer with friends. The interview was taking him that far from Paterson. There were no familiar buildings to remind him who he was. He was unmoored but also freed. On that drive along barely paved roads, busy work meant to load Cindy's file, something opened up in Jamie. He wasn't the beat cop on patrol. He was the police officer assigned to investigate a murder.

Getting out of the car, he felt different. Adjusting his hat, patting his front pocket for his notebook, then walking to what looked like the smallest house he'd ever seen. Pale blue. Empty window boxes. A propane tank in the rear. No car anywhere. Dropped in the middle of a dirt track and not even a street number, just the strange, simple address. Island Patch Road.

It was a wonder Cindy stayed as long as she had, which, according to Gil, was until April the previous year. By then, she had her driver's license, if not a high school diploma. And, of course, her fake ID. And Brad's apartment to move into. For that week or two until Brad revealed himself, she must have thought she had it made.

Jamie knocked softly at first, increasing the power in his fist after a few failed attempts at an answer. A heater with lines running inside was pumping, so it was likely someone was home. Waiting for a response, he noticed a stream behind the fencing. It brought him back to an afternoon catching sunfish with his mother's last boyfriend. Doug had weighed the fish in his hands, then instructed a nine-year-old Jamie to throw the sunnies back. The unexpected memory was interrupted by the door opening. A woman with soapy hands regarded Jamie. She looked to be in her mid-thirties.

"Are you Marlene Sutter?"

"I'm Marlene."

"We spoke on the phone. I'm from Paterson," Jamie said, indicating his badge and experiencing that mix of pride with a slice of embarrassment, knowing that he'd pressed his chest forward.

"This is more stuff about Cindy?"

"Yes." Jamie waited but the woman stood idly with her hands at her sides. "May I come in, Mrs. Sutter?"

"Marlene," she said. "Call me Marlene."

He followed her to the kitchen where assorted dishes sat in a rack to the right of the sink, taking up almost all the counter space and threatening to tip over. Not sure what to do in the moment, Jamie offered to help dry them. Like the interview with Lorraine, he felt invasive in the home.

"I'll just leave them in the rack."

With that, Marlene squeezed her hands on a striped towel, then threw it on top of an overturned bowl and headed towards her living room. She pulled a balled-up afghan off a small easy chair and folded it quickly.

"Here," she said. "You can sit here."

"Thank you."

"They came to tell me personally, the police. That's how I found out. A nice man from the town here. I guess that's how it's done. Your department makes a call to the local police station. We don't get that much activity here. I think he was uncomfortable. I felt sorry for him, to be honest. He was very nice. A real gentleman."

"I'm sorry," Jamie said. "I really am."

"She'd just turned eighteen. Not even a month before."

"Do you have pictures of her?" He hadn't planned to ask that question but thought it would be something to focus on and get the conversation flowing though he wasn't entirely sure how best to pivot to RJ's and have Mrs. Sutter confirm that her still teenage daughter had been dancing in bars and what she'd known about it. Get a statement on who she thought might be responsible for setting that up. It was easy to see why Gaines hadn't gone into any of that.

"I'll get them." Marlene regarded her hands, only recently dried. "You stay here. I'll be right back."

She returned with an album and a plastic bag of loose photographs. Those appeared to be more recent. Cindy and her friends at the beach. Cindy getting ready for her junior prom. Jamie noticed a dark-haired girl next to her in several of them. Had he been right, imagining Sandy's coloring?

"Who's that one girl with your daughter?"

"Which girl?"

"Here." Jamie pointed.

"That's Sandy. That's her best friend."

Hearing the present tense was jarring. He looked over at the dishes, away from Marlene, not wanting to see if she noticed how she was speaking about Cindy. Jamie understood in the smallest way that Marlene inhabited the in-between space where the unbearable thing life had thrown at her wasn't fully processed. She wasn't yet in her new reality. And then the name Sandy. He'd wanted to bring her up and was pleased how she'd come out naturally in the conversation. Better to get back on track with the interview and away from the increasing tightness he felt and how he'd never been trained to deal with Marlene and her grief. He wasn't hardened or stoic, the stance he'd seen modeled by older officers discussing their cases. Her sadness made him uncomfortable. The perfect time to ask how he might locate Sandy.

"Does she live nearby?"

"I don't know where Sandy lives exactly, but I think she's close to Cindy, around the same area. She's a few months ahead of Cindy. Left school a little earlier, moved in with her boyfriend a little earlier. The girls were similar. Different timing, that's all."

"So you're saying that you don't have an address. Do you have her number?"

Marlene shook her head.

"No number. Last time I spoke with her, she called here. You know. Recently."

Marlene took a moment for herself.

"Her last name's Cicero, I believe. Sandy Cicero. Something like that. I don't know the spelling."

"Her boyfriend's name? Could the listing for the apartment be in his name?"

"I have no idea. I don't know his name, or anything about their apartment."

"Where are her parents? Local?"

"They'd be in the book, no?" Marlene said. "Probably Jefferson. One of those towns. The girls weren't in high school together but the kids around here all get together, you know, socially."

Jamie wrote every part of it down. The questions he'd asked. The unhelpful answers. He went back to the photographs. Cindy in a school play, wearing the padded shoulders and cinched waist of a 1940s dress.

"She was Adelaide," Marlene said. "Miss Adelaide in *Guys and Dolls*."

The pin curl wig wasn't especially flattering, but the girl was obviously Cindy. Still so pretty.

"She kept in touch with her teacher. That Mrs. De Carlo. The drama teacher. Maybe she has something that would interest you."

Cindy's high school drama teacher. Jamie forced himself to add the name into his notes while Marlene smiled and nodded at her contribution.

"She was a teenager. At that age when we weren't expected to get on so well. But I know she thought the world of Mrs. De Carlo. They had a nice relationship."

Jamie suspected he was trudging over areas that'd been covered, but Marlene enjoyed the conversation. She'd have kept going with it.

"Tell me about Brad."

"Brad?"

"Did Cindy know him long?"

She began coughing. A dryness had caught in her throat. Marlene excused herself, padding towards her neat, compact kitchen where she ran the faucet into two glasses, handing one to Jamie when she returned. He took a small, polite sip of tap water.

"Brad," she said. "I'll tell you about Brad. Lucky as hell he was in jail that night. That's what I'll tell you. Lucky as hell."

TWENTY-THREE

THE PLAN WAS FOR JAMIE TO SPEND THE MORNING WITH Andres and Gianelli reviewing the file to prepare for another of the second-round interviews. A developing theme for Jamie. Go follow up on the questions the first guy messed up with. That was the call he'd received. This time the meeting would be with Brad Rogan. Gianelli was distracted when Jamie got to the office and not all that interested in Brad as a witness. Instead, the detective busied himself recreating the crime scene.

"This is what I don't understand. The under-the-counter safe or drawer or whatever you call it. That was never opened."

"Craig Low said it wasn't used to keep money. That it's where Randall kept his gun. The day bartender said the same thing. That he never used it for cash. He only half-knew the .38 was there. His exact words, 'half-knew'."

"Right, so the gun was out for the night. It was in Randall's pocket 'cause he already walked Lorraine to her car, plus he had the night deposits, so the gun was going home with him."

"Right," Andres said.

"So, the drawer wasn't opened during the robbery. How did the guy robbing the bar know there wasn't money there."

"You don't know he didn't look. The drawer was closed, but it might have been opened at some point," Andres said. Clearly thinking while he was talking, he added, "But that doesn't make any sense. It's a robbery. It's chaotic. The drawer got stuck. It didn't open and close easily. The wood on the side was all splintered. If it was opened at some point, who would have bothered closing it?"

"Yes!" Gianelli yelled. "Yes. You see where I'm going. It was under the counter where those secret drawers always are. But the guy robbing the place isn't interested in looking."

His partner slanted his eyes to a spot on the floor where a half inch of cellophane glowed in the sunlight.

"Let's think about this for a minute. Guys who rob bars are usually in kind of a hurry. I mean, have you ever gone on a call and seen a place that wasn't a hellhole? Nobody's ever straightening stools and sweeping broken glass on their way out. Okay? And things at RJ's pretty much went to shit, so he's wanting to get out extra fast," Andres said. "But then you got him hiding upstairs, he's planned the whole night. Why not rip the drawer open and see what's there?"

"Didn't do that. Didn't bother. Either he panicked or there's some other reason," Gianelli said.

"Either way, the drawer was never opened," Jamie said in a soft voice. He was thinking along with the two detectives, adapting to their process. Playing with ideas that didn't give clear answers but added to the stockpile. Another piece to the larger puzzle.

Andres and Gianelli became silent, working a new and complicating fact into the accepted scenario. With nothing to add, Jamie looked around the office and over to their fishing picture. The pier was vaguely familiar, possibly Greenwood Lake during the day. Jamie thought he might have passed it on the way to one of the many bars he went to with Steve.

Eventually, they moved on from the drawer, discussing the timing for Jamie's meeting with Brad. Even though he'd been in jail the night of the shooting, the boyfriend was considered an important enough witness, worth another talk.

"They already took his statement. Not a lot of good information there," Andres said.

"All I'm saying." Gianelli made this point slowly. "What I'm saying is that maybe—maybe—when we talk to him again, we make sure to have more background on him, see if we can trip him up if he's lying. That's all. That is what I am saying."

"He was in jail, for Chrissakes. I mean, is there a better alibi, 'cause I don't know. That seems like the best one to me."

"Yeah, he's got an alibi. He wasn't there. So maybe he didn't shoot the two of them. It wasn't the whole jealous boyfriend thing. But it could be something other than robbery. The supposed robbery. Could be drugs. Could be he was dealing. Could be he had her dealing." Gianelli raised his hands. "You never know."

"The supposed robbery," Andres said, giving Gianelli a look.

The two of them went back and forth. Jamie listened, hanging on their words. Their demeanor. The way that Andres and Gianelli made arguments off one another.

"And why do you always say that? Supposed robbery. Like what else, other than some wild card drug theory, might it have been?" Andres said.

Gianelli was back at it. The crime scene. Jamie read the expression of someone reenacting the logistics over and over in his mind.

"It don't sit right with me. The idea that she got shot first. That's not how those things work. He would've been pressing Randall. Finding out where the money was. I mean, what'd she have? A night's worth of tips? A bunch of dollar bills. Maybe a five or a ten from some drunk."

Andres didn't answer Gianelli. His facial expression said he was picturing the inside of RJ's, the exact spot where Randall would have been standing, the guy with the gun pressing him for money. The night's deposit, whatever else was on hand. Jamie started to picture that too. The inside of the bar, the two of them still alive. Along with Andres and Gianelli, he moved through the dark tunnel of the two murders and felt a raw shiver in his spine, imagining the fear they'd have had.

"She'd have just been standing there," Andres said finally.

"What've I been telling you," Gianelli said. "I don't like that *construct*. It don't sit right with me."

From the forensics, they'd determined that Cindy was shot first. She'd fallen to the ground and Randall was on top of her. That's why Catherine Rose only saw one body when she'd been the first on the crime scene. She'd been traumatized and confused. She'd seen a lot of blood and the jacket she knew to be Randall's on the body smack in the middle of that mess. She hadn't registered anything else. She'd run out into the frigid night. Screaming for help. Not even noticing Cindy.

Jamie wanted to return to the photograph and the dock and the mountains in the background that were probably the Ramapos, and the speedboat on the New York side of the lake. Get his mind away from the crime scene he felt unnervingly close to. Get his mind away from Cindy in her junior prom gown. But he needed to think hard about what could have happened. Care deeply about what those last final minutes were and how they were experienced by the two victims. The all-consuming need to know leading him to some answers. That was his job. The way that Andres and Gianelli operated.

The two detectives shared a glance. They'd suddenly remembered Jamie was meeting with them for a reason.

"Okay, cowboy," Andres said to him. "No boyfriend for now. We'll keep him on ice a bit. He's probably squirming. Even if he had nothing to do with it, he was a piece of shit. Even the girl's mother said that."

"That's what everyone says. Pretty much. Got Cindy dancing when she was still seventeen. Beat her up a bunch of times," Jamie said. He didn't need to look at his notes to remember the statement from Marlene Sutter. The time a neighbor finally had enough and called the cops. He was fairly sure that was October.

"Yeah. Let him wait for the follow up. See what information comes in so we can try to trip him up with it."

Gianelli seemed satisfied with his judgment. There was so little else.

TWENTY-FOUR

AFTER HIS AUNT RO PASSED, JAMIE GAVE HER OLD BED-
room set to the Cosgroves across the street and helped Bill restain it with
a satin finish. The bedframe and dresser went into a tiny room at the
back of their house, a gift for their preteen daughter. Jamie then moved
into the larger of the two bedrooms in what had become his own house
and set up his old one as an office. The desk was where he studied for
criminal justice tests and did his taxes and where he'd recently set aside
one drawer for files with documents to read over. Reviewing his work was
important for his assigned cases but also kept him busy around the house.

Being occupied filled the space and let him skirt the things he
preferred not to notice, like how small his aunt's physical life had been.
How quickly the evidence of her ever being could disappear. Sometimes
he felt her there with him. More times he felt her gone. Jamie glanced at
the digital time flashing from his nightstand. He couldn't recall the last
time he'd wound her porcelain mantel clock.

The soundless TV was waiting for him when he went downstairs.
That and Nugget. Jamie turned on the volume and finished dinner with
the dog at his feet, then got ready to meet Steve and Dan. His drive took
him to the club they liked on Route 23 when they were bored with the
Eagle's Nest.

Aldo's was a square box of a building with a near black exterior.
Jamie couldn't have said what color it was painted. A roadside board
listed cover bands in block letters and happy hour pricing. Aldo's was
anything but a cop bar. The previous Friday, a tip from an anonymous
caller sent the Butler police looking for guns and they'd emptied the

club in the process, a scene Jamie was glad to have missed. He hoped that'd been the last of pointless hoax calls. He needed to relax and shake off the week. Not only work. He was angry that Missy had ended what they had before it started. He'd wanted to see her that weekend. Driving out of Paterson, a night at Aldo's ahead of him, he'd realized how much he'd wanted that.

No more than two steps into the club, the air was damp and sweaty. Jamie, freshly showered and cologned, didn't see an easy path to the quietish lounge area where Steve had said they should meet. He skirted the crush near the stage, avoiding the light show and the full 50-watt amps of a band that called themselves Crystal Ship. Fronted by a copy of Jim Morrison in worn denim and a black leather jacket, they broke into the opening chords of "L.A. Woman" as Jamie fought his way to the bar. It wasn't until he'd ordered his second Jack and Coke that he felt a tug on his sleeve and was suddenly flanked by his friends shouting over each other.

"This isn't the best dance music," Dan said.

"Yeah? Since when is that a thing for you?"

"Girls dance," he said. "I like to watch girls."

That's how it was at bars with Steve and Dan when it was noisy and jammed with people. They drank more than they talked. And looked around. Jamie tried not to see if there were any drugs being swapped. Ignoring the spectacle of large bills passed around in plain sight, he turned to the entrance and the woman taking cover fees and stamping hands, her long teal nails visible from the farthest corners of the bar. All the while a bouncer stood behind her making eye contact with every new patron.

Jamie left Aldo's around 11:30 with a nursing student named Cheryl. Her place was closer to the bar than his house and meant less driving after he'd had a few drinks. Not that he was legally drunk, but Jamie didn't want to get stopped and have to show his badge. He followed her VW until reaching a series of streets lined with garden apartments, snow blanketing the lawns, but the paths neatly cleared. Her heels teetered as she fumbled with gloves and her pocketbook, Jamie right behind her once they were at her door, leaning into her back as she giggled and pressed her key into the lock. Taking his hand, she led him to a living room cluttered with soft bound textbooks, stacks of looseleaf papers and cassette tapes. She removed her coat and shrugged as it slid off the couch where she'd tossed it. A tall blonde wearing what looked like a black leotard with a shiny green skirt.

Until Jamie had noticed her watching him from across the bar, he'd been thinking almost the whole time about Missy. And when he wasn't thinking about Missy, he was thinking about Randall and Cindy and the phone call from Sandy and everything that Gianelli and Andres had said to him. He was beginning to burn with the case. All he'd done was add names to the file. What he wanted was to understand what happened that night. Then he saw a pair of eyes waiting to catch his and walked over to introduce himself.

Jamie awoke around 7:00 a.m., tired but he didn't go back to sleep. He rolled on his back and stared at the ceiling's standard white paint. The landlord special. A match for the dome fixture centered above the bed. A view he'd seen many times. He wanted to leave without any conversation and avoid the next morning ritual. He just wanted to collect his clothes and go home, which was probably rude, but not impossible. Nugget would be hungry. He had work to do around the house and notes to look at from his files that made him feel important but also, he felt, he was narrowing in on some real clues and insights. That was what he told himself as he quietly closed the front door, stepping out of the strange apartment and into an icy daylight.

For all his effort, he knew it hadn't mattered whether he'd made any noise. The nursing student he'd convinced himself he'd left sleeping probably knew the minute he stood up. Even with his careful movements, the mattress bounced as it released his weight, though she'd kept her eyes closed. Jamie knew how it worked. No wrapping herself in a robe and inching towards the hall in time to find him fully dressed and pulling on his boots. All the awkwardness papered over.

As he neared his car, he saw his outline reflected in his windshield. The glass was smeared with salt and didn't give Jamie a mirror image. He didn't need to see his face to know he was someone angry and hurt. Missy. She was the first thought he'd had that morning. Jamie hadn't thought of anything else. Clearly not about the nursing student who maybe wanted more than their good time. Maybe hoped for a boyfriend. He hadn't left her even the thinnest note saying that he'd let her sleep and promising to call. He knew better than that. Knew better but it wasn't unfamiliar and he was ashamed.

TWENTY-FIVE

JAMIE FOUND HIMSELF BACK AT ALBERTO'S. HE ORDERED beef and potato empanadas again. They were decent enough and he didn't know what else Alberto was capable of making. Jamie hadn't seen much variety on the grill.

Safe inside the pocket of his jacket was the list he'd taken from Gil. Most of the names had been crossed off in disappointing blue ink. Jamie's last shot was around the industrial edge of the neighborhood. Gil had pushed the not-terribly-hopeful prospect, even after Jamie told him all the plants and warehouses had been closed at the time of the shooting.

"Most of them don't have midnight shifts. Almost none of them. And they've been checked."

"Some of the regulars. They don't live in the exact neighborhood, but they're around during the day. I talked to them. A few of them told me about the night watch. Someone on security."

"The area's been canvassed."

"By cops maybe no one wanted to talk to."

It wasn't just Gil's persistence sending Jamie back to the luncheonette. The possibility that an overlooked security guard might prove to be a witness was all he had. He thanked Alberto for the empanadas, then began to steel himself. He wanted answers. Someone had to have seen or heard something. Someone had to know and he needed to be the one they could trust.

RJ's was sandwiched into a few streets that tried to be a neighborhood. Two-family homes with their above ground pools and tolerance for what came with a location bordering Getty Ave. The gas stations, a wholesale fabric outlet, a forklift dealer, the requisite auto repairs, there were four of those, and a stocky, standalone building beneath a sign that simply said "meat." Stuck in the mix was RJ's, the local go-go bar. Lunch during the day for all the men who worked nearby. Guys from all over at night.

The homes had already been picked clean by patrol officers hoping for real information. One woman said she'd gone to her window out of curiosity when startled by a loud noise but hadn't seen anything. She'd been awake feeding her five-month-old and heard what she'd decided was a tire backfiring and couldn't recall the exact time. It wasn't warm enough for flung open windows and serviceable acoustics. Still, there wouldn't have been air conditioners blocking the view. If anyone else had bothered to look.

Jamie had read all those reports. He left the residential area, pushing forward in search of better luck, crossing the main road towards a string of warehouses and factories hidden in part by a high concrete wall. A late afternoon sun washed over the classic brick mill that occupied a sizable portion of the block. Most of it had escaped the wrecking ball and stood as a landmark, dividing commercial and pure industrial. Jamie walked to another row of buildings around the corner. Those had once been textile companies and textile-related companies. He could read the words Grundy Brothers Cutting on the still-standing fence outside what was now Chem-Spray. Jamie had an appointment with a machinist who worked a particular graveyard shift there.

According to Gil's information, Tomasz Kaminski came from Poland with his half-brother Marek in the early 1960s. He spoke broken English and asked for his friend, Vincent Miletti, whom he called "Mr. Vincent" to sit in on the interview. Tom, as he was known, understood everything, but relied on his friend to answer for him. That was apparent to Jamie, from the first question.

"What shift do you usually work?"

"Shiiift," Tom nodded.

"The plant shuts down on the weekends. Unless there's a big job," Vincent answered. "Which there wasn't."

"But Tom was here, at the plant."

"He was told to check," Vincent said.

"Check?"

"Make sure there was nothing going on. No one in the parking lot. No broken windows near the office."

"So, he works as a machinist but also he's a night guard?"

"Something like that. It's taking turns on weekends. It doesn't cost the firm a lot of money for security. The guys that work it get over-time pay."

"He doesn't mind?"

"He gets paid."

The area he covered was part of an industrial complex. Chem-Spray stood next to buildings newer than the historic textile plants near Mill Street, yet even these were aged and neglected. The end of the block was largely vacant and more like eerie remains than anything worth guarding. It wasn't the place for an elderly immigrant from Łódź with a broken-down Buick to be patrolling for trouble. In fact, it was exactly the kind of parking lot where Jamie had field training. The whole point was those lots invited drug deals and break-ins.

Jamie remembered being driven to the backs of shopping areas, factories, anywhere that was empty and waiting. Getting there sometimes at midnight, sometimes at 2:00 a.m., maybe later. Mixing it up. Never making it obvious when the cops would be around. The play to switch off the cruiser's headlights and coast in almost total darkness. It'd been unnerving for him the first time. Jamie being someone with a gun sitting next to another officer.

"He could come across something pretty dangerous. More likely than not that he will," Jamie said.

"He says where he came from, this is nothing," Vincent answered.

"What does that mean?"

"I never asked."

Together, Jamie and Vincent walked to the window that looked onto Getty Ave. Tom was right behind them.

"I take photos from here sometimes. It's a pretty clear view. Out past the strip and the tops of those last three houses, you can see some of the Falls."

The ancient glass framed the urban landscape in a soft artistic light. A city moving through time at its own slow pace. From the elevated view, even RJ's appeared benign.

"Did Tom ever go across the street? Stop in before or after work?"

"That's not how Tom spends his money."

"What about you?"

"I've been to RJ's. But not on the weekends. Not on the night you're interested in."

"And that night? Tom was doing his patrol?"

"He was in the parking lot, outside the factory and he didn't see anything."

"But he heard a car door slam," Jamie said.

Vincent turned to Tom. The older man's eyes were shut in a deep concentration. When he opened them, he motioned and mumbled to his friend.

"He says that he heard a car. Mostly he remembers the engine gunning and then tires screeching. It was loud and he was glad there was no trouble at the factory. Whatever happened, it was on the other side of the wall."

"He heard that from here?"

"Tom says that's what he remembers. It was loud. Very loud."

"What time did that happen? Does he remember that?"

Vincent conferred with Tom who tapped the Casio on his wrist.

"He says it was probably close to two."

The loud engine and tires, the carelessness in leaving the scene with no thought to whether he was drawing attention to himself. What else had he been careless about? Running out. Perhaps not covering his face. Who else would have heard the car? Someone close enough to also have a good look.

TWENTY-SIX

JAMIE'S ROTATING SHIFT WAS TAKING HIM BACK TO THE
Eastside. The patrol near Barnert Hospital often meant trips to the ER,
often right after breakfast. A lesser-equipped hospital, their staff handled
overdoses and gunshot wounds and victims of other violent crimes.
Working that ward was usually a dreaded assignment, but that day it kept
Jamie off the purse snatching detail downtown. He watched as Gary
shook out the gray wig.

"It's my turn, you lucky bastard."

Gary didn't seem all that unhappy. He was nominally part of the
wider, RJ's investigation but he truly feared Bachman, having spent some
after-hours time with the sergeant at Tocci's, the older cops' bar that
Jamie had only gone to once on Henry's last birthday. Gary had been
more often, trying to get in with the ranking officers, but stopped a
few months back, telling Jamie that Bachman was a sour drunk without
elaborating. He'd have also overheard the sergeant's recent yelling at
Jamie for going through the neighborhood around RJ's "with a fine-
tooth comb" as if he was going to find something. That would explain
Gary dumping his report onto Jamie's desk. They were putting their
witness lists together to present to the investigative team, meaning Gary,
who'd be working undercover at the bus stop next to Jacob's, left his
copies with Jamie.

"What's this?" Jamie asked, chewing on an egg sandwich and
holding up a single sheet of paper.

"My report on the very last patron. Gerald Corbett. Bit of a regular.
He was in the bathroom when the lights started going off and he basically

had to bolt, still pulling up his fly. Said it seemed like someone was in a hurry to close that night."

"Who was hitting the lights?"

"The witness said he only saw Cindy. Randall wasn't around."

"All his shit check out?"

"Pretty much. He's a foreman at Tanis Construction. Been there twenty-six years. No debts. Wife's got MS and he's home with her most nights, except on Saturdays. Nothing on him really. No motive. Wife said he was home the usual time. Calm. Normal. Story is, he had a cheesesteak for lunch, all the peppers and onions. And he got hung up in a stall."

"So, he didn't see Lorraine or Randall?"

"The witness said he saw Cindy and didn't mention anyone else. Believe me. Bachman grilled me on that."

"No follow up? To square with Lorraine's story?"

"What's to square? As far as Bachman's concerned, Lorraine left, and if she didn't notice this Corbett, so what? His wife is sick, he has no motive. He didn't see anything and Bachman isn't big on wasting resources chasing after nothing."

"And Cindy was hitting the lights?" Jamie said, repeating the information. Not really asking a question.

"Maybe she wasn't as good with the routine as Randall. Didn't think to check for any stragglers." Gary laughed. "Closing wasn't really her specialty. Not why they hired her."

Jamie took the last bite of his egg sandwich and pried the lid off his coffee.

"She's dead," he said quietly.

In a few minutes, Gary was wearing the woman's coat Jamie had worn to work downtown, holding a large pair of low-heeled pumps.

"Wish me luck," he said.

Jamie waved him on. Then he walked out of the squad room and found Elizabeth at her desk, flipping through a worn paperback.

"Here to give me some of your reports?"

"Not yet," Jamie said. "Not ready to have much of it filed."

"So, what do you need?"

Half the department was chatty with Elizabeth and the other half, where Jamie counted himself, avoided getting drawn into her office critiques. He handed her a slip of paper with Cindy's full name. Cindy Jane Kaczorek.

"Got any complaints with her name on it? Would have been around early fall last year. Maybe October. Anything in '78."

"Against her? For what?"

"She'd have been the complainant or a witness. Boyfriend stuff. A neighbor made the call. Heard yelling and probably a slap or two."

"A neighbor?"

"You can pretty much tell when someone's getting hit in the next apartment."

Jamie's added clarification was taken from a piece of family lore he wished he hadn't known.

"That is for sure," Elizabeth said. She held up the paper with Cindy's name and considered it. "I'll take a look."

"You can leave the file on my desk."

TWENTY-SEVEN

HE HELD THE NEWSPAPER, MULLING OVER THE ARTICLE.
A veteran of the Vietnam War, a member of St. Paul's Episcopal Church of
Paterson and the Orange Lodge. No photo of Randall Low, but he remembered
clearly what he'd looked like.

The write-up didn't tell the whole story. Randall was the guy who'd screwed
things up reaching for his gun before he knew what was going on and setting
everything off. Randall continued screwing things up because he mattered. RJ's
and their dumb as shit softball team. There were plans for a memorial tournament
dedicated to the family. Posters were going up around town. Into the spring, at all
the practices and games, everyone would be saying that jack shit was getting done.
Randall was a guy they cared about and there'd be growing pressure, boiling hot
pressure. The barroom shooting would never just sit there, one more file in a sea of
files. It would never simply go away.

TWENTY-EIGHT

JAMIE LEARNED THIS AT THE ACADEMY WHEN AN AD-vanced skills class had an FBI expert come in and give a talk on interrogation. Witnesses don't like to lie; they prefer not to, so there are always needles of truth. Telling the truth, even a fraction of it, makes them feel better. They don't consider themselves liars. They just didn't tell you everything. Statements were what Agent Loden called haystacks.

"Look for the needle. Then start connecting it."

Standing at Chem-Spray's window, Jamie had noticed some things more interesting than the vistas Vincent photographed in black and white. The two-family homes across from RJ's had an unfettered view of the parking lot. The position of the corner streetlamp allowed light to hit the curb cut and apron leading into the lot, even with the rear hidden behind hedges and a thick wooden fence. After seeing that, he'd rummaged furiously through files and found the name he needed. The sole witness with viable information. The woman who said she'd heard one large bang and thought it might have been a car backfiring or a blown tire. She said it'd been too dark to see anything. That was her statement. Still, she'd taken the time to look.

The Brandsher family lived on the second floor of a house on Sycamore Street. A bird's eye view of RJ's parking lot and the north side of the building. Eileen Brandsher's needle, her sliver of truth, was that she'd been awake with her baby. She could have said she'd been sleeping but that would have been completely untrue. So, she'd admitted she was in her living room, but she'd also said she hadn't heard anything beyond what would have been the first gunshot, and that now seemed to be a lie.

She had to have heard the screeching tires. Possibly she'd heard all the gunshots as well, facts that would have come out if the person who'd taken her statement had pressed her. If she hadn't admitted to hearing the shots and the car gunning away from RJ's, there might be even more to her story.

Jamie hadn't called ahead. He introduced himself when she answered the door. When he offered his card, she waved it away, looking past Jamie and scouting for who might see her. Then she stood aside, allowing him in. Eileen took a seat at the kitchen table and offered Jamie the chair across from her. The baby that was so fussy at night was down for his nap. Jamie spoke clearly but didn't raise his voice, though he thought a bit of dramatic effect might be helpful.

"We have a witness from one of the plants, says he heard tires screeching," Jamie said.

Eileen looked at him blankly.

"Must have been pretty loud for him to have heard that all the way on the other side of that concrete wall, separating their parking lot from Getty Ave. Maybe you want to think back. Get a better recollection of that night."

"I told you," Eileen said. "My husband was asleep. My other two were asleep. Tyler was fussing and I got up before he started crying. I was sitting with him, giving him a bottle. That's all I did. I didn't hear anything. I didn't see anything."

"Your witness statement says you heard a loud bang."

"Yes, there was that. I told the officer I spoke with I thought it might have been a car backfiring."

"At almost two in the morning?"

"People drive cars late around here."

"Nothing else? No other shots? No car door? Loud engine? Screeching tires?"

Eileen was silent, rubbing a thumb on the inside of her wrist, deep in thought.

The more she refused to answer, the more convinced Jamie was. He saw a lonely, bored woman who'd been up with a baby who woke for feedings like clockwork. Trying to be quiet and let the rest of the house asleep. Too late for TV. Why not peek outside and see what was going on? Maybe watching the dancers leave with this one or that one. Maybe she liked to see if she recognized a face from the neighborhood. A husband spending too much money at RJ's.

He waited, taking in the apartment. The refrigerator was papered with homemade Valentines. Cutouts made from red and pink cardboard with crayoned messages. Wanting to focus on something less personal, he found a pair of cross-stitches framed and hung on the wall across from the stove. They were old, like someone a generation back had done them and passed them along to Eileen. He favored the larger design with its border of bluebells and what resembled a cottage beneath the simple words, "Bless this House. Oh Lord, We Pray. Keep it Safe by Night and Day."

"Who did the needlework?"

"That's from my mother."

"They used to sell ones like that at the five and dime. They were copies, I guess. If you looked close, they were only paper."

"Yeah? What made you look close?"

"It was a Mother's Day gift."

"That's one's a real cross-stitch."

"Very nice," Jamie said. "A nice blessing."

He kept his stare on the wall behind her and waited. Soon, she tapped a cigarette out of a half-finished pack of Parliaments and played with it but kept it unlit, holding it in her fingers like the former smoker that she was.

"Why me?" she asked. "Why not go out and ask one of the other neighbors?"

"Because it was so loud, someone else on the block must have heard it all, too?"

"Yeah."

"You're the only one who's told anything at all to the police."

She nodded, drawing the left side of her face into a smile.

"It happened so fast. I heard the shots and went to the window, still holding the baby. Maybe that wasn't smart. Could have been someone shooting nearby, but you know. Late at night. You don't think."

"Of course. Did you notice what time it was?"

"It would've been after one. One-thirtyish. That's when I usually go to the window. Back and forth. I'll sit and look a bit, then walk with the baby."

Though Jamie wanted to pinpoint the time, he decided to give her space to talk.

"I get a little bored, up at night. I got into a habit of sitting at the ledge and looking out around closing time. Those girls. They have an exciting life, don't they? Even if I don't always see their faces, you just know they're so pretty. It's something to watch."

"Would you recognize any of them? The girls? Who they normally left with?"

"That night, I saw the owner walk the tall one, the one with the long brown hair to her car. That wasn't unusual. I've seen that a lot."

"What exactly did you see?"

"They left the bar together, walked over towards the lot, then not too long after, he went back into the bar and her car pulled away."

"Do you remember what she drove?"

Eileen shook her head.

"What about the blonde dancer?"

Jamie placed a photograph of Cindy on the table that Eileen scanned and seemed to recognize.

"Once I saw the blonde girl leaving with the owner. I only saw that once. But then, I don't sit and watch every night."

"She left with Randall? You're familiar with him?"

"Oh yeah. From sitting and watching. I recognize him. The girl, I only did get a look at her face that one time. Like I said, I wasn't at the window every second. I've seen blonde hair on occasion but can't say for sure if it was her with him, other than that once when I saw her in the light. You know, the two of them leaving the bar and then driving off together."

"When was that?"

"Maybe a month before the shooting."

"He walked her to her car?"

"She drove off with him."

"You know that?"

"I saw them leave the bar and walk towards the back and only one car left and I'm pretty sure there was a passenger in it."

"Okay. The night of the shooting, what did you see, after Randall went back into the bar?"

"After he went back in, I didn't see anyone else go into the bar, but it happened I'd left the window for a while. Then I heard those shots. It lasted just a minute, I think, but maybe longer. It felt like forever. You can't see the side door perfect from here, but I saw the guy come from behind RJ's running. The side and then the back of him. Right past the light, before it goes dark. It wasn't much but I could see his build, I guess you'd call it his silhouette. Like his outline. Big guy. Broad shoulders. That's what I remember. A military guy."

"Did you see a uniform?"

"I couldn't tell what he was wearing."

"What makes you think he was in the military?"

"You know. Broad shoulders. Even running, he kept his shoulders back. He wasn't like the ones around here. The guys walking around, skinny from drugs. Stooped over, looking for a car to break into. This guy was powerful. He's a big guy," Eileen said. "Real big. I wanted no trouble with him."

"Did you see anything else? His face?"

She shook her head.

"So, you didn't want to talk to the police."

"I didn't want to be in any trouble with that man," she said. "Besides, you know, talking to the police, all it does is get you pegged. There are people on this block that'll do that."

Jamie took a moment to look at the cardboard hearts. So much fallout from the Hurricane Carter case, keeping the Paterson police in the news and under scrutiny and less and less popular out on patrol.

"I do hear that," he said, holding her gaze so she'd understand the words weren't merely a script for him. "Only tell me what you saw, not what you think I want you to tell me."

"Okay."

"I get that it was dark. But you saw his shape, right? What about the car?"

"Maybe it was a sedan. I think it was on the longer side. He drove off so fast and loud and I was a little, I don't know, maybe just beside myself at that point."

"So, you don't remember the car. That didn't stand out to you. But you're certain the guy you saw after you heard gunshots was in the military."

"My father was in Iwo Jima," she said. "Not that he got the medal he deserved, but that's another story."

She gave Jamie another of her half smiles with that, making it clear if she was going to talk, she'd be sharing her opinions.

"He's fifty-three now, my dad. Still straight as an arrow. That guy I saw, could've been the same age, served in Iwo Jima. Maybe younger, could've been in Saigon. Who knows which war? He's got the same straight-up back."

Jamie flipped his notebook closed, fit it into his shirt pocket and stood.

"You came here looking for answers," Eileen said. "Well, I'll tell you. That guy was someone to remember."

Jamie had no more questions to ask. He already knew that Randall walked Lorraine to her car. She'd told that to Bachman. It was something he did every night. That piece of information confirmed Eileen had been doing her usual watch. But the rest of it? Cindy didn't have a car so maybe she did go with Randall one night. What did that prove? Too many maybes. And then a guy who looked like he was in the military, but nothing else. As much as he believed Eileen and found her as decent a witness as Tom, it wasn't much to write up.

Eileen had a day to get back to. Jamie followed her along a worn path set into the carpet. A store-bought Valentine was taped just above a front door that was shellacked and thin and opened onto the street. A wonder Eileen hadn't heard more. Loud voices. Names yelled out. Jamie couldn't help himself. He'd hoped for all of that.

"Well, thank you. This was very useful. And, obviously, if you remember anything else from that night, please call."

He handed her his card. A gesture he'd become more comfortable with. A smooth transition to fully end the conversation. Eileen took it without giving it a look and laid it on the entry table, next to a potted fern and her pile of mail.

"I know what I saw," she said. "The man that was running. I know what I saw."

TWENTY-NINE

A FEW DOUBLE SHIFTS EARLIER THAT WEEK MEANT Jamie had Thursday as an off day. A day that should have been spent running the vacuum over area rugs, checking the gutters for ice, hanging out with Steve later that night and generally doing all the things that got Jamie's mind away from the precinct and his files. Instead, Jamie had plans to meet Gil at his apartment. The invitation had come a few nights before at a Totowa bar when Jamie had also been off-duty and meeting with Gil even though they'd more or less exhausted whatever information Gil could possibly turn over and he'd switched to framing potential theories. Gil hadn't come up with one yet, but the case was under his skin. They had that in common. While Jamie didn't quite share everything with Gil, their talks were easy. It was understood the information and theories would not go two-ways. Gil didn't seem to care. He liked being close to it. Maybe getting sad with it too. That night had Gil switching topics.

"You go to target practice?" he'd asked.

"Of course."

"What do you shoot there?"

"Mostly revolvers. My basic service piece and I have another Colt. Some rifle shots. Why? You like shooting?"

"You ever shoot bow and arrow?"

Jamie pressed against the back of his stool as he took a harder look at Gil, who hadn't seemed drunk.

"What cop takes a bow and arrow with him on a shift?"

"You know I meant targets. What about clays? Ever shoot those?"

"A few of the guys in the precinct shoot skeet."

"It's different than skeet," Gil said. "With skeet, your ready position is different than clay. The stock is below your elbow, at your hip. When you're ready to call, you raise the gun. With clay, your gun is already in shooting position at your shoulder, and when you call for the target, you pivot."

"That's what you like? Clays?"

"I've really only shot clay. What I'm used to. You know guns. How your body goes with them depends on what you're using and how you're using it."

Gil insisted on another round, and he spent half an hour describing clay pigeon shooting and how it was unpredictable, all the different trajectories, angles, speeds, elevations, distances and target sizes.

"It's like live shooting. Except they're not live, of course. "

"Unpredictable," Jamie said.

Their talk led to Jamie driving to Gil's that Thursday morning. The plan was meeting at his apartment. Gil wanted to use his new car for the trip. A two-tone Cadillac. The perfect factory crimson finish and a white vinyl top. Gil's Coupe DeVille was a gas guzzler, big and flashy and the car Jamie never expected him to drive. Not at all rumpled like Gil. Not an unfortunate GMC car, a Pacer or a Gremlin, leading Jamie to wonder about the mechanics of the law firm where Gil's father and brother were partners. The financial parts of that.

Jamie brought along a double-barreled shotgun that had been in his family and which he deep cleaned and cared for, though it was a gun he rarely used. He had no idea what Gil had thrown into the trunk of the Cadillac.

It wasn't just the car that smelled new and clean that morning. Gil was slick with a sharp, spicy aftershave. Nothing that hinted of morning sips of Jameson or forgetting to change an undershirt.

When they got to the Foodtown shopping plaza, Gil paused at the stop sign, fiddling with the radio until the signal returned with the rapid-fire sounds of the morning talk show. "You get to the base of the mountain and the reception is for shit here," he said.

They listened to a call-in program the length of the drive, going west along the route Jamie had taken to see Cindy's mother. Jamie considered how he'd fallen short. The interview with Marlene Sutter hadn't been fruitful at all and it wouldn't have been wrong if Gil brought him back. He continued sorting through questions that might have led him to Sandy as they went past the Sparta exit, then a few minutes further to Andover.

Once off the highway, there were similar two-lane roads, though where they were headed was a members-only shooting club. Jamie had only been to target practices, mostly in Haledon or Garret Mountain at the Sheriff Department facility. He understood he wasn't going to a pistol range. He'd been flipping through the brochure as Gil drove. *A secluded, year-round outdoor experience on one of the most desirable and challenging shooting layouts in the country. Over 4,300 acres of bucolic farmland.*

It wasn't the Windsor Farm's sign as much as the sudden change in landscape that announced their arrival. The stone fences and manicured lawns. Passing through the entrance touched an eagerness in Jamie, reminding him how much he liked long guns.

"This is amazing," he said. "Bet you can shoot anything and everything here."

"Pretty much. The recoil doesn't get to you too much with that double-barrel?"

"I learned a lot about balance when I was boxing. It helps with the recoil. I can hold my ground," Jamie said.

"How far'd you end up with that?"

"Almost all the way. But then, you know, life happens. My Aunt Ro was sick. I stopped going to the gym. Took too much time away from her. And then after, I don't know. I felt differently about a lot of things. Went for some new stuff. Classes at William Paterson. The police academy."

"I get that," Gil said. "Going for some new stuff. You did that right."

The drive into the complex was exactly as promised. The ponds and mossy paths flanked by mature oaks. The private road leading to the white-columned main lodge.

"So, all this, the whole club it's just target?" Jamie asked. "No one goes after the water birds?"

"Nope. Clay is fast. It has that feel of field shooting, going after ducks and pheasants, only they're clay rounds." Gil shifted the car into park. "You know, I'm not one to shoot anything else."

They were met in the foyer by an instructor named Bryan wearing an oilcloth vest and booming "Hallo" with a British accent. No one like Bryan was pictured in the brochure, but seeing him wasn't a surprise. They were led out, passing by a set of berms at the upper pistol range, and more shaded knolls, going farther to the clay area. Bryan went over the basics. Mostly what Gil had told Jamie driving there.

"You don't move the gun, you pivot. Right? You know that. When we get closer, I'll go over the stations where you'll be shooting."

There were twelve they'd be using that day. Jamie was told how to call for the target. It was understood that Jamie didn't need much instruction beyond that. He knew about boxing and he knew about shooting and the energy it took to hold a stance. What it took to support the weight of a gun. Balance and stability. You can start with balance, but it's stability that lets you hold the balance. You can start with a decent stance, but if you can't keep your stance, you can't hit your target. *And if you're not even starting in the right place, you're basically fucked.*

Boxing coaches and shooting instructors. So many years of training in Jamie's head. Jamie settled his hips and fixed his hand on the grip before hoisting the shotgun. Once he called "pull" there was nothing else, only the trigger beneath the crease of his finger and the open, rough gray sky, then a sphere of iron-red clay shattering into a burst of flakes and dust when he shot.

The day was quite a workout. Not only shooting. Moving along, from one station to the next. As they walked back, again passing the pistol range, Jamie told Gil he'd teach him with his Python.

"Next time, I'll show you."

"That'd be great. Always wanted to hold a revolver. Like really hold one. In-the-movies kind of shooting."

"It's not really like that," Jamie said.

"Yeah, maybe not to you."

Jamie couldn't argue. Guns, the ones Jamie owned and shot, didn't really match with the Windsor Farm's rolling hills and fields. The gentle streams. No doubt seclusion, the kind necessary to shoot every possible firearm was the whole point of the club's location. That also made the day peaceful and meditative, walking back and forth over a pebble brook, watching Cooper's hawks and kestrels circling the tops of distant mountains. Occasionally, the birds would come close, then ride a thermal column and he watched until each was just a pinpoint.

Jamie could forget a lot being there.

THIRTY

IT HAD BEEN COLD, STANDING ON THE HARDENED ground of the shooting club. The February thaw hadn't lasted the day. A light drizzle began as Jamie left Gil's complex, driving the Datsun away from West Paterson and roads called Boulder Run, Rustic Ridge and Highpoint Drive back into his neighborhood. By then, the rain had progressed to an icy sleet that caught in his collar once he was out of the car.

Beyond the cold, he'd been holding the double barrel for a long time, its recoil pounding into his shoulder. His mindset didn't feel much better than his arms after he'd been cornered into a brief discussion on how the case was going. Gil knew Jamie couldn't say much and asked in a general way if things were moving.

"It's on pace. Slow. But that was expected," Jamie had answered.

There wasn't much else Jamie could have said. That homicides like RJ's were difficult. Andres and Gianelli had a full caseload of their regular assignments and a bunch of foot patrol officers out getting rote statements for them. None of it added it up to much that was promising. His response had felt thin and hollow and it lingered with him long after he'd dropped Gil at his apartment.

It was still sleeting when Jamie was done with his shower and coaxing Nugget into the yard one last time for the night. The dog hesitated, but eventually braved the few steps it took to get to his favorite bush, and then a quick return. Getting rigorously toweled by Jamie before he could shake himself off all over the kitchen floor.

A canine, Jamie remembered, as he pulled clumps of ice from the little dog's fur. The instructor at the Windsor Club talked about his canines, the two he took with him for ducks and what he called "other waterfowl." English pointers. But Bryan also said his dad had been a lorry driver for the London Railroad and that he'd grown up in prefab house because much of his neighborhood had been destroyed by Luftwaffe bombs. He'd chatted a lot. Calling his dogs "canines" was part of the culture. Using the correct terms. The way he'd said stock, not the butt of the rifle.

"You're a canine," Jamie said to Nugget. They both headed to the living room.

He was in jeans and a T-shirt and a stubborn chill lingered from the minutes he'd been standing in the open doorway waiting for the dog. Jamie rubbed at his upper arms, noticing the sleet falling even harder. It was louder than the television and Nugget's noisy claws tapping across the wood floor. The dog seemed agitated. The icy rain shook the trees and bushes, but mostly it slapped against the front door. Jamie realized it was a knock.

He didn't have a peephole and it was too dark to bother with the curtains covering the room's lone window that was blocked by shrubs anyway. He considered going for his gun, sitting on the dresser upstairs. The pellets of sleet made it useless to ask who was there. And if someone wanted trouble with him, they weren't going to knock. Instead of cracking the door, he pulled it wide open, as if it was a sunny afternoon with the neighborhood kids on their bikes, sprinklers running back and forth over freshly mowed lawns.

She'd been standing outside for a while, her loose hair soaked by the freezing rain. No clip holding it off her neck. No barrette. No soft blonde waves, only long, wet strands. He stood back and she hesitated before coming in. Like Nugget, she needed to be toweled off.

"I have to ask you a favor," she said, moving inside slowly, aware that she was dripping water onto the floor. "Can I stay on your couch tonight?"

Not sure what to say, not entirely sure what Missy was asking him, Jamie observed her quietly, reading her for clues he couldn't find. She had no bag of clothes. There was only the beige purse he recognized from their one date.

"I looked you up. Found your address," she said. "I'm kind of between places. I thought, if it's okay. It's just for the night."

Her cheeks and the tip of her nose were bright red. He wanted to take her face in his hands. Instead, he helped her with her coat, led her to the bathroom and handed her extra towels from the kitchen. After she'd closed the door, he went upstairs and retrieved the army cot from the attic. It'd been years since the house had a visitor like this. The rare but memorable late-night appearances from Barbara and her three boys. Aunt Ro had called her "my lady friend." She and the boys would show up maybe once or twice a year beginning when Jamie was twelve. The boys were younger than he was and there was only the one cot, but they never fought over it. They took whatever blankets and pillows they'd been given and worked out how they'd sleep. Usually this was way past midnight and the boys were tired. The next morning, Jamie would find his aunt cooking bacon and corned beef hash and sausage while occupied with the boys. Going over the times table with them and asking them to spell random words and then trying to convince Barbara to stay a bit longer. But Barbara always went home as soon as the boys were fed. By that time, her husband would have sobered up and she needed to leave. And nothing Aunt Ro said ever changed a thing.

Jamie wasn't sure why Missy was there, but guessed whatever the story for her was, it wasn't all that different than Barbara's. Maybe not the wrong guy. Instead, maybe the wrong crowd. Based on their last phone call, he'd picked up that Missy had fallen into what he'd call bad company, the kind that drew in girls or young women who didn't have much. They'd quickly get into places where they had to be smart and careful. Something happened to Missy and she'd gotten to where she had to be even smarter, even more careful. Avoiding some real trouble by finding her way to his house. He wondered if he ought to be concerned about drugs or some other awfulness he couldn't wrap himself around.

He left her alone once the fitted sheet was secure across the cot's thin mattress, which they'd arranged in total silence. He'd never entertained a woman in that space. Once he'd taken over the larger bedroom and replaced its worn furniture, he left his old room without thinking of it too much. The desk drawers were filled with personal files and marked-up manuals from the academy and notebooks for his courses at William Paterson. A man's office. Still, the shelves were lined with high school wrestling trophies and the model cars he'd labored over before discovering sports and then girls. Thankfully, the gag poster of Lynda Carter he'd been given one birthday was gone.

He'd gone through all of his teenage years in that house. The walls were solid enough. The doors less so. After pouring himself an inch of Wild Turkey, Jamie slowed his way back to his current bedroom, passing the room where he'd left Missy with the cot and fresh bed linens and one of his smaller flannel shirts. Jamie knew the house. Its sounds. How far from the door he'd have to stand to hear Missy softly crying herself to sleep. Jamie brought a court management and policy book with him to bed. The material was boring enough to help him doze off and kept him from staying up the night thinking of Missy.

At daybreak, Jamie awoke and instead of heading to the bathroom first thing, he took a folded uniform shirt from his dresser and listened for new hums and noises in the house, thinking it already sounded busy. He went downstairs to find Missy furiously scrubbing the pan he'd left soaking in the sink and forgotten once the whole night upended, its stainless-steel bottom cleaner than he'd ever seen it. He brushed by her on his way to the refrigerator. She smelled heavily of Ajax and not of the Wind Song she'd worn on their one date, which he remembered vividly.

Missy moved in quick bursts, soon attacking the top of the gas range with a yellow sponge while telling Jamie she was going to look for someplace else in the afternoon. Thanking him. Apologizing for having bothered him so late. She wasn't like that.

"I'm not," she said. "Really. I'm not about drama."

Missy was again clarifying who she was. On their date, she wasn't a party girl. In his kitchen, having showed up in the middle of a sleet storm, she explained that she wasn't a drama person. Jamie wasn't sure who she was, but he knew she didn't have anywhere else to stay.

The other thing was that Missy wouldn't eat breakfast. When Jamie set four pieces of bread next to the toaster, Missy waved it off.

"I get so much for lunch at the restaurant."

Jamie scrambled eggs, feeling himself getting testy with Missy. Growing angry. How thin her coat was, how she was refusing breakfast. She'd taken a small juice glass and filled it halfway with milk, sipping gingerly. To Jamie's eye, she wasn't actually drinking, prodding his burr of anger.

"Look, do whatever you want. Run up a tab and pay me back. We'll keep it to the penny if you want. But here are the rules. If you knock on my door and ask to sleep here, I get some say in this. You don't have to tell me what's going on. You can or you can't. Up to you. But this is what I say. You're going to stay here for a week or two until you figure out what you need to. And you are going to eat here. You can keep a ledger, square away what you think you owe me. Okay? Are we good with that?"

Missy was silent.

He placed his hands on her shoulders, turned her and walked her to the stairs so they were both facing the tiny bedroom where he'd grown up.

"This is where you're going to stay for now," he said.

"I'm going to look for someplace this afternoon."

Jamie thought again of Aunt Ro's lady friend, the one who always left in the morning. She went back to whatever propelled her and her three boys out of their home in the middle of the night as if that was all to be done. It was clear Missy wouldn't say what she had run from, but it didn't matter. People needed time to settle their thoughts. Settle their lives.

"No," he said. "No, you're not. You're staying here until things smooth over. Whatever needs to be smoothed over. It's not a big deal. I'd do the same for any of my friends going through a rough patch."

"Us," Missy said. "This is complicated. We can't be us right now. It would get more complicated."

Jamie couldn't imagine how anything could be more complicated than Missy living in his spare room. The ache that he had for her. How intensely he wanted to kiss her and not stop there. There was, of course, more. If he wasn't bringing her into his bedroom, he wouldn't be bringing anyone else there in the foreseeable future. Not while she was sleeping on the cot.

He went to the cabinet for a salad plate, pushed half the eggs onto it and added two pieces of toast. He could hear her breathing. Normally he walked Nugget after breakfast, but he knew Missy needed some space. He needed some space. Neither of them had a clue where this might go. Not really. He strained to hear her chewing as he opened the side door, the dog's collar jangling.

THIRTY-ONE

DRIVING WITH HENRY, JAMIE DIDN'T GET THE SORT of banter he'd had at the academy with recruits his own age. Even the instructors had been regular guys with their war stories mixed in with ad-libbed jokes. Jamie wouldn't get what he needed that morning. No distractions from his thoughts about the night before.

Henry tried. He asked if Jamie liked to shoot pool as they drove through Eastside Park, looking at the skinny young men carrying duffel bags who'd probably just stumbled out of Barnert Hospital. Within a year or two, they'd be spending their nights at the edges of the Passaic River, sitting on logs and gathered around fires built using wood pallets. Fully homeless. Drinking rotgut.

"They're lucky we're not looking for users today," Henry said.

"I don't think we're finding any stolen cars in the park."

"Yeah, we're not."

Jamie steered towards McLean Boulevard, then looped back onto Broadway.

"You see that blue car up there? With the vent window smashed in."

Henry was pointing to the left lane.

"Yeah."

"They teach you that in the academy? How to spot a car that's stolen?"

This was typical Henry. Stating the obvious.

"He hasn't done anything though," Jamie said. "No violations. Can't do a Terry stop."

"Yeah? I say he's driving too fast."

The blue car, a Chevy Nova, had stopped at the light and they were sitting directly behind it. Not much was visible inside beyond the driver's plaid jacket.

"Damn," Henry said. "Nine out of ten times they try to run it."

The siren went off as the light changed. In an instant, the Nova began to speed up.

"What'd I tell you? He's going over the limit. I'm calling it in now."

The chase took them through the winding streets near the river. Jamie slowed to avoid parked cars and the possibility of a driver's-side door swinging open, but the Nova went on, blowing through stop signs. When the car was finally forced into a dead end, the driver kept the motor running, occasionally revving the engine.

"Okay. He's resisting. You back me up. And keep your gun out."

Henry grabbed a bullhorn.

"Stay in the car and keep your hands on the wheel," Henry yelled.

Jamie was surprised at how deftly he'd handled the arrest. Maybe Henry had no other ambitions, but as a patrol officer, he knew what he was doing. It went fine, with the snarling twenty-year-old arrested and the stolen Nova impounded, but the darker parts loomed for Jamie. The bullhorn and the loud commands and their guns drawn and the possibility the four-inch blade he'd come across in the pat down could've been pulled on him. It left Jamie a little shaken into the afternoon and leading into his meeting with Bachman.

In the sergeant's office, Bachman sat with his fingers tapping, as if there was a keyboard only he could see on the blotter, while Jamie gave a review of what he'd come up with. The interview at Chem-Spray. Eileen Brandsher's observation.

"She was very clear about the military."

"Well," Bachman said. "That sounds like a good theory."

He pushed back in his chair, careful to make only a small recline.

"An *interesting* theory. Someone from the military," Bachman said. "That witness, you say her name is Brandsher?"

"Yes," Jamie said.

"Did she, this Mrs. Brandsher, see anything else? Give you anything more?"

"No. I think I was . . . lucky to get that much."

Jamie regretted that last sentence. He should have avoided the word lucky but there wasn't another that felt right, so he'd said it. He wanted to be smart. Effective. Not lucky.

"Right. It's fortunate she told you anything."

Lucky. Fortunate.

"So, no facial characteristics? Exact height? Make of car?"

"No," Jamie answered, setting in stone how little he'd come up with.

"What? She didn't say his rank? What unit she thought he might be in? What military theater? World War Two? Vietnam?"

Jamie's report included everything the witness said. It was his job to write down whatever he was told, trivial and not trivial. He reminded himself of that while he sat on the tenderfoot side of the grand cherry desk, heat moving across his face and his ears probably reddening. The minutes stretching out.

"Look, you know how many of the guys sitting in the bar that night were probably vets? Hell, Low was a flight officer. Made it home from Vietnam."

Jamie did have more angles that he was considering. The name of Cindy's high school drama teacher, a woman her mother had said she'd stayed close to. Jamie realized how futile that lead would sound if it were offered. He hadn't even bothered contacting her. Not yet. At most, the teacher might lead him to Sandy, and that was another whole problem. Nothing for Jamie to do but wait and have Bachman finish the conversation.

"That's the thing. It's late at night. No one around really. And in the rare case someone was around *and* that person actually saw something useful." Bachman took a moment to breathe. "Those'll be people out late without a good reason. Probably not someone who likes to talk to cops."

Jamie had known it would be tough. Hardly any witnesses. The surrounding neighborhood distrusting the police. But still, that couldn't be all. The department's full interest had to be more than going through the motions, ever ready to pack it up. A case destined to go nowhere. Jamie had a growing sense of injustice. Cindy and Randall were real people. They had been wronged. Seriously wronged.

"You did good with the Mod Squad work."

That reference pulled him back. The code name for his undercover assignment that could only have been thought up by a cop almost fifty. What amounted to Jamie taking turns with Gary wearing a gray wig and impersonating a grandmother to catch muggers and purse-snatchers. He'd made eight really good arrests in the past month. So far, he'd only banged up his knee the one time, wrestling with a seventeen-year-old. It wasn't much to bask in and steer him off patrol and into Narcotics or Auto Theft or the assignment that was top on his wish list. Violent Crimes.

Jamie didn't normally hang around the office trying to win points, asking about the PBA events Bachman organized, or what he thought of the Giants, the team the sergeant was known to favor. Or whatever else would be the right suck up question.

This time felt a little different. Jamie wasn't so quick to stand.

"What do you think?" Jamie asked. Andres and Gianelli were always juggling theories, testing them to see if they sounded the same said aloud, or if they'd only been plausible rumbling in their heads. They'd study any solution remotely conceivable. Bachman, Jamie realized, had never offered his thoughts beyond how tough the case was going to be.

"I think some guy went into RJ's to rob the place. Had the whole thing planned, hiding upstairs until closing time. But plans are just plans. Likely things got out of hand once Randall pushed back. He had the gun in his pocket, not tucked away in a drawer. That's gonna ratchet it up. Or maybe the guy's a loose wire, would have been nervous anyway. And dangerous holding a gun."

He lifted a pile of papers from his inbox.

"This," he said. "This is what I hate. You work to get a promotion and this is what you get. Papers to push around."

With that, Bachman stood like he was going to shake Jamie's hand or personally escort him to the door as he had recently. But he made none of those moves. Instead, he grabbed at his stomach and grinned.

"You sit behind your desk long enough and this is what you turn into," Bachman said. "The ladies. They like it better when you're lean and mean."

Jamie wasn't sure how to respond. Like Jamie, the sergeant still lifted weights. Bachman wasn't all that different than the man he'd been posing in any number of group photos hanging in the squad and conference rooms. He'd always managed to find a place front and center, his biceps visibly straining against the sleeves of his uniform shirt. Whatever Bachman had meant being genial, Jamie waited too long with an answer. Bachman was focused on the row of tightly shut windows that framed the back wall of his office with their view onto Washington Street, where everything seemed to be dull and ashen and wet.

"Be careful what you wish for, Palmieri."

THIRTY-TWO

MISSY LIKED TO COOK AND BAKE AND CLOSELY FOL-
-lowed the handful of recipes and techniques she'd picked up from
station chefs and prep cooks and anyone with time for her. One of
the skills she'd learned was how to crack eggs and there was often an
unmistakable crunch in one or more bites that she was seemingly unaware
of. Her sweaters and the scarf she kept tucked into the sleeve of her
coat were the same pattern, made from textured yarn in varying colors.
She had crocheted them herself. Jamie knew all this because for the
past week, she'd been living with him. He woke to see her hair perfectly
styled and shining in the kitchen. The Farberware percolator plugged in
and steaming.

They were awkward around each other. Sometimes the silences were
painful. But Jamie wasn't unhappy that she was there. For her part,
Missy kept the newspapers opened to the classifieds, on the lookout for
someone renting a spare room. A hint she was done with large apartments
full of ever-changing roommates.

"You gotta be careful with that," Jamie told her.

"This looks okay. It says, 'female preferred.' Maybe it's a woman,
running the ad."

"And maybe it's not."

She pressed her lips together, sitting across from him, hands off the
paper and folded in her lap.

"Look," he said. "You're already set up here, so don't rush it. Save a
few dollars so you can get a better place for yourself. With decent people
renting it."

She looked blankly ahead. Naïve or maybe not naïve.

"Otherwise, what's the point of having stayed here at all? If you save up some, you can find a better place."

She nodded.

She didn't dress warmly enough. She didn't eat enough, in his opinion. She wasn't careful about where she was looking to rent, never mind the total strangers she'd find herself living with. He hadn't asked yet what it was exactly that had brought her to his house. He assumed she'd get around to it. Three days after showing up on his doorstep, she'd hauled in a small suitcase bursting with clothes and a cardboard box he'd carried up to the second floor for her. After that, the scent of peppermint frequently floated from the bathroom.

Missy was currently working as a hostess and occasional waitress at Casa Romano, a reliable family style restaurant off Wagaraw Road in Haledon. She had a pair of black knit dresses that were identical, which she hand-washed in the utility sink and brought to her room to dry. She draped them over the rail at the foot of the cot, which Jamie knew, having caught a glimpse inside the spare bedroom one night when the door was cracked open. He'd walked by swiftly, as if he hadn't been looking sideways, hoping to see more than laundry. Like Missy partially, or fully, undressed.

"Us," Missy had said. "This is complicated. We can't be us right now. It would get more complicated."

She'd managed to assert that much. He wanted to brush his lips over the top of her head. Instead, by eleven, he was saying goodnight to her and quietly closing the door behind him, getting ready to dig into his files. He'd moved all the paperwork into his own bedroom with a folding table where he spent too much time reviewing notes and interview summaries. Staring at them as if more information might magically appear. He thought he might find overlooked gaps he could then fill in.

What sentence had he failed to follow up with? Could he possibly meet again with any of the witnesses? The case and its status had taken on a life within him.

That week, at the meeting of the working group, the conference room had been put together auditorium-style with rows of metal chairs for every patrol officer and detective that'd been assigned to the case. Bachman had given the update while Miucci sat in the back, flipping through the *Paterson Morning News*.

"We knew this was going to be a tough one. Tough to solve, but also tough on us. A lot of people knew Randall Low. His dad and his brother. The softball team. If anyone deserved to get this solved, it was Randall."

Bachman looked down, possibly referring to his notes.

"But the manpower. That's the concern. A case like this eats up a lot of manpower. Boots on the ground. Door-to-door in the neighborhood, not really yielding anything. Actually, not yielding one solid piece of evidence."

Jamie had felt those words keenly. The lead from Eileen Brandsher not qualifying as anything.

It would be a tough decision to change course. That was Bachman's claim. It would resolve with the higher-ups eventually handing down their edict. That'd happen. Andres and Gianelli pulled off the case officially. The patrol officers who'd been given assignments going back to their other work.

Bachman hesitated before adding a thought.

"Right now, the case isn't closed. It's never closed. There comes a time to slow it down and start dragging in the loose ends. Hey, you never know. Maybe one of those loose ends will be the key."

Jamie had wondered what the widow would be told. Perhaps she'd get the same official line. They'd keep the case active. There was always the possibility of a witness coming forward. Then again, he wondered if they informed her of anything at all.

Jamie turned off the gooseneck lamp he'd positioned on the folding table and put the files away. He'd made a list of everything he planned to do in between his other assignments. Mostly that was waiting. Waiting for Sandy to call back so he could arrange to meet with her. Waiting and waiting for Sandy. Actually, that was more like hoping.

THIRTY-THREE

TRAFFIC FOR JAMIE WAS HITTING MORE THAN THREE red lights on his drive into work. He was used to cars and buses funneling into downtown and didn't think much of the increased double parking until he was half a block from the city lot, a full ten minutes past his normal arrival time. Being that late, he had trouble finding a spot close to the front for his Datsun. Sam, one of the more senior attendants, was on duty, deep into the "Meadowlands Entries" in the sports section, and making Jamie question the safety of his 280ZX. It was the municipal lot, but it was also Paterson.

Sam called to Jamie from the guard booth, its window conveniently half-opened and letting out smoke.

"What'd you think of this name? Sally's Whistle."

"I don't really play the horses," Jamie said. "But I think you're supposed to look at more than their name."

It was a brusque answer, but Jamie didn't have time to talk racing.

"I know what you're supposed to look at," Sam said. "I've been at it with the horses since before you were born."

By Jamie's calculations, that would give Sam a twenty-six-year plus losing streak and explain his career.

"Well, Sally's Whistle sounds like a good name," Jamie said.

"I like the fillies. Always looking for one with potential."

Jamie walked quickly down Ellison Street, away from the impulse to tell Sam not to waste his time and his money. It took a lot of energy and a lot of effort to get the right luck. Jamie was beginning to catch on to that. He pulled up his collar as he turned the corner at the intersection with Washington. The cold wind caught in the open space, whipping dust from the sidewalk. Jamie tightened his grip on his coat, figuring he'd try to avoid too much foot patrol. If possible. He imagined Henry would agree.

The plan to stay in their squad car fell apart when they were called to a grammar school in the Riverside section around lunchtime to follow through on a stabbing. Henry watched as Jamie chased and then arrested a fifteen-year-old but at least that brought them back to the station. Instead of a holding cell, they took the teen to the interrogation area to wait until officers from the State Juvenile Detention Center arrived for the transfer.

The compact room wasn't made to be comfortable. The steel table. The stools attached to the floor. A stark place for the slight figure hiding beneath a thick, black sweatshirt. Handcuffed. Confined. Henry began to make small talk with their suspect, then told Jamie he ought to leave, only one of them needed to be there.

"You sure?"

"Yeah. I'll sit with him. You go do whatever you need to upstairs. Catch up on your papers."

Henry kept his comments brief, but he seemed to know more than Jamie would have guessed about his work on the RJ's case, and how much time Jamie wanted to throw at it.

"You like Snickers?" Henry asked the quiet boy named Kevin. The question echoed in the room along with the unwrapping of candy bars as Jamie left.

Once at his desk, Jamie bent over his typewriter getting the specifics of the juvenile's arrest into acceptable form. Those tended to need extra care since every detail was considered important. There'd be the decision to charge as an adult or find some easier resolution. He reviewed his wording, a jar of correction fluid wedged in his palm.

Once he was done with the report preliminaries, Jamie returned to the witness statement taken from Craig Low. The register tapes indicated the bar had done three hundred in business that Saturday and Craig said that was in line with the previous weekends. All the money they'd taken in that night gone. Jamie held the report against the various theories he had on index cards. He compared that to what the evidence teams had made of the crime scene.

Randall had his gun drawn, but shots hadn't been fired by anyone until the killer was up close. And Cindy was shot first. Randall's gun hadn't discharged. The most popular theory had the killer upstairs, hiding until the bar had cleared out. Sneaking up on both of them, giving Randall enough time to pull the gun, but not to fire. That was a a theory favored by the higher ranks like Bachman and Miucci. Andres in particular didn't like it, nor did Gianelli but neither had a better one. Nor did Jamie. Only the general sense it was a robbery that went south pretty quick.

The squad room wasn't the best place to consolidate his thoughts. Jamie labored, trying to ignore the smell of cigarette smoke that clung to Gary's uniform and tended to waft over every now and then. There were also the sounds of papers flipping on the desk behind him. Ron Sargysan just back from vacation was returning a week's worth of phone calls, which he did loudly and while clicking on the tab of his cartridge pen.

It wasn't until Henry returned to the third floor, handing over the juvenile's prior record that Jamie noticed the time. Then he put in an extra half hour, reading details of the teen's previous crimes, surprisingly few, but all of them violent, before signing off. As he rose to leave the station, he was already thinking of the weekend ahead and the disruption of having Missy at the house. Could he leave and go barhopping with Steve? He guessed he could. Jamie really didn't want to. Even though he and Missy weren't dating, they were both off that Friday. Jamie didn't know what going out *not as a date* would be. He'd never considered horseracing. He'd never been. Sam with his systems and dreams of trifectas and other big payouts had planted a seed.

When he got home, Missy was with Nugget, leafing through a *Glamour* magazine. The cover was familiar, he'd noticed the issue days before neatly centered on the coffee table beneath that week's *TV Guide*.

"Have you ever been to the Meadowlands?"

"The Meadowlands? Like, for what?"

"The racetrack."

Missy moved her lips, but words weren't coming out. She seemed poised to remind Jamie of their relationship, which wasn't one. That's what Jamie expected, cutting her off.

"It's the weekend. People *do* things on the weekend."

Missy drew the magazine into her. Shielding herself. He knew he could be forceful at times. He couldn't help it.

"Would you rather go to Rails, down the street? Their specialty is Weissbier. That's beer with raspberry sauce. They serve it warm. Does that appeal to you?"

Missy shook her head.

"Karl came from Berlin. It's a real traditional place."

He was waiting for her to respond and found himself filling up space.

"Did you know they used to have mandatory lights out in Paterson during World War Two? The factories made planes, parts for the war. They thought the Germans would bomb here. A sub was spotted off the coast near Seaside," he said. "A U-boat."

Jamie was spewing a lot of random information. He realized he might be as nervous as he was pushy. Unsure how the weekend would playout if his Plan A didn't work.

"So anyway, my Aunt Ro was never a fan of me going to Rails."

He could have added how annoyed she'd been when he'd won the Oktoberfest stein-lifting contest. How a few years after that, he'd been given Nugget from Karl's sister who'd made a point to sit with him one night in the week his aunt had passed, boisterously describing the ten-week-old puppy who'd been raised on blood sausage and was at that time named Krieger. *"German for warrior. The pick of the litter!"*

He tamped down those stories and all his anxious chatter, giving Missy time to answer.

"The racetrack sounds fine," she said. "Is it dressy?"

Jamie didn't know. Racetracks were for betting and drinking out of plastic cups and smoking cheap cigars. But he'd heard Pegasus, the restaurant overlooking the Meadowlands track, was more of a sit-down place with dinner and cocktails and that was where he meant to take her.

"Maybe a little," he said.

Missy wore the pretty dress she'd worn on their only real date with one of her hand-crocheted sweaters.

They drove through the dark lots that dotted the Sports Complex, navigating the many service roads until they reached the track. There was valet parking and a glass-enclosed elevator brought them to the upper level, making it feel like more of a date than he'd intended. Sam, with a perpetual cigarette hanging from the side of his mouth, his fingers stained yellow with nicotine, forever bent over the dailies, had made Jamie think of the Meadowlands and that going there might be a good idea. There was more to the night than simply harness racing.

Jamie led her to Pegasus East with its à la carte menu which he thought would be preferable to the buffet served in the other section. Off to one side of the restaurant were betting tables and further down there were places to stand and watch the track below through oversized glass panels.

"So, we watch from inside here?" she asked.

"Racing begins at eight, so we'll be in the middle of dinner then."

Missy looked around. The other dinners were older. Men in double-breasted suits and tailored overcoats and women in silk dresses and a few furs slung on the backs of chairs. She moved closer to him and dinner at Pegasus began to seem like less of a bad idea.

"I think you'll like watching the horses."

Around 8:30, while Jamie and Missy waited for their entrées, the tables around them began to empty. Everyone else seemed to have timed the evening differently, crowding around the betting tables and viewing windows and clutching their drinks. Jamie asked Missy if she wanted another Chablis.

"Thank you, no."

Jamie nodded to the waiter, raising one finger and pointing to his almost empty Jack and Coke. He wasn't in a hurry to watch trotters.

"What made you want to be a chef?"

Missy rolled her neck. It had become a reflex she turned to, when he focused his attention on her.

"I didn't know I wanted to be a chef, but then when I was in Jacksonville, I got a job at this French restaurant. The owner used to let me stay after my shift to watch all the preparations. Jules, he was the owner. He would notice me watching and have me try things. He showed me how to hold my wrist and whisk a hollandaise sauce."

A single white rose sat between them on the table. Everything was cut glass. The vase. Even the salt and pepper shakers caught light from the restaurant's tiled ceiling and fanned a rainbow glow.

"How did you pick Jacksonville?"

"I didn't pick Jacksonville," she said. "I think Jacksonville picked me."

"Really? How so?"

"We were going to Daytona, but the car broke down in Jacksonville and that's where I found a job and that's where I ended up."

We. Jamie wondered who that meant.

"I liked it. I liked Jacksonville. The people there are nice. So nice and friendly."

"Why did you leave?"

"My mother. She was in a car accident. Not a bad one. I mean, it was a bad one, but she's fine now. I came back to help her. My stepfather was out of the house by then."

She was too shy to talk about her finances, but it was fairly clear she'd used all her savings to get to New Jersey and help pay her mother's medical expenses.

"So," Jamie said. "Who did you go to Jacksonville with?"

"I had a boyfriend when I left for Florida," Missy said. "But not for too long."

Their dinners arrived. Jamie had ordered for her once she said she liked lamb chops. Their plates were arranged with snow peas and potatoes lyonnaise. Missy didn't hurry to try any of it. She moved her shoulders to Frank Sinatra's, "Fly Me to the Moon," taking her usual careful sips of wine.

"A cook," Missy said out of nowhere. "A cook is someone who follows recipes. I want to be a chef."

"A chef doesn't follow recipes?"

"A chef makes recipes."

Her cheeks reddened when she said that. Jamie knew, without being told, that she was repeating something she'd heard. Something Jules had told her.

"A chef can make beautiful dishes. Cookies are angels. Salads that are tiny gardens. I see meringues, and they're like the most perfect clouds."

"It sounds like Jules was a good person to work for."

"He was really good to me. He was always teaching me."

She speared a lamb chop with her fork and passed it across the table to Jamie. He noticed she had two left on her plate.

"There's nothing like Le Morvan around here," she said. "The nicest restaurant is where I have my hostess job. Sometimes I waitress when it's slow, but that's not what I really want."

Behind Jamie, a huge shriek rose high over the music and restaurant noise.

"Someone won big," Missy said.

Jamie turned fully to the scene of a woman jumping up and down on impossibly thin heels. The men around her were grimacing and staring at their own tickets. Crumbling them tightly and tossing them.

"Someone picked the longshot," Jamie said.

"You think? That's the best, isn't it. Winning like that."

"Playing against the odds."

Jamie looked out the closest window where he had a partial view of the oval-shaped dirt, the striped poles, the floodlights, and the starting gate. The next race would be coming up soon. They had time to place bets and press their faces to the glass and fill themselves with possibility.

"We should buy tickets," he said.

"We should buy longshots."

Jamie pulled the program from his inside pocket and handed it to her. He smiled. "You pick."

THIRTY-FOUR

"THIS IS WHAT I HAVE SO FAR. YOU DON'T HAVE TO AN-swer me if it's something you already know. I'll be the one recapping what I have for you."

Gil twirled the Jameson in his glass. The clinking of ice cubes was appealing to Jamie, though playing with his drink wasn't a habit he had himself.

"They're selling the bar," he said. "Not exactly selling. They just stopped paying. Craig stopped paying. It's only him now, not 'they' anymore. So, the seller had a mortgage and he's taking it back. Not a true foreclosure. They came to a deal."

"Does that mean anything? Financially?"

Gil smiled at Jamie. "I guess not. And if it did, I might be breaking the attorney privilege. Even though I'm not an attorney."

Jamie thought Gil was as smart as any lawyer he'd ever met. Not that he'd met that many who'd impressed him. The kinds of cases where Jamie was a witness were drunk and disorderlies, petty thefts, and nickel bags of pot. The lawyers who showed up for those weren't professionals you'd trust your life with if you were charged with a capital crime or needed sound legal advice on a business deal. None of them dressed as nice as Andres and Gianelli.

Gil's ability to gather information had essentially passed though Jamie continued to meet with him, letting him rehash what he'd already disclosed. Like Jamie, he looked for whatever he might have missed the first time. He also liked to parse through Cindy's life and occasionally found new information there. Conversations he'd remember.

"It's something I noticed. Something I was thinking about."

He paused, taking a break from talking and purposefully moving the cubes around his glass. The ritual of staring as the ice melted and took on different shapes seemed to soothe him. There was a ceremony to Gil being in the bar.

"She seemed to go for the guys that were older and had a soft edge. Never leaving with them but sitting down talking in between her sets. She liked the protective guys that gave her big tips and told her to get a job waitressing or answering the phone at some nice company. They'd tell her to go someplace 'where there ain't a lot of bums like us around to bother you.'"

"Which guys were they? Names Gil? Got any names?"

"All of them. They'd give that Dutch uncle advice after they'd been pumping quarters into the jukebox for songs that got her moving the way they liked. "Suzie Q" or anything by Donna Summer."

"Where's this going?"

"Cindy told me she was planning to go to Atlantic City, but she didn't say with who."

"And you still don't think it was a guy she met at RJ's. You think she would've been going with that mystery guy she was seeing. The one who was helping her get away from Brad. After he hit her."

Gil winced as Jamie mentioned Cindy getting hit. Jamie made a note to follow up and get the report for the call in from the neighbors. Get their names and then an interview. Ask if they'd seen someone new near the apartment sometime in October or even early November. And then? And then what? A description of someone and still no name.

Jamie wanted to tell Gil he had plans, that he still had leads and the case wasn't a brick wall. Not yet. But Gil was onto another Jameson and it wasn't long before he was talking about the rabbit again.

"Once I walked out of the basement, out of their idea of a party, I knew I'd get shit. Clean the bathroom floor with a toothbrush. Iron all their underwear. Stupid, meaningless shit. Whatever. I went to Mexico. My parents, once I deciphered the payphones in Guadalajara and called them, they were just happy to know I was alive. Happy I'd be coming back. Dropping out of college wasn't that big a deal after they'd spent a few days convinced I'd died of an overdose in the gutter somewhere. Thinking I'd been rolled for my wallet and they'd never know what happened to me."

He turned and looked at Jamie straight on.

"Here's the thing. If I'd stayed, I'd never get that rabbit out of my mind. How I could have saved it."

Jamie noticed Gil said could instead of should and mulled over the difference the words made to the sentence. Then he lifted his finger, let the bartender know he wanted another round. Gil was staring into his tumbler, which was empty. Speaking into the bottom of the glass.

"She was a girl filled with dreams. Dreams, hopes, and plans."

THIRTY-FIVE

THAT WEEK WAS MOSTLY FIRST SHIFTS FOR JAMIE AND even after stopping at the gym, he still would be home for the six o'clock news. Missy said she'd get off "on the early side" but that often meant around eight. She hadn't specified if she'd have his dinner waiting. That was part of the tumbleweed of an arrangement they had going on, which was loosely defined and shifting. Mostly, she cooked and would leave something on the counter for him. A casserole with heating instructions that were easy to follow. A plate covered in foil with breaded cutlets. Her meals were decent. Not amazing, but solid. If he hadn't been able to head out the past weekend looking for girls at Aldo's, or the weekend before, he was getting fed.

Her car wasn't on the street, as he knew it wouldn't be, and he felt a small pang anyway. Walking into the mostly empty house, he bent to pet Nugget and was hit with a new smell overwhelming the kitchen. Tangy and sweet, what he took to be cinnamon. He found a tray of still warm muffins on the counter with a note from Missy saying, "just baked" as if that were a necessary thing to tell him. Finding them left Jamie confused and unsure if she was going to make dinner. Were these supposed to tide him over? When had she actually left for work? It was hard, having another person in the house, both of them with erratic schedules, and often vague plans for how they were supposed to organize their lives around each other.

Jamie picked up a muffin, soft and crowned with a crunchy, brown sugar streusel. A river of blueberry compote ran down his chin. It was the kind of not-entirely-cooled off, falling apart baked good that demanded a fork. He grabbed the tray and went to the sink, leaning forward and finishing the first. Once he'd pulled the top off a new quart of milk, he returned to the sink for another two muffins and then changed into sweats and fell into a peaceful sleep. It was after eight o'clock when he heard Missy's voice.

That had been his want for the past two weeks. Waking to Missy and rolling towards her, his fingers brushing her bare thigh. But Missy wasn't lying next to him. She was standing at the side of his bed, rustling his upper arm gingerly, with Jamie barely registering movement.

"Jamie."

"Huh?"

"The phone. There's someone on the phone for you."

He propped himself up, feeling the deep ether of early evening napping and a possible headache.

"Do you want to take the call?" she asked.

He wiped his mouth with the back of his hand, awake enough to hope there weren't crumbs or dark smears of fruit. With another part of his brain, he knew he had to get up.

"Go," he said. "Go tell them I'll be right there."

His voice came out harsher than he'd meant. Missy backed up and hurried from the room. She was so light, the stairs didn't make a sound. And when he got to the wall phone, she faded from the kitchen.

Jamie was sure to grab the pad and pen he'd left for this very moment, catching the time from the clock on top of the stove. The receiver rested on the counter. He lifted it. Before he said "hello," the dial tone was obvious. The line was dead.

It was exactly 8:27. Less than two minutes had ticked by since he'd been downstairs. Missy was staring at the television. There was only a half-wall separating the rooms and she'd been trying hard not to listen. Jamie could tell. But how could she not be curious?

"I'm guessing you didn't get a name."

"No," Missy said. "She didn't say her name and I didn't want to be rude."

Nosy. She didn't want to be nosy. Didn't she want to know if Jamie was seeing anyone? Didn't that matter to her?

"Was that for work?" she asked. "It sounded important." Missy was standing, a hand tucked into her back pocket. "I only answered the phone because it rang so much and you were upstairs."

"It's probably Ginny. Steve's birthday's coming up. She likes to throw parties."

There were girls and women that might call him at night. Like Steve's sometime girlfriend, Ginny. The call could have been from her. Or a neighbor needing a favor. Have Jamie watch their house if they were going away for a few days. The voice Missy heard could have been anyone's.

Jamie knew, he just knew it'd been Sandy. And if it wasn't, that was the only one he wanted it to be.

It was a weariness, not quite desperation. Jamie thought it might be time to meet with Connie De Carlo. All he had was the phone number for the high school. He would leave a message at the switchboard for Mrs. De Carlo that the police wanted to speak with her. Even to him, that sounded blunt and he weighed driving over unannounced. It might be better, less unnerving in person, to ease his way into the explanation. Jamie considered the two options. It was all he could do. Either way, he slated a few hours on Thursday or possibly the following week. He calculated that Missy would be at the restaurant then anyway, not sure why that mattered.

THIRTY-SIX

PARTNERING WITH HENRY WAS OFTEN A SLOW-PACED shift, but Jamie always drove the cruiser and almost always got the arrest. They'd left the squad room together before splitting off at the top of the stairwell.

"You go ahead," Henry said, which meant his usual men's room stop.

Jamie stood and paced near the lobby's flag stand. A map of Paterson, circa 1941, was on the wall, framed in gilded mahogany. His mother would have been eight and his Aunt Ro thirteen. Her brother, Jamie's father, would have been twelve. He tried to pinpoint Fulton Place and then Paxton Street. Family information was sparse, but he did have addresses for their childhood homes.

"Got all your gear together?"

Henry had never been Jamie's field advisor. As far as Jamie knew, he'd never been anyone's field advisor. Despite his years of seniority, Henry was technically Jamie's equal, since Jamie was a full patrol officer. But Henry liked to be helpful. Or to feel experienced.

Jamie twirled a set of keys around his index finger.

"All set."

They settled onto familiar brown vinyl, the radio crackling as Jamie hit the ignition.

"We're in the Fourth Ward."

Jamie had seen their schedule but didn't comment.

"I need to stop at the pet store first," he said.

Henry didn't even ask why.

Krauser's was in one of the city's still busy shopping areas, crammed between Leonard's Pharmacy and DiCicco's, a bakery and salumeria. The wind that day was just right, catching DiCicco's soft, yeasty bread. Their Pane Toscano was a favorite around the department. Jamie planned to combine a stop for breakfast rolls with his quick run next door.

"I'll be back in five," Jamie said as he pressed on the brake, leaving the car double-parked with Henry rooted comfortably in the passenger seat.

Hurrying through Krauser's, he passed the aquarium supplies and low-lit tanks with guppies and tetras. Then it was a display of leashes and harnesses and around the corner, open hutches of pink-eyed guinea pigs and noisy cages of gerbils. An entire aisle covered in pine shavings. When Jamie got to the stacks of dog food in the back, it struck him. The pine shavings.

RJ's upstairs hall was where they hosted special events. Large, boisterous parties with excessive decorations. A New Year's Eve bash in the the weeks before the murders. They'd been preparing for an upcoming Country and Western Night, featuring music and a jamboree motif. That was in the investigative report from the responders who'd showed up with the first call from Catherine Rose. Curiously, there hadn't been much hay in the bar area. No trail leading to the bodies.

It was assumed that Randall had been in the basement, then returned to the main level, about to close for the night. Checking his inventory was a routine he was known to follow and the assumption squared with the crime scene. They'd found nothing unusual in the crepe-soled bottom of his shoes nor any evidence that Cindy had left the first floor. Yet there'd been dozens of bales stacked in the lounge, with hay spilling onto the landing and on most of the upper staircase. Bachman in particular insisted the gunman had hidden in the upstairs hall, then snuck down after the bar closed. But where was all the hay the shooter would have dragged in with him? That part of the working theory had to be wrong.

"You want a bag for this?"

Jamie had set a case of dog food on the counter before reaching for his wallet. A case of dog food that wouldn't fit into any bag he could imagine.

"No, thanks."

Jamie needed to think. What did it mean that he could rule out the best theory the working group had? That the killer wasn't someone who had snuck in, someone who surprised Randall. Did it matter that the killer had to have come into the bar after closing, or been someone who was already there, inside and known to Cindy and Randall? What could this shred of a clue mean?

Back on the street, the cold air of mid-winter wasn't enough to shake a coherent thought into him. There was never enough clarity. He popped the trunk open and found a place for the dog food, carefully moving the unit's standard issue rifle and a package of road flares. Inside the car, he found Henry sleeping.

THIRTY-SEVEN

*IT WAS A BALLSY MOVE, GOING TO THE FUNERAL HOME.
Showing up in a rumpled shirt and slacks, looking like a guy who might run a
forklift during the day and hang out at RJ's staring at young girls at night. The
service was quite a few weeks after the murders. A light turnout. He hadn't really
expected many of her customers at Gorley's for the closed casket remembrance.*

*A girl he guessed to be Sandy was there along with a longhair he guessed to
be her boyfriend. Mid-twenties, wearing a patterned shirt and designer jeans. He
didn't match the description of Brad Rogan, who was useless to him anyway. The
only other man in the reception room looked about as rumpled as he did except that
man's shirt was a ticking stripe. He figured him for an uncle or the mother's current
boyfriend, since he'd been interacting with the Gorley representative. At one point
an envelope was exchanged. He understood what he saw was probably payment for
the burial arrangements but imagined for the briefest moment the hand-off was the
very thing of particular interest to him, though that item wasn't what he'd come for.
He was at the funeral home looking for a person.*

*There were two men to choose from and he could only follow one home. He
picked the patterned shirt. For backup, in case he picked wrong, he trailed the
striped-shirted man until they both reached the amenity table. He took a wrapped
butterscotch from the diamond-glass dish and slipped it in his pocket.*

"I'd like to offer my condolences," he said.

Thank you."

*Because of Cindy's career, discussing how each of them had known her
would be delicate. He'd known that and took his time, edging towards the floral
arrangements. A spray of white and pink roses with a satin sash and "Angel"
scripted in gold lettering stood sentry before the casket. Other flowers were in vases*

placed nearby. Chrysanthemums and lilies and green button poms and lots of baby's breath. He made a point of reading every card and then, in a great show, made the sign of the cross. As he turned from her casket and faced the room, he saw a woman in the first row with a blonde updo and those unmistakable blue-green eyes. The familial resemblance he hadn't counted on. A black cat running dead in his path.

He moved quickly, back to the demilune table with its pamphlets and candies where the man in the striped shirt had stayed idling.

"Family?" he asked.

"A friend," the man said. "Friend of the family."

He shook his head. "Helluva thing," he said. "Helluva thing."

There was a long—but not uncomfortable—pause. The other man filled it by introducing himself, holding out his right hand.

"Gil," the man said. "Gil Christian."

THIRTY-EIGHT

IT HAD BEEN YEARS SINCE HIS AUNT WORKED THE floor at the Florence Shop and as a teen, his visits there had tapered off to where he'd only stopped by a handful of times, even after she'd made senior management. He didn't imagine he would recognize anyone at the women's store or that anyone would know him and there were malls with better options, but the shop was a mainstay downtown and for Jamie, the only place he'd even considered. In the well-lit aisles, he was greeted with clothes meant for women of his aunt's generation. He passed by millinery and a costume jewelry counter full of clip-on earrings, then an alcove for fashion dresses with its discretely placed sign offering "complementary alterations."

When Jamie first hatched the idea, he'd been certain he could easily blend in and shop on his own. He persisted with that tact, sliding hangers along racks, and checking tags on random blouses, until realizing he had no idea where to find the clothes he was looking for and that even if he did find the right clothes, he wouldn't know the size. Small? Extra-small? Coming upon an entire petite department, he was mystified and forced to approach the first woman he saw wearing a gold employee pin. As he'd expected, the woman didn't seem to know who he was and he found her not only unfamiliar, but curt, particularly once Jamie asked for help with a pair of pajamas. Jamie would learn that the lingerie department was tucked way, way in the back, off to the side, and that "pajama" or "nightgown" was likely the code men used when looking for some of the clingier, flimsier negligees.

At the rear of the store, he was met with mannequins wearing those slinky pieces. Peach chiffon and shimmering silver and lace and thin spaghetti straps. Jamie had meant to buy real pajamas. The kind with a top that buttoned like an Oxford shirt paired with elastic waist pants. The actual definition of pajamas.

"They're for my sister," Jamie said. "What's the smallest size that you have?"

The woman eyed him.

"She's not built like you? She's small?"

He could have said his mother was slight and that his sister had the finer build of that side of the family. But when he thought of Missy, he saw her slim hips measured against what he guessed was her B-cup, well aware that wasn't how anyone would describe a sister, even when buying her clothes. His mouth suddenly became dry. The White Rock girl, Jamie thought. *Have you ever seen the White Rock girl? She's like a pixie, really. What size would that be?*

After he'd selected a pair of mint green pajamas with white piping that looked warm and comfortable, he was led to the sweater department.

"Turtleneck?" the woman asked.

He imagined Missy would disappear into a turtleneck, but maybe that's what she needed.

"Okay," he said. "One of those. And also another one. Maybe the kind that buttons."

He let the woman helping him choose the colors.

"Can you make sure it's soft? Not itchy."

She held out a white sweater, a halo of wool that brought to mind rabbit fur and marshmallows and Steve's mother's toy poodle, a little dog named Toy.

"It's angora."

Jamie was mesmerized with its feel and losing all pretext of having a sister. He'd used the excuse because it felt easier than explaining Missy. A girl. Young woman. They'd recently met. Gone on one date. She was living at his house and he wasn't sure why. It was platonic. He wasn't sure why that was either. Stroking the sweater meant for Missy, he felt confused and exposed.

"Do you want these all together in one box? I think I can put them in one of the small coat boxes. Will that do?"

He told the woman that would be fine. To put the white sweater on top. He wanted that to be the first thing Missy saw. The first thing she'd touch.

Jamie came home to a house he was still getting used to. Even with Missy away at the restaurant, it had taken on new energy. A female energy. All her pretty soaps in the bathroom. Jamie managed the shopping trip and still had time to kick around. He went for a six-mile jog circling through Hillcrest, came back and showered. The waning daylight as he put on clean sweatpants reminded him of high school. It was that slot in the late afternoon when there would've been wrestling practice. He placed a call to Mrs. De Carlo.

"She's in her classroom working with students. Can I have her call you back?"

Jamie hated to say he was a police officer. It might sound as if she were in trouble. He didn't want to alarm her for what he meant to be a casual meeting. All he wanted was Sandy's information and Mrs. De Carlo seemed like his best chance.

"Tell her this is a routine call about Cindy Kaczorek," he said, trying to strike the right balance. Routine meant she shouldn't worry. Cindy's name meant she ought to return the call. He gave his name as Officer Palmieri. A simple message.

He set the TV to Channel Seven and *The 4:30 Movie*. Vincent Price week. *Theater of Blood*. Background noise. With the screen's patchy light behind him, Jamie climbed the stairs to his old office. As much as he could, he'd turned the space over to Missy. After setting her up with the cot, he'd taken a trunk from the attic and cleaned it for her. The box from the Florence Shop that he'd left sitting on the wool blanket a reminder he'd already been in once that day.

He took two composition books from the desk and brought them to his room with the folding table and the files he'd made up for himself, primarily copies of reports on RJ's. Forensics and interview summaries. He needed to review his notes from the last semester, a stab at getting ahead for an upcoming course in psychology. Instead, he went to his write-up on Brad Rogan.

They'd met at Addie's. Brad came directly from work wearing overalls, his hands lightened with cement dust, his hair blow-dried and gelled. He was driving a truck and delivering pallets in Port Elizabeth and told Jamie he was a stereo salesman in between positions. Cindy's mother had described him as slick though sitting at the diner, he looked brought down a bit. Of course, there was Cindy and what her death had done to him. Even if he had been detained that particular weekend. He didn't need to be a person of interest in the case to be ripped up by it.

"Got her clothes, still in the apartment," he'd said. Those were his first words to Jamie, before he'd been asked any formal questions.

They both ordered cheeseburger platters. Jamie took notes while Brad spoke. How he'd met Cindy. How great she was. According to Brad, it was her idea to start dancing. She liked the stage. She'd been in plays in high school. If she could get some experience, then maybe go work at a club in New York, she might find a way to work on Broadway.

"That was a dream, you know?" Brad said. "I wasn't gonna be the one to tell her that wasn't the way it worked."

"No," Jamie said.

"So, she danced. She made money. But she wasn't like, loose about anything. Just Cindy wearing her outfit."

"And that didn't bother you?"

"Why would that bother me?"

The interview paused when the food arrived. Brad ate his burger slowly, putting it down often to pull a napkin from the dispenser and wipe at his mouth. A small pile of crushed paper was pushed to the side of the table.

"So, what happened the night your neighbors called the police on you?"

Brad turned away and reached for another napkin. This time, he was pressing it to his eyes.

"Take your time," Jamie said.

Jamie's notes didn't really tell the whole story. They were flat. Nothing he'd written captured what it was like to sit across from Brad and hear him tell a pared down version of the fight that brought the police to their apartment. He didn't blame Cindy, but as he saw it, he wasn't to blame either. He was drunk. He didn't know what got into him. Really, if Brad had to blame anyone, it was the neighbors. According to him, it always sounded worse listening to other people fight.

"Louder because, you know, you're paying attention to just that. What's going on next door. Nosy people hear things differently."

"Did Cindy start seeing anyone after that?"

Brad rolled his latest napkin around in his fist.

"What are you talking about? Cindy wasn't seeing anyone when she was with me. I told you, she was never loose."

His face tightened, quick and defensive of the person he'd been portraying as Cindy.

Gianelli had reviewed the notes and thought it was a good follow-up. Checked off the right boxes. Still, Jamie thought there was more underneath. Brad, too casual about Cindy dancing. Not suspecting she'd been seeing someone. He read through the interview repeatedly, looking for the questions he missed and trying to recall Brad's exact demeanor when asked if he thought there'd been drugs behind the shooting. He probably could have manipulated her into dealing, but Brad didn't have a record and RJ's had too many off-duty cops to be a place for any sort of real business.

It was almost six when he put away Brad's interview, aware of the time and Missy getting home and finding the box he'd left for her without a word of explanation. Wondering if she'd wear the pajamas that night and if he'd see her in them. Whatever she planned to do with the clothes, whatever she thought of his gift, it didn't come out during dinner, although to Jamie, she seemed light and secretly pleased with herself. Slipping in a Fleetwood Mac cassette when they were finished and ready to clear the table. Missy moved effortlessly through the kitchen, stretching Saran Wrap over a leftover chicken breast, and Jamie still worrying about gift-giving and how he would have worded a note card if he'd have thought of it earlier.

"Are there extra vacuum bags?" she asked, bending to wipe the floor around Nugget's water dish.

"Is the one in there full?"

"Uh huh. I couldn't find where you keep new ones."

She pulled a small plate from the refrigerator and set it on the counter.

"I brought you an apple crisp," she said. "Leon, he's the part-time pastry chef. He's always trying to get me to try out, like, everything."

The little rituals they'd carved out were in place and the night went that way. Folding towels and sheets, a rerun of *Hawaii Five-O*. Missy said she was tired and left in the middle of Johnny Carson's opening monologue.

It wasn't until much later that Jamie heard her padding through the hallway, past his room and in the direction of the stairs. Then there were more noises he strained to identify; the light suction of the freezer door followed by running water. After a time, he noticed she remained on the first floor. Perhaps there ought to have been rules about her privacy, where Missy was able to have a glass of water by herself. But there weren't specific guidelines pushing back on his unbearable urge to join her.

Once downstairs, Jamie took a glass from the cabinet, filled it with ice and ran the tap over it. He drank leaning on the counter, alert to the sounds in the adjoining room. When he walked in, she didn't turn. She set her glass on an end table and went to the mantel decorated with family photographs and his aunt's carriage clock. Missy chose the double frame with a picture of Jamie in his scout uniform and the studio portrait of his mother taken for her high school graduation. Both of them sepia toned. She took her time on each before she ran her finger along the frame, tracing the stamped brass design and then the worn velvet backing. She returned it to the mantel, stepping back a few paces to make sure she'd centered it. Within the cave of the living room, quiet and dimly lit, she never acknowledged Jamie. She never asked if the portrait was his aunt or his mother.

He'd never told the story aloud. Not to Debra. Not to Steve. The sudden aneurysm that changed his life. The ambulance and police cars at his house when he came home from school in fourth grade. A day in late April like any other. And then not like any other. And then soon after, this house became his home. His Aunt Ro's house on Maitland, where he'd been sent by whatever relatives were in charge and where he'd lived ever since.

In the weeks Missy had been living there, their way of being together shifted as they adjusted to each other. They'd become comfortable with their silences. Then some internal mechanism—a mainspring, a coil, a ratchet wheel—would turn by a hair.

Back in their own rooms, Jamie sat at his folding table desk, not tired at all. He kept his focus on the closed door. Transfixed.

THIRTY-NINE

IT FELT AS IF THEY'D JUST HAD THEIR LAST MEETING AND again, the working team was brought back into the conference room. The metal chairs were lined up as before. Most of the officers stayed quiet, letting the on-and-off knocking of worn pipes set the background noise. That's what the heating system was good for. It wasn't sturdy enough to warm the room or their seats.

A green board had been rolled to position behind the podium, flanked by a pair of flag stands. Names and dates were written in a generic block. The salient facts. Ballistic report information up in the right hand corner. Bachman set a stick of white chalk into its resting place, then ceded the space to Detective Lieutenant Miucci, who was the liaison for the press, and also one of the senior officers overseeing the case. About midway in the chain of command.

Sitting with Jamie were Andres and Gianelli, Gary, John Greene and his longtime partner, Fred Gerritsen. A few other patrol officers who'd done some witness interviews of the bar crowd and the neighborhood. Captain Ulrich, who Jamie hadn't seen in any of the prior meetings, had taken an aisle seat, adding a pointed layer of meaning.

Miucci began. "We all remember that case a few years ago? At Finley's?"

Everyone remembered. It was a rhetorical question.

"A fight started. A bouncer, Bobby Warner tries to break it up. Everyone shuffles to the back of the bar, then they push themselves through the rear door. There's a gunshot. Warner dies in the emergency room."

Miucci paused. Checked his cufflink. Someone cleared their throat.

"Not one person saw a gun. No one," Miucci continued. "And that was legitimate. Not a bunch of guys who didn't want to get involved. Everyone loved Bobby. Wanted the guy caught. It was a crowd of people, too close to see what was going on." He took a minute. Miucci wasn't chastising the department for their work. He was framing the perspective. "That kid last year," he went on, "has his brand-new license, first time driving to the mall. He's about to walk in with his girlfriend to see a movie. Eight o'clock on a Saturday night. Creep leaning against the wall beside the main entrance. A few people saw him hanging around, waiting there. He walks up to the kid, shoots him in the chest. Twenty witnesses saw the whole thing. Then the guy turns and runs down an embankment. A couple of people see him in the parking lot heading over to some pine trees. Got a detailed description of him from every one of them."

An angry silence filled the room.

"No motive, no reason for this seventeen-year-old kid to be dead. And no arrest for this waste-of-a-human life that shot him." He cleared his throat. "Never found him."

That shooting was local, even if outside the Paterson jurisdiction, and a personal thorn for Miucci. The victim was a teenager. Miucci walked away, returning the front of the room to Bachman. The sergeant weighed in on the ballistics report, the only firm evidence. Added to that, "the hard work of the guys on the street. Going through the neighborhood, sometimes checking with witnesses twice. Making sure they got the whole story."

The assembled men looked at each other. It was tough, what he was saying. But they had to be realistic.

"It's coming on almost two months now," Bachman reminded them. "We're not calling this a closed case. Can't do that until the suspect is either caught or dead. But it's time to wind things down. Paterson PD isn't made of money."

The meeting ended with Andres and Gianelli officially off the case. Jamie and the handful of patrol officers with him were told they could work on it between other assignments. Finish up whatever interviews they had scheduled.

There was nothing Jamie could offer. A phone call from Sandy he'd never said a word about. Convinced she'd call back and he could get a better story together, that hadn't happened and it was looking more and more like a dead end anyway. All he had was his recently scheduled meeting with Mrs. De Carlo, Cindy's former teacher who'd called back and said she'd be delighted to speak with him. As if that were a coup to brandish in the investigation of a bar shooting. Gianelli clapped him on his upper arm as they walked slowly out of the meeting.

"It happens," he said.

Jamie nodded.

"You did some good work. Learned a few things," Gianelli said. "Got a feeling we'll be seeing you again."

FORTY

JAMIE WAS SURPRISED TO LEARN MISSY LIKED TO PLAY Scrabble. She'd opened the breakfront off the kitchen looking for dish towels and found the trove of old games stored there. Trouble. Monopoly. Battleship.

He'd only played games with Aunt Ro. No one else, not even Debra in the two years she was his girlfriend. His aunt had been strong willed her whole life and often sharp-elbowed and he couldn't imagine facing off at that level with anyone he was going with. But Missy already had the box in her hands.

"I have a Lazy Susan we always used."

He reached into the upper shelves of the cabinet and produced a round of solid wood. The writing pad he kept by the phone in case Sandy ever called finally proved useful. He skated it across the table for Missy to keep score. They played for almost an hour, ending when Missy placed "tithe" down with "h" landing as a triple letter.

"Tithe?"

"Tithe."

"The only dictionary I have is upstairs. It's a paperback."

Missy gave him a sideways stare. With her tiny, pushed-out ears and wispy energy, the slightness of her. Small boned. She was small boned. That's the description he'd been searching for in the Florence Shop.

"It's a real word," she said. "I didn't make it up."

She hadn't known the exact meaning and her cheeks reddened when she'd been forced to admit that. He wanted to explain how he'd played with his aunt. How she challenged him and never, ever let him win. Not at any game. Not even Hearts or Gin Rummy. He hadn't meant to be aggressive with Missy, who was picking up the small wooden tiles, folding up the board.

Jamie reasoned they were both tired. He had work at seven. Missy had whatever she did in the early part of the day, which Jamie wasn't sure he knew. Cleaning. Food shopping. The house was immaculate. He was well fed. She worked a full-time job. He knew her days were filled.

Soon, they were both upstairs, Missy's hand on the door's round knob about to enter his old bedroom.

"Goodnight." Jamie's voice was soft.

Missy half turned, only her left side facing him, her eyes cast down. She waited. They shouldn't end the night angry with each other. They should be able to fix the awkwardness. He felt the thing unsaid between them digging into his side. The silence hovered while neither moved, Missy finally breaking it.

"Goodnight," she said.

Sitting in bed, he tried reading the court management and policy text he'd been studying the first night Missy had shown up. That night had felt off because he had no idea what to think. This time, Jamie had the unsettled feeling of having done the thing that made it all wrong between them. A prickling realization he tried to ignore as he reviewed the section's first sentence.

We are an independent branch of government constitutionally entrusted with the fair and just resolution of disputes in order to preserve the rule of law and to . . . .

Jamie was struggling to concentrate and get to the next paragraph when Missy knocked on his door, then opened it, revealing she'd changed into her mint green pajamas. He was given his first full-on view of her in the Florence Shop's pairing of soft, breezy pants and silky top, a vision from some black and white film. She took the briefest step forward, not moving past the frame. Her face stayed a question while neither of them spoke. The pause that began in the hallway pulsed as they waited, or maybe that was the blood in his ears. The opportunity for Jamie to apologize a ripe plum that he chose to ignore.

Jamie was sorry. He was very sorry but he didn't know how to explain why he'd become fiercely competitive over a boardgame. Rudely insulting Missy. The air needed to be cleared, Jamie knew that. But it was so much better to pretend it never happened. He wanted Missy to do that with him. Intending to wait her out, he filled the lingering silence trying to read Missy, her head cocked to the side, inscrutable. He could only imagine his facial expression, baring his pitiful longing for her to take care of this.

"I'm not mad at you."

It was the only thing she said.

Jamie, with a burst of relief, patted the sliver of mattress next to him. A reflex. Like that, he'd forgotten she wasn't in the category of Debra or a girl he'd brought home from Aldo's or somewhere like it. Coaxing her next to him was surely a breach of their unspoken and maddeningly evasive house rules. The night was just getting worse. A new tension caught him, knowing how far he'd gone. Curiously, she moved into the room. The light seemed to follow her.

For as many times as Jamie had dreamed of those pajamas, dreamed of unbuttoning her top slowly and sliding it off her shoulders, he was breathless with surprise when she bent over him. Everything compressed into that moment and the night in her foyer. Jamie stopped to steady himself, brushing away the hair at her nape and then kissing her neck.

Somewhere in the middle of the night, he'd remembered to set his alarm. It went off at 6:20 a.m., not waking Missy. He wanted to let her sleep but he wanted to say something to her before he left.

When he was in his uniform, he poured a coffee for her. Mostly she drank milk, so he made sure it was light. He left the mug on his dresser, then rubbed her face with the back of his fingers. Her eyes began to blink, registering the early sun and taking in the new room she was waking in. Her voice groggy. Her face a faint grin.

"We're even more complicated now," she said.

FORTY-ONE

HE'D LET NUGGET OUT FOR A QUICK RUN AROUND THE yard after breakfast and knew it was a cold one. It was colder still as he scraped off his windshield. Inside the car, he was forced to peel off his work gloves and blow on his hands. But it wasn't the slow-to-heat Datsun that occupied his drive down Maitland. As a stream of windows began to brighten and the neighborhood awakened, Jamie processed how quickly the night had ended. He was flooded with Missy, as he'd known he would be. She'd be getting ready for the day, eventually making her way back to the spare room and pulling on her jeans. Once again, life inside the brick-faced Cape Cod was shifting.

Hillcrest was full of homes like his. Front stoops with Clarke's Dairy boxes, open and waiting for deliveries, as if that was all there was to living there. So many had absorbed divorces and imposed sales from other financial disruptions and deaths. A few actual foreclosures.

The changes at his house after his aunt's passing had become plain soon enough. The dead-end had grown accustomed to a series of unfamiliar cars parked at the curb on Saturday and Sunday mornings and the occasional weekday. A turnover of women leaving early. He knew his neighbors had seen that, taken note, and he'd been given a pass. But having Missy living there, on his tiny block of borrowed jumper cables, Girl Scout cookies and gossip, he wondered if that was different, really different from all the other disruptions and if this one would matter. There was what he was allowed to do as a young, single guy and there was what Missy wasn't supposed to do openly. Now that they were even more complicated, as Missy had said, it was something Jamie knew he ought to consider, given that what he wanted was to be with her. He turned over options of how he could keep Missy at the house. Convince her to stay indefinitely.

They hadn't spoken of anything like that during the night. What they'd said to each other had been whispers. When the train rolled by around one, they'd both agreed it was a good sound though Missy said she liked falling rain best. Then Jamie dozed with Missy next to him, already asleep, the quilt on top of her moving in even measures.

He rewound the night until it was fully daylight and he was downtown, the yellowed columns of the municipal lot officially greeting him. The Colt Building was solid as ever. An anchor for him. Jamie took the three flights of stairs focused on his oxygen and marking the run down to the second. A holdover from the conditioning coach he'd had at the academy. He'd averaged a good pace even though the morning he was sprinting to wouldn't be eventful. He expected the chiffon dress to be waiting on his desk, Gary having put in his time the week before.

Elizabeth handed him his daily. "And the sergeant wants to see you. I didn't get to write up the note."

"Did he say what time?"

"Now, I guess."

Meeting with Bachman could mean new assignments added to his work at the bus stop near Meyer Brothers and driving around the Fourth Ward with Henry. Jamie considered the sergeant had noticed his diligence in pursuing witnesses. Tomasz at the chemical plant had led to Eileen Brandsher. He'd put those pieces together. As far as Jamie knew, he was the only one to interview anyone who'd legitimately heard or seen anything and, in the end, he'd obtained two statements. He tried not to feel prideful. Neither had been all that useful and hadn't been mentioned at any of the briefings. The summary Bachman started with told him as much.

"Tough case, that RJ's," Bachman said.

Jamie nodded.

"Sometimes better to let those go," Bachman continued. "You get some crappy lead, go after the wrong fellow. Looks like the department is taking the easy route, pinning it on someone. Everyone looks bad. Sometimes you have to let those go."

"Yes."

"Here's what I learned at places like Yongsan-dong. Treat these setbacks professionally. It's never personal."

Jamie heard that line at the academy. The code to not feel anything.

"Anyway, it's good to get your mind on to the next one. The best way to clear it all out. This new one's a bit interesting. The complaint is that stuff is falling off trucks at a particular warehouse behind Getty Ave. A little faster than usual," Bachman said.

His white uniform shirt, crisp and decorated with sergeant stripes, said as much about Bachman as his Muscle Beach arms. Jamie figured he'd been on the force almost twenty years and was someone to listen to.

"Not a few VCRs or stereos here and there. The extras that always come off around the holidays. This is like the real shit. Whole shipments."

"What kind of merchandise?"

"Good question. Excellent question."

Bachman was engaging him. Jamie tried to care about warehouses and thefts and not obsess over unsolved homicides and how the RJ's case he was being pushed further away from was more than a file; it was Randall and Cindy's murders. The wire mesh glass behind Bachman attracted his attention, as loud, wintry gusts swept the panes.

"We don't know. Here's the kicker. It's an FBI case. They're the ones to open the file. We're just in for backup. Who we know in the neighborhood. Our favorite dirtbags, the ones we go to if we need to barter for information."

Jamie leaned forward.

"You don't necessarily meet with them, the Feds," Bachman continued. "I'll be farming some stuff over to you. So, keep that in mind. You got this new file. Not anything to work on yet but expect to be busy."

"Okay," Jamie said. "I will."

He didn't know how to answer Bachman without sounding small. Childish. Backup for the Feds. He felt like a cartoon. If that's how he'd come off, the sergeant had moved on, waving a white envelope at him.

"Drop this off when you're back downstairs."

"Right. With Elizabeth?"

"Yeah, with Elizabeth. Jesus. Talk about letting yourself go." Bachman shook his head. "She's due for a replacement."

Jamie reached for the envelope, making an uncomfortable eye contact with the sergeant. The comment was sharp. Too sharp, as if Elizbeth was someone who was personal to him. He wasn't quick at all with the smiling comeback expected of him.

"Are you paying attention, Palmieri? For Chrissakes."

"I'll drop it off right now."

"You do that. And the next thing you do is, you go finish whatever you have to finish. Because it's time to be done with that Low case. You got that?"

You got that? The command left no doubt he needed to get going on new things. He had scant hope of finding Sandy's information from Cindy's drama teacher. Those were the realities. There was no way to justify the time it would take Jamie to meet with Mrs. De Carlo and he'd have to plan on using his off-duty hours. He budgeted roughly two hours, cutting out most of his workout but he could do a run in the twilight.

After his shift, he drove down Route 80, then onto an artery of small, local highways. The last one he took was more a country road, parts of it unpaved and sprinkled with loose gravel. He'd had to pull quickly to the side when a blue F-150 came barreling towards him from the opposite direction. Jamie's Datsun almost landed in the tall grass and weeds on the road's shoulder. A few yards away, stuck in the thicket, a barely visible mileage post steered Jamie to Cindy's high school.

It wasn't Paterson Catholic, but when he opened the entrance doors, Jamie was suddenly back. Rows of double-tiered lockers on both sides of the wide front hall. Trophy case after trophy case led the way to the administrative offices. That late in the day, the janitor's trash barrels and wide brooms were already pulled from their closets.

At reception, he was given directions to see Mrs. De Carlo. Jamie showed up in uniform and no one questioned him or asked for identification. His boots were hard on the all-purpose linoleum he'd last walked in gym sneakers. He made the first left turn and then second left as he'd been told and found Room 224. Through a window framed high in the door, he saw a girl wearing a cheerleader's jacket sitting next to the teacher's desk. Jamie paused, waiting for his turn, although he was a police officer and what could be more pressing than a murder investigation? A double homicide.

The woman at the desk caught sight of Jamie and made the kinds of movements that signaled the end of her conversation. The girl and Jamie passed each other, she leaving and he walking into the classroom.

Mrs. De Carlo was someone who struck with a first impression. Her precise, rust-colored bob. Her blouse, her skirt, the gauzy scarf tied at her neck, everything matched her hair. Jamie didn't know all that much about women and clothing. His aunt's mode of dress was probably a style called utilitarian. But Jamie knew right away that Mrs. De Carlo had a flourish with her statement shade of red.

She held out her hand, welcoming him.

"Officer Palmieri," she said. "I'm Connie De Carlo."

After shaking hands, she returned to her desk, clearing papers and setting aside a stack of stapled reports. Jamie stepped back, falling into his regulation stance. Legs partially apart, hands together resting at belt level.

"Oh, sit please," she said. "Look at me. I think I'm a little nervous."

Jamie took the chair next to Mrs. De Carlo, still warm from the junior or senior who'd just occupied it.

"Mrs. Sutter," he said, "Cindy's mother. She says that you kept in touch with Cindy."

"Yes. That's true. Cindy liked to call me. I called her too sometimes. She was a really special student. A very talented girl."

"Talented. How so?"

"Her talent? Cindy had a real stage presence. I'm the school drama teacher. I've been doing this for years. Many, many school plays. So many."

"And Cindy was special?"

"Cindy was special."

"Did Cindy ever mention anything to you that was personal?"

"I knew she took that job as a dancer. I didn't want to judge her, make her feel bad for it. But we talked. She knew my opinion."

"What about Sandy? She had a friend named Sandy. Do you know her? Know where I can reach her?"

Mrs. De Carlo slowly let her hands find the ends of her scarf, rubbing the fibers.

"I appreciate that whatever she told you was meant to be in confidence. But everything you know is important for us to also know. For the investigation," Jamie said, trying to sound as textbook as he could.

Jamie purposely avoided the word, murder. Mrs. De Carlo occupied her day with the world of her students. A sea of cheery posters brightened the walls. Auditions for *Gypsy* would be opening soon. A Wednesday afternoon bake sale. These were not the things of death. Cindy's violent death. Jamie listened closely until he heard a familiar slow exhale. The one that Eileen Brandsher released. It'll happen now, he thought. He'd prompted her just enough.

"I don't know what any of this is about, but if Sandy's name came up, I can tell you this. With Sandy, there was always trouble. Cindy did reveal that much in our calls."

"What kinds of trouble?"

"Whatever kind there is. Some people seem to attract it."

"Do you have any information on Sandy? Anything?"

"If I knew where Sandy was, which I do not. But if I did know, I'm not sure I'd care to be involved all that much. Her whereabouts are something that I might not tell you."

What had been a polite conversation, a pleasant one, had turned on a dime. Jamie had no idea why. He'd driven all that way on the thinnest hope he'd be led to Sandy. He'd tried so hard to ask the right questions.

"Okay, then. Can we talk about Brad, her boyfriend? Did she talk with you about leaving him? For someone else? Was there anything she said that you recall?"

"This," she said. "This is what *I* told Cindy. That she was getting out of the frying pan and into the fire."

"Right."

Mrs. De Carlo looked away from the tips of her rust-colored nails and straight at Jamie.

"Do you know what I'm getting at?"

"I'm waiting for that. I'm here to listen to you. Whatever you want to tell me." *Whatever on earth that might be.*

"Well, what I am going to tell you will be difficult. Because of your position. But I am going to trust you with this because I have no choice."

"I hope you trust me," Jamie said, having no idea what was going on and feeling less and less surefooted as each minute ticked off on the same basic wall clock of his own high school days.

"I hope so too," she said. "Look, I've been doing this for years. I've been a teacher for twenty-one years. First English Literature, then Drama. And the ones that I'm talking about, the ones that we will be discussing, they seem to enjoy teaching courses like that. That's where they find the girls they're looking for. Sensitive girls. Girls that like to read Blake and Shelly. Nowadays probably Edward Albee. Sylvia Plath."

"Poets?"

"Yes." Mrs. De Carlo smiled. "Poets."

She pressed her shoulders back, then relaxed them, resuming a confidant pose.

"They always find the girl with a problem. Not too difficult to do that in high school. Find the girl that feels different. Unloved. Not getting asked to the prom. Her mother drinks. And they make her feel special. No one understands her. But they do."

"Did that happen to Cindy?"

"Not here, if that's what you mean. It's simply the background. My expertise. I've seen those men sift through the system. They get caught and suddenly they've secured a position at some other school in some other state. That's how it works. The girl would have been considered willing. The parents solely concerned with their daughter's reputation. Fifteen, twenty years ago, a girl who willingly went off with her English teacher was considered loose. Especially her married English teacher. A high school girl doesn't get much looser than that."

"Well, I mean, there are laws against that." Wearing his uniform, his pad in hand, Jamie felt the sudden need to defend a system he was pretty sure didn't work all that well.

"There are laws, but well. The relationship is never forced. Not in the common sense. I've seen this for a lot of years. I mean, maybe the times are different now, but are they really? A month ago, the district hired a new teacher for Advanced English. He's from a boarding school in New Hampshire. Suddenly had the urge to uproot his wife and two-year-old son."

"Tell me about Cindy."

"Well, with Cindy. This, I think, is so ingenious. She was living with Brad, kind of a shit, we can say that. And then finally one of the neighbors called the police on him. Finally. I'd been telling Cindy to do that since she moved in with him. I wanted to, but I had to be careful with her trusting me. Anyway, the police did get called. I guess they investigated."

Jamie was listening and writing as pieces of things he hadn't expected to hear began to move past his notes and into his consciousness.

"Then what do you know? Who shows up a few days later? One of the officers who'd been called to the apartment. What would you call that behavior? Reaching for the low hanging fruit? Cindy, a girl about as vulnerable as you're going to get. Her boyfriend is a shit. And this man has a badge. He's the hero."

"Is that what Cindy told you?"

"Again, this is what I told Cindy. I told her this new guy was worse than Brad. With Brad, she knew what she was getting. This other one, this older man. He wasn't looking to help her. Worse thing that could've happened to her would've been taking up with him. At least she took that advice and cut off their relationship."

Jamie had been taking in the story and getting all of it down. It wasn't until he stopped writing, Mrs. De Carlo finished, that he fully understood what he'd been told.

"He was a cop?" Jamie needed that spelled out for him. "The man that was going to help Cindy leave Brad was a cop?"

"He was a cop," she said. "He wasn't the man that was going to help Cindy leave Brad. He was the man who *said* he'd help Cindy."

"Did you ever get a name? Of the officer."

"No, Cindy was very clear that was taboo. His position was delicate. Their relationship wasn't one he wanted known."

Jamie felt clammy and pale. There were more questions he needed to ask. Other things he needed to know. He couldn't think of one.

"Does this surprise you?"

"It does," Jamie said, fully aware that wasn't the professional answer he should have given.

"I guess you never thought about it."

"No, I never did."

"No, you wouldn't have." She stopped, pinched at the bridge of her nose. "I'm sorry. I don't know why I'm going on like this. You didn't do anything."

Jamie wondered if it was the uniform or if it was him. No different than any other guy on any given Saturday night. Eager for the girl who'd had one or two drinks more than she could handle.

She smiled at Jamie, wide. And once again, welcoming.

"She really was special. Dazzling often."

"I've been told that." Jamie was glad he could be honest and not just say the expected thing. He'd heard so much from Gil.

"Of course she was seventeen. She was impatient. And like others, maybe more so with Cindy, she went with the wind. Whichever way it was blowing."

That was something Jamie couldn't respond to, though he was starting to suspect it played a part in what happened at RJ's.

"There are a lot of nice teachers. Not all of them like the ones who hop from school to school. I'm sure that's true of you and your fellow officers. I'm trusting that."

She could. She could trust him. But he wasn't sure he had the words to make that real to her.

FORTY-TWO

HE WAS DYING TO GO HOME TO MISSY, BUT JAMIE HAD to get to West Paterson first. It was too early for the bars and Gil was home. Jamie was greeted at the door as if his appearance was no surprise at all to Gil. The apartment had the smells Jamie expected from the school cafeteria. A frozen dinner. Salisbury steak?

Like Mrs. De Carlo, the choices of who Jamie could trust were narrow and the amount that he could share limited. He didn't tell Gil anything outright, gliding over the specifics as if he were posing a theory he'd recently come up with.

"What if it was someone that Randall would never suspect. Someone with authority. Someone from the County Sheriff's Department. Or a cop. Like, that's a stretch, but let's say that's why he let the guy in. He figured he was trustworthy. He didn't come from upstairs. But he was able to get into the bar, after it closed because he was someone Randall would trust. So go with that, what kind of investigation would that turn into?"

Gil was disheveled as ever. A haze of indifferent grooming. Caught as he was at home, even his glasses were crooked. He'd maybe had half a bottle of Jameson, judging from the looks of his apartment, the evidence of his drinking all around him. But he was sharp. He didn't have to think long at all.

"A sheriff's officer? A cop? That would mean no investigation," he said. "Fold up shop and go home."

"Oh? You think that'd end it? It's just a theory I was toying with."

"Really? Theories are good to kick around. Get you thinking about new angles. I read this in a P.I. novel once. It stuck with me it was such a cool detective thing. Let me see if I can get it exactly."

Gil stretched his arms stick straight and palms to the wall, as if he was preparing to bow.

"Here it is," he said, catching Jamie's eye to make sure he was listening.

"That's how the devil works. He shows you what looks like virtue. He gains your confidence."

Pleased with his presentation, Gil pressed his hand across his waist and dipped into an actual bow, surprising Jamie with his balance.

Though Gil ought to have been drunk, that wasn't what happened to him after half a bottle of Irish Whiskey. He hadn't even begun. He'd soon be smoothing his hair and clothes and going off to whatever bar he had in mind for the night. Ordering Jameson after Jameson over ice would eventually get him full-out drunk. Jamie thought he could use a drink of his own then. What Mrs. De Carlo had dropped into an already bewildering mix of facts was opaque and nameless. With the right fuse, it could turn into a bomb. Gil, his best sounding board, was telling him what was probably true. RJ's was over.

What Jamie had learned about Cindy wasn't information to be shared. It was seriously not to be shared. Jamie had known that the minute he'd sat in his Datsun gripping the steering wheel and staring blankly at the concrete block high school. He wore the same blank stare in response to Gil's quote from a paperback, one that proved easy enough to read.

"Be careful," Gil said. "Just be careful."

He doled out that final counsel stone cold sober.

Jamie hoped Gil drove as clearly as he thought. He suspected a good number of local bartenders knew Gil well enough to take his keys and call a cab around closing time. It was a consideration that occupied

Jamie as he stepped into the night with the sound advice he'd been given and not a clue what he would do with it, though he knew what he ought to do.

From the parking lot, a glittering valley that could have been North Arlington or Manhattan unfolded like a cluster of stars. Drawing lines through pinpricks of light was how constellations emerged. Like a dot-to-dot puzzle. Jamie craned his neck towards the real night sky. His habit was to search for Orion, but everything around him was dark and clouded over.

She was waiting with his dinner. She had moistened paper towels and placed them over a pork loin in the oven with the heat off. While Missy fussed with the roast and a cucumber salad and a saucepan that smelled of garlic, Jamie took the tie off a wrapped loaf of bread and felt for the heel that he tore into four even pieces. Just the rustling of the plastic had the dog running into the kitchen, straight to his bowl.

Missy served Jamie first, far more timid than she'd been in the morning. He hadn't even chewed his first mouthful of green beans, when she raised her face to him.

"Is it still okay for me to be here?"

Her halting voice betrayed how very unsure she was. It had something to do with his coming home later than he ever had. It had *everything* to do with his coming home so late. That was the kind of coincidence that would make her insecure. She couldn't know what their new relationship was or if it was one Jamie wanted. For all Missy knew, he'd achieved his goal and planned to move on. Thrown in, as an extra bonus, was that he'd come home tasting of the two shots he'd had at Gil's. None of it made for a conversation Jamie was ready to have. He hadn't made the adjustment of leaving the day behind and opening himself to being alone with Missy. A full pivot probably wasn't possible. RJ's, Mrs. De Carlo, Gil's warning. None of it would stay tightly sealed within a box for anything but a few fleeting moments.

"We can be honest. I mean, we, us. We happened so fast," she said.

This was the honest thing. His most pressing concern was that he couldn't have her leave and get a room somewhere so that he'd be full of worry over her. Her finances. Her safety. Maybe it wasn't his place to worry, but he would and he couldn't have that with everything else rushing through his mind. He needed to know that she was safe. He didn't have any space in his head to even consider what she might want.

There was more. He liked having her at his house and very much wanted her there.

He moved from the green beans and on to the pork loin. Chewing slowly. Buying time. Realizing it was actually three shots he'd had with Gil. A sudden memory of his aunt came to him. She'd begun to work on him when he was sixteen. Rules for who he should and shouldn't hang out with, then routing him into more of a commitment at Lou Costello's. That was the exception. She'd never been one to give Jamie direct advice. He'd learned by listening to her talk about the choices she'd made. The things she'd done wrong and the things she'd done right. She'd ditched her gentler philosophy when she'd needed to work fast, and Jamie understood then, the power he could wield over Missy if he chose to press her. It gleamed like the blade of a knife.

"This is a good place for you to be right now. It may not make sense. I know it probably doesn't make sense. We are so new with each other. But I think it'll be okay. As long as you're happy, stay here and let your life settle a little."

Do that. Just do that for me. I can't worry about you with everything else that's going on. I really can't. And I can't figure out my feelings for you. Please don't be complicated. Just do what I want. Make this easy.

When she didn't answer, he reached for her hand.

"This will be good for you. I want this to be good for you."

There was no history or context for Jamie to tell Missy about Mrs. De Carlo and Gil's warning and how much he craved the uncomplicated; the salad and green beans and pork loin and the smooth surface of her being happy with him. Letting his fingers lightly circle her wrist, he chose to believe that she was.

Missy waited until Jamie let go of her hand, then went to the stereo to flip *Hotel California* to its other side. She returned to the table and sliced the rest of her roast and said she'd used a combination of tarragon and mustard and the release began working its way into him. Like those first few weeks out of the academy, meeting up with friends for drinks on payday. Nothing ahead of him and nothing behind.

FORTY-THREE

"LOOK WHO'S HERE!" GIANELLI SAID, HIS VOICE BOOM-
ing a little too loud in the garage.

Bachman had sent Jamie down from the squad room to meet the
two detectives. Starting with the FBI case that wasn't really much of
anything, he'd been giving Jamie more duties beyond his rotating patrol.
Jamie followed the pair towards their Monte Carlo. Andres dropped
behind Gianelli so he could walk with Jamie, catch him up on this
new investigation and what was known so far. The three of them were
heading to a crime scene that a pair of responding officers had gone over
earlier in the day. They'd reported a home break-in on Linden Road. The
victim was a female aged thirty-two. The time of day, the report of a
raspy-voiced assailant, fit in with the facts of several ongoing cases.

Andres and Gianelli did more than scrape together evidence. Jamie
knew that. He'd feared he was on his way to sit for an interview with the
woman who'd been sexually assaulted. He was sure he could handle that
if given more time to prepare. He'd want a night to study his psychology
texts and was much relieved when he learned that Andres and Gianelli
had already spoken to the woman at the hospital where they waited
with her until counseling arrived and then had a brief sit-down with
her relatives. Having read the initial report and found it lacking, they'd
decided to go back to the house to pick over the crime scene. They
were meticulous.

Jamie's assignment was to rake through a few adjacent properties
looking for items that may have been discarded. As if he'd memorized

the report, Andres recounted, "the suspect was said to have run out the back door, making his exit in the direction of Manor."

"So, I'll check the yard. See if any of the bushes or shrubs look trampled. Follow the path."

"There you go. See what you come up with. Ground might be too hard for shoe prints. But you can find gloves, tools, tape," Andres said.

"We found a wallet once," Gianelli said, turning from the passenger seat to face Jamie, who'd drifted into his usual listening, letting the two detectives banter.

"Yeah. They're not all master criminals."

"You know what's still bothering me?" Gianelli said.

"About what?"

"About the bar shooting."

"That's out of nowhere," Andres said.

"Well, I think about this in particular, how she went first. The guy was shot second, fell on top of her. That's why the manager was confused when she ran in and saw the crime scene. Didn't see the two bodies."

"What does that mean?" Jamie asked, piping in. "I mean, what's your theory."

"No theory yet. Just that it ain't right. If it was a robbery, they wouldn't have been so quick to shoot her. A pretty girl."

"The whole thing's not right," Andres said.

"Yeah. There are these little things that nag me," Gianelli said. "I can't get my hands around it."

The discussion of RJ's thinned to a thoughtful silence.

At their meetings, Jamie had shared Eileen Brandsher's interview, but he'd kept that light since Bachman had dismissed her as neither a credible nor a relevant witness. He'd been mute when it came to Sandy. His latest find was that Cindy had been involved with a cop. Mrs. De Carlo was clear on that. Gil said he had to be careful. Really careful.

What Jamie knew was that it was near impossible that either Andres or Gianelli would have pursued Cindy. And beyond that, none of it, not the affair, not the murder, could have happened without the other one knowing. Their tight connection as partners, their deeply connected lives. A single preferred cologne for both of them. Aramis. Jamie held that thought as they continued onto Vreeland Ave.

When they got to the house, all three began circling the exterior. Responding officers had done their review of the residence and left the property intact. Jamie found glass on the back stoop with most of the shards on the linoleum entryway, indicating the breach was from the outside, just as it was written in the report. He left Gianelli and Andres to meet with forensics who'd arrived late and were still dusting for fingerprints. A few homes away from the Linden Road address, Jamie retrieved a coil of rope that'd been laying in the center of the yard. The tag from Goodman's Hardware still imbedded in the core.

"It's what I said before. Geniuses. We're dealing with geniuses," Gianelli said.

They left after collecting the rope and a black knit hat that could have been anyone's. Returning to the station, Jamie was sent to the hardware store to sift through credit card receipts.

"Call us if the guy says he needs a warrant," Andres told him.

Jamie couldn't square it. Spending more and more time with Andres and Gianelli and the respect he had for them, yet he was paralyzed and it was all his own doing. He hadn't trusted the legitimacy of Sandy's call or how he'd handled it, and that first mistake was getting piled on with the accusation that a police officer had been involved with Cindy. Even if it hadn't been either Andres or Gianelli, it wasn't a drop in the bucket to suggest a cop as a suspect. That would ripple through the department with a huge potential for backlash. He couldn't even calculate the fallout that'd come to him.

On the other side of his arguments were Andres and Gianelli and how the murders nagged at them, even if they were no longer officially in charge of RJ's. He just needed to give himself a little more time.

He was still wary of Missy leaving, but when he got home, she was comfortably settled in the living room wearing the old flannel shirt he'd given her the first night she'd stayed. He squatted next to her, ready for the day's constant state of alert to start fading. Praying that it would.

"I was looking at your cars," she said.

"Cars? I only have one."

"Not upstairs."

"Well, those are different."

"Most of the models are Mustangs. Why didn't you get one?"

"You know, I don't know. I still like Mustangs, but I really liked the ZX when it came out last year. I didn't overthink it."

Jamie huddled next to her and then, like pulling at the first loose threads of a sweater, it began.

"What if I told you about a situation. There's a woman and say her husband or boyfriend gives her a hard time, so eventually the cops get called. They get there and do some talking. One of the officers talks to her, the other takes the husband and talks to him. That's how it works to make sure everything is all calmed down. No charges are pressed because that doesn't usually happen, but the cops do the best they can. Defuse whatever's going on. And then after that, the woman gets a visit. You know. A visit. Checking up to see if she's okay. Maybe this visitor thinks it's a good time to try to strike up a relationship. Get something going."

Jamie bent to untie his shoes, giving Missy some time to consider.

"Like what do you think?" he asked.

"What do *I* think?"

"Yeah. I'm just, I don't know. I'm just asking you."

"The guy who goes visits. Who is he?"

"He's a cop. One of the cops that showed up when the call came in."

Missy reached for his collar pin, rubbing the silver-plated initials slowly. PPD. Paterson Police Department. Jamie had been so relieved to find Missy home, he'd gone to her and hadn't thought to change. His uniform wasn't meant to be worn with the story he was unexpectedly sharing.

"I guess there are those kinds of cops out there. I've heard, like if a girl gets pulled over at night. Maybe she's had a few drinks. Smells of beer or whatever and the cop says he can fix things if she's friendly enough. I mean, do you know guys like that?" she asked.

Jamie was silent. They both knew the answer. The names of those cops didn't circulate around the station. They didn't have to. Everyone knew. Yet, those were the guys at the center of every award dinner and pool tournament, considered good cops and trusted partners.

"Why are you asking about this? Is this a rumor?"

Jamie brought Missy close to him, her face in his chest, his chin sitting lightly at the ponytail on top of her head.

"Well, it's more than a rumor."

Missy pulled back, a crease down her forehead he'd never seen.

"Why are you asking about this?"

Jamie didn't know. He moved to the center of the room, unsure how far he should go with his story and pacing with new thoughts. He passed the family photos and the carriage clock, once, then a second time, the hands on the clock not moving.

"I'm thinking a lot, okay? I have a lot on my mind now. Like, here's something. Why did you come here that night?" he asked, his tone full of accusation. "I mean why here? Why did you trust me?"

"Are you the cop that went to that girl's house?"

Jamie took a moment from pacing, his face dropping. "No! Of course I'm not. You know that."

Missy's forehead was still creased in confusion. "I don't know what you're asking me. Or telling me. What are you telling me?"

"The whole thing has me thinking about you coming here and trusting me."

"What whole thing?"

With the living room so small, Jamie had circled the floor three times, fueling his agitation. "Why did you trust me?"

"I don't know. I thought you were nice and you're a cop and I did, okay? I trusted you. I didn't think you would strangle me. I was pretty sure you wouldn't."

"It's not just strangling. There's other bad things."

Missy tapped her chin and looked from Jamie to Nugget who was alert with their raised voices.

"I'm not the idiot you seem to think I am. I know what a guy who yells a lot is like. Guys who are bullies. And I know about guys who don't yell and act like they're perfect and it's like everything is fine with them until it's not. So, I know what they're like. Okay, you weren't like any of them. You're not a bully but you don't act all perfect." She steepled her fingertips, watching him with a curious expression. She sighed and ran a hand through her hair. "You're messy," she said.

"I'm messy?"

"Yeah, you're messy."

"How? How so?"

"Like the way you think you're the only one who knows what's really going on and I had no idea how to handle my life until you came along."

"I don't think that. I know you can handle yourself. I just worry about you."

"Well, I worry about you," she said. "Like now. You're all upset."

"It's just work. I'm sorry. I had a lot go on today."

Jamie brought his lips together. How easy it would have been to go deeper, past the line he'd been skirting. Instead, he picked up his shoes and brought them to the foyer. It was time for dinner, and he'd happily let Missy revisit her day at Casa Romano or detail the recipe for whatever she'd made that night. He'd seen the Kraft cheese on the counter and hoped it was spaghetti and meatballs. When they got to the table, the crease was gone from her forehead but she wasn't quite done with him.

"I wasn't wrong," she said. "I wasn't wrong to trust you."

She took his hand and squeezed it, surprising Jamie with how much comfort that gave him.

FORTY-FOUR

TWO OFFICERS VISITED THE APARTMENT ON JASPER Street on the evening of October 24, 1978, after a woman called to report a loud argument taking place nearby. When he'd arrived, the other officer was already at the scene, listening at the door. He'd joined him and the two eventually knocked.

The young woman answered and was upset there were two policemen on her doorstep and asked if it was illegal for a couple to argue. He explained that they just wanted to be sure everyone was okay. She hesitated but let him inside. The other officer took her boyfriend out to talk.

He'd sat her on an ottoman and knelt on the carpet while he spoke to her. He didn't plan to take notes. She said that she and her boyfriend had been fighting over money. She was embarrassed having to talk about it. Three days later, he'd driven to the apartment during the afternoon while the boyfriend was out but she, working nights, was still at home. He said it was a routine follow-up. He wanted to check on her. She was younger than the ones he was used to. And prettier. So much prettier.

He'd been staying away from that game for a while, but she'd been so gorgeously disheveled that first night when she answered the door. In his mind, she'd enticed him. It was a gamble, but he'd gone there and was able to take the right approach with her.

Her lips. Her lips had been incredibly soft.

The other officer had been transferred to the Sheriff's Department. A promotion that was immediately arranged in the wake of the first phone call about the Polaroids. Then the entire folder was removed from the police files, though it had never contained the relevant parts. How when they'd met in October, she'd tugged on the top of her blouse, avoiding his look. Then he'd leaned forward and took her delicate wrist into his palm. "Don't be embarrassed," he'd said. "I hope you're not embarrassed, talking to me."

He eyed the report one last time, tore it into shreds. It would be odd to burn even a single pail of garbage in March. But what the hell did he care what his neighbors thought.

FORTY-FIVE

MISSY HAD TAKEN A FEW CLASSES FROM A WOMAN IN
Midland Park, she and several ladies who lived in Ridgewood, those other
students being the young wives of lawyers and stockbrokers who wanted
a handful of "go to" dishes for their dinner parties. Duck à l'orange.
Assorted canapés to pair with cocktails. Then she'd won tickets to a three
night "Gourmet Cooking Class" at Houlihan's Old Place, one of the new
restaurants in the mall. She'd gone to those between Thanksgiving and
Christmas where she'd learned to make her meringue.

"The ad was in the paper and it seemed perfect. I was nervous
entering. I'd never won anything before."

Jamie thought of the racetrack and the woman with her longshot
ticket and Missy winning the three-night cooking class of her dreams.
He didn't think she needed special lessons as much as she needed to lift
weights. Believing he could strengthen her biceps, he bought her a set
of two-pound dumbbells he found in Korvette's sporting goods section.
Once home with them, he held the largest saucepan he could find in his
left hand and one of the weights in his right. They seemed even though
he couldn't imagine what it would feel like for her, carrying pots filled
with steaming water. Most chefs were men. Missy had told him that and
Jamie had known why straight away.

He moved the coffee table and placed Nugget high on the couch,
away from Missy and the floor around her.

"These are called curls. I'm going to teach you to do curls."

Missy readied herself as he placed his hands on her hips.

"Balance your whole body," he went on. "Okay, now we'll start with one. Hold it like this," he said, placing the tiny weight in her palm and letting her fingers close over it. "Right. Now turn your wrist so that it's facing up and then bring the weight to your shoulder," he said. "Perfect. Just like that."

Missy's face was a burn of shy accomplishment. She lowered the dumbbell, letting the weight pull her arm down.

"You'll hurt your elbow like that. Don't let the weight fall. Keep control while you're holding it."

She nodded.

"Let's try it with two. We'll do both arms at once."

They worked for fifteen minutes, Jamie concluding he really needed to get her to a gym and onto a Nautilus machine. After her lesson, she collapsed on the cushion next to Nugget, stroking his side while Jamie went for a beer.

"He gets a lot of time on the couch for a dog that's not allowed on the couch," she said.

"That's more of an old rule. My aunt's rule."

"She didn't like dogs?"

"Not at all."

"So, Nugget's your first dog?"

"Actually, no. My aunt wanted me to have a dog. She got me my first one."

Missy raised an eyebrow.

Jamie flipped the story in his mind. For his tenth birthday, when he'd been living with his aunt for almost a year, she'd gone to the pound and adopted Toby. Long after the dog was a fixture in their house, well into Jamie's teens, she'd still instruct Jamie on how to treat the little pug. *You're bigger than him. No roughhousing. Watch you're not yanking his ears.* As he got older, he'd hear her words and form a vision of his grandfather. The scraps he knew. How the man treated women. How Aunt Ro hated her father. Jamie's father's father. He had no idea how he even knew what he knew. Then there was his aunt's lady friend. The mornings Jamie woke with those three boys scattered around the house and the lady friend in Aunt Ro's room. After his aunt cooked their eggs and pancakes and filled bowls of cereal and the boys ran off to find whatever they'd brought with them and whatever Jamie had that might fit them, the energy began its leach from the house. Barbara drumming her fingers on the kitchen table, explaining why she had to get back home. Jamie had been told never to look at her face. To pretend that there wasn't a bruised cheek or swelling eyelid to be seen.

"My aunt thought it would teach me responsibility. Walking and feeding and caring for a pet."

She wanted me to have a gentler side.

Missy nodded. She was holding Nugget's face in her hands, so tenderly, as if he were a newborn. The dachshund's eyes locked on hers, retuning a deep love.

"Nugget has a moustache and a beard," she said to Jamie. Bending closer to Nugget, she whispered, "You're such a funny dog."

FORTY-SIX

JAMIE HAD ONLY TESTIFIED IN COURT ONCE. HE'D BEEN nervous, certain he wasn't a very good witness. His only statement, that he'd seen the defendant speed walking towards a car that was waiting outside Martone's Jewelry and Watch Repair with its engine running. The defendant had got into the back seat and the car snaked away, all of which caught his attention. He'd been in the process of writing down the plate number when an elderly man stepped from the front door and stared at him in confusion. Fortunately, no one was hurt in the armed robbery. Jamie wasn't really on the case, the police had been called when the owner pulled the store's alarm the moment the perpetrator ran out. The responding officers had the call logged in and they were the ones to open an investigation. Jamie was solely a fact witness as the DA had told him. "All you have to do is say what you saw. What you did. What you wrote down. That it was contemporaneous with your observations."

The public defender had tried to get him to twist his words but wasn't very practiced or particularly skillful, asking him if he wore corrective lenses and his level of education. Whether he'd taken any prescription drugs prior to the incident.

It would change. He'd have better cases assigned to him. Drug busts and organized gambling, all with the potential for stiff sentences. Better cases came with defendants who'd have better attorneys. The kind that could trip him up just asking him to say his full name.

Sometimes, Jamie would go to the courthouse on his breaks, or he'd try to get to the city parking lot a half hour early and sit in on a proceeding before getting to the station. He preferred the hardwood benches in the back so his arms wouldn't brush against the spectators sitting closer. Parents and girlfriends and accomplices who eyed every movement in the courtroom intensely. Even in the rear, he had a decent enough vantage point watching the motions and unconscious signals of the witnesses. Which ones had clenched hands. Fingers fiddling with zipper tabs. The nail biting. Tissue shredding. Overly rigid posture. Then the demeanor and tone of experienced detectives. No sweaty brows. Solid professionals. Seasoned. Jamie felt they were seasoned.

After a time, he found the courthouse a place to quietly sit and relax. Occasionally a case would be interesting. A murder scene deconstructed for the jury in detail. An elaborate drug sting. Mostly he sat and watched the rotation of court reporters he'd begun to recognize, the bailiff checking the microphones. It had an evenness that was soothing. Here was a place where judges wore black robes and ruled with their gavels, surrounded by gleaming, polished wood and a large relief with Lady Liberty and her scales of justice as a backdrop. A place where it all came together. Where order was promised.

That afternoon, a lawyer from Pat Virgilio's firm, resplendent in an Italian wool suit, was arguing for an extension of the trial date. Additional witnesses had been located and needed to be deposed. It would be a hardship for the defendant if the case was not adequately prepared. He had the rich baritone of Robert Preston in *The Music Man*. A voice destined to charm and sway juries. Jamie could have closed his eyes and napped it was so peaceful. So reassuring. The perfect stability he craved.

FORTY-SEVEN

FOR THE PAST SEVERAL DAYS, GARY HAD BEEN OUT OF the office on a new case. A late-night murder in West Milford had the department working jointly with the suburban detectives. The victim, Drew Steinle, had lived in Paterson. The case was considered a drug deal gone bad. The crime scene had been sealed and investigated by the team in West Milford but then a pair of detectives from Paterson were sent in for their own review. The ballistics report no doubt sent to the city lab and Gary brought in to find scraps of information on Steinle. Who he was involved with. Where he was getting his drugs. Anything to link back to the deal that had ended with his getting shot.

This was a notch above the backup work Gary had handled for RJ's. Because he was generally given so little beyond his foot patrol duties he paraded his latest assignment through the office, letting Jamie know whenever he'd be out, "going over to the scene." But other than a few showy moments, he was roughly trying to be a good team player.

"You looking for any more overtime?" he asked once Jamie was comfortably seated at his desk.

"Not really. Gotta bunch of work here and I jammed myself up this semester with classes."

He could have added he had a new girlfriend and that he was losing his mind over her. That he couldn't bear to be away from her. That he had to steel himself from thinking of her every waking minute. There was also his obsession with RJ's and that was no small thing.

"A lot of stuff going on the next month or so. But in the summer, when the Meadowlands concerts open up, let me know."

"Sure will."

Jamie rose to get a few files from Elizabeth. Those would be the last he had to cross-reference for dates to manage the timeline of his master report to Bachman. The final pieces before closing out what was officially the Low-Kaczorek homicide file. They called it a slowdown of the investigation on record, but Jamie knew Bachman and the higher ups in the department were viewing this a cold case, even if officially it would remain listed as open. Jamie knew he should follow that route and return his attention to the burglaries and car thefts that were his daily fare and whatever top-level felonies he might assist on. He just couldn't shake what he'd been told by Mrs. De Carlo, even knowing there was nothing tying that information into RJ's. Nothing Mrs. De Carlo said changed the analysis. A double homicide that began as a robbery. The clearance rate when the victims weren't previously known to the killer was always slim. One of the most basic facts. The probability of solving any murder dropped precipitously with each passing week. Another hard fact.

His theories were just guesses. More pressing was the page in his notebook and the lines in his own handwriting that were smudged and illegible. Had he jotted down "witness" or "woman?" He read back the paragraph to put the blotted words into context when the creaking of Gary's chair broke his focus. Then the loud shutting of drawers. He'd be leaving soon, as he'd made sure to tell Jamie earlier, spelling out the details. The West Milford detective was going to be the lead on an interview with Gary sitting in.

"So, I'm off," he said.

"You going straight home or coming back?"

"Not sure. Not sure the witness will even be there. Having some trouble tracking her down. Steinle's girlfriend. She answered the first call, said she'd speak with police. But it's spotty."

Drug investigations were like that. Unreliable witnesses. The RJ's murders had neighbors and bar patrons who'd been locals. Fixed in their homes, their jobs, their routines. Even if they hadn't seen anything there were reports of their interviews written up, thickening the file.

"Sandy Santasiera," Gary said. "That's a name. Gotta wonder what a girl named Sandy Santasiera looks like."

A stapler that didn't really work clicked as it was forced a second and then a third time. Pens dropped and phones rang, and balls of paper landed in the trash. The squad room and all of its noises slowed. Everything was filtered through a thick liquid, as if there could be no other sound beyond what Gary had said. Jamie was absolutely still, staring at the notepad he'd been looking over, though it was impossible for him to read because he'd become instantly lightheaded. His neck, his upper arms, even his cheekbones tightened, certain he'd heard Gary wrong. Certain he was hearing the name only because it was in his mind so often, but also certain he'd heard correctly. It took a moment for him to remember where he was. Gary was halfway to the door when Jamie pushed up from his desk and sprinted to the corridor.

"Wait!"

Gary's face froze in surprise.

"So, tell me. What's the deal on your case?"

"What's the deal?"

"Just asking," Jamie said. "I didn't mean to brush you off so quick. It sounds like a good case. You got in on a good case."

Gary was too proud to really care that Jamie had run over in a fury, hitting his leg on a file cabinet as he grabbed Gary's jacket sleeve.

"Execution style shooting."

"Really. Really interesting case for you to be on."

"It's exciting."

"What were the ballistics?"

"Pretty big gun. One shot to the back of the guy's head. A .44."

Before Jamie went for his next question, Gary added, "The slug was in bad condition. Deformed. Gun could be the Smith & Wesson that Clint Eastwood uses. Could be the same one as Son of Sam. The Charter Arms Bulldog. They don't know." Gary spoke with an expertise Jamie guessed to be freshly minted. "Still, a .44 caliber gets attention. That's a pretty serious gun."

"If it was a Model 29, that's an expensive gun these days," Jamie said. "So, that'd be a different kind of shooter than someone with a Bulldog. Any ideas about that? Did they find drugs on the guy? Money?"

Jamie was almost panting with his questions. Gary took a minute and began adjusting his belt, batting his flashlight back and forth. Slowing with his answers.

"Just, kind of, that was his reputation. What else could it be?"

"And the guy who got shot lived in Paterson?"

"Adams Street. Complex on Adams Street."

Jamie clapped Gary's arm. The we're-all-cops move that'd been done to him by Bachman. Gianelli.

"Good luck," Jamie said. "Good luck with your interview. Hope she's there."

"Hope so, too."

Gary boasted a knowing grin. "She sounds like a wet T-shirt girl, you know? You ever see that movie, *The Deep*? I'm thinking this girl does those contests. Figure that's what she'll look like."

"The girl? At the interview?"

"Yeah, the girl. I mean, she won't look exactly like that at the interview. Just the type."

FORTY-EIGHT

JAMIE FINALLY HAD AN ADDRESS TO MATCH THE NAME he'd been searching for. There was that from Gary's file and maybe more would develop from the interview. In his mind, RJ's looked less and less like a robbery. Gianelli's drug theory was a noisy possibility. Still, all he had were loosely related pieces that weren't coming together. Sitting at the kitchen table, he'd made a list of the information he'd collected so far for the file he was keeping at home.

He sipped seltzer and read back his notes.

A man heard screeching tires, so whoever left RJ's hadn't planned the murders. It was something that went wrong.

A man who looked to be in the military was seen leaving the scene. But there was nothing else. The witness hadn't given more of a physical description or even an approximate age to attach to the suspect.

One of the cops who'd gone to Cindy's apartment on a call from the neighbors followed up looking to get more from her. But according to Mrs. De Carlo, she'd cut that off. And did crossing the line with a girl who danced at RJ's mean all that much? Just as Missy had heard, Jamie knew cops that stopped young women, offered them deals if they had pot in their cars. It wasn't what everyone did, but he'd never heard of anyone thrown off the force for it.

Even so, he wished he knew which cop it was. Surprised when he'd learned from Elizabeth there wasn't a file on Cindy Kaczorek for an assault. Brad hadn't known which neighbor made the call and he'd already moved. Jamie thought about the outcome from screening the streets around RJ's for information on a double homicide. It wasn't much. Going to Cindy's old address to find the right neighbor, asking if a cop took their statement and if so, explaining why he needed the name of that cop, or at least a description, that didn't seem like the best use of his time.

Sandy.

Everything other than Sandy looked like the scraps of information he'd expected. Negligible things that went nowhere.

Sandy.

Mrs. De Carlo didn't trust cops more than she had to. She wouldn't give out Sandy's address, but why? Where was the danger?

Sandy.

Her boyfriend had been a drug dealer. Not a surprise. The ballistics report said he'd been killed by a different gun than the one used to shoot Randall and Cindy.

Sandy.

She'd called him once, possibly twice, with something urgent to tell him.

FORTY-NINE

HE MADE A LIST OF THE SALIENT INFORMATION FOR THE file he was keeping.

A man heard screeching tires from roughly the area believed to be RJ's parking lot somewhere around 1:30 a.m. on the night of the murders.

A man who looked to be in the military was seen leaving the crime scene. No other identifying information was provided by the witness.

One of the patrol officers assigned to collect witness statements on the RJ's murder case had gone looking for a previous file on one of the victims relating to the report of a domestic dispute at her home several months before the murder.

The ballistics were different at the West Milford crime scene. There was nothing on the surface to tie the shooting together with the homicides in Paterson.

Only ten of the twelve Polaroids were turned over by the victim when they'd met at the location in West Milford. A fact he'd only discovered after the shooting.

The officer seeking the file on the domestic dispute seemed concerned when told that no such file existed. An important point to note: that officer had been kept off the West Milford investigation.

FIFTY

MISSY WAS SCHEDULED TO WORK EXTRA SHIFTS THAT
weekend and they both had Tuesday as an off day. By 11:00 a.m. they
were on the Palisades Parkway, passing by Exit 4 where Jamie had done
overnights with his Boy Scouts troop. They were driving further, much
further than his old campgrounds along a route Jamie had drawn that
would take them across the Bear Mountain Bridge and then to Hyde
Park. According to the map he kept in his glove compartment, the
Culinary Institute of America was north of Poughkeepsie, and where he
was taking her to lunch.

The school and the restaurant had been highlighted in the paper. In
the days that led to the end of winter when there wasn't much to do, the
entertainment section ran stories he usually ignored although this time
he'd taken note. It was hard not to see a full-page feature titled "The
'Other' CIA." Mostly, the article gave tips for getting reservations and
reviewed the dining experience. Jamie asked Missy if she'd heard of it.

"Escoffier," she said. "I think it's part of the training kitchen."

"It sounds exclusive," he said. "For a restaurant with students doing
the cooking."

She never brought it up again, but Jamie thought about the classes
she'd taken in Midland Park. The meringue she whipped furiously. How
alert she'd been on their first date at Homestead's and then when they'd
gone to Pegasus. He'd called for reservations and learned they'd be
able to tour the school.

"You should see the whole thing. We'll check it out. Go have
lunch. Maybe you can do a weekend program there."

She'd gone quiet with his suggestion, but he kept the reservation, reading past her indifference. It'd been the right call. She'd bubbled with excitement getting into the car. It was the first time he'd seen Missy in the white angora. She surprised him, wearing the sweater; her hair in barrettes on both sides, her bow-shaped lips coated in an especially dewy gloss.

"I hope you like the restaurant," she said as they passed above the Hudson River. The expanse around the bridge was vast and the cliffs barren. Entering Westchester, he noticed her eagerness giving way to a nervous fear and she occupied herself running a nail over the ruffled hem of her dress. A soothing, metronome movement.

"This must look nice in the spring, when the leaves are out," Jamie said.

"Even right now is nice. It feels like a driving adventure."

Taking Missy to lunch at Escoffier wouldn't just be good for her. Roaming the campus would be a getaway for Jamie. He needed the distance from Paterson and the urge to drive up and down Adams Street. Gary had reported his interview was a no-show though he'd quickly moved on to a warrant that'd been issued, so he "and the team" could go look around some more. Jamie tried to appear interested, but not too interested when Gary shared his update and drifted onto side topics. A single name had surfaced from the couple's landlord. Shelly, who seemed to live there briefly. A lead that went nowhere for the West Milford detectives and meant nothing to Jamie. For the one afternoon, he could give it all a rest.

Jamie steered the red Datsun along New York Route 9 North, passing a squat building with a large antenna.

"Did you see the call letters?"

"I didn't."

"WPDH, I think. Maybe we can get some decent reception now. Is it okay if I switch to the news?"

He'd played the soundtrack to *The Last Waltz* for the length of the ride. A favorite they shared. Missy had lost herself occasionally and relaxed with music, but he noticed as they listened to a traffic report that her hands returned to her hem, the soft rubbing with her nail.

A few miles past Poughkeepsie, they approached a grassy quad crisscrossed with sidewalks and surrounded by buildings that all had "hall" in their names. A campus chapel. A classic bell tower. A blend of woodlands and academics on the east bank of the Hudson River. Students roamed the grounds in white uniforms, a few carrying knife kits.

Jamie held Missy's hand as they checked in for the basic tour available to guests before dining. The school had been a Jesuit seminary. Its former use explained the stained-glass windows in the restaurant.

Their lunch was a five-course meal. Jamie inwardly gasped, thinking that would be three days' worth of food for Missy, but she seemed unfazed as she examined the menu. They started with vichyssoise because Missy said she wanted to try it and Jamie couldn't say no to her, not even after he was told this was the chef's signature cold potato soup. David, their student waiter, explained, "He's using Yukon Gold Potatoes which he pairs with leeks." He said this directing his focus on Missy. Maybe because he knew she had scheduled appointments with admissions. Maybe because of the angora sweater. David rarely looked at Jamie, so he missed the unrelenting glare.

The soup tasted exactly as Jamie expected but it was tolerable and he tried not to disappoint Missy. No jokes that he'd be fine if this wasn't a recipe she tried at home. As their meal went on, David continued to clarify course selections and ingredients he thought Missy would find interesting. Their plated salads were prepared with seasonal greens, sliced pears, and a sherry vinaigrette. Beef Burgundy was the main dish, followed by a selection of petit fours for dessert. The final course was a cheese plate to share, centered on a Roquefort made in-house.

When David left, Missy leaned into the table and whispered, "Did you ever have cheese after dinner?"

Missy's appointment to see the full school included a more in-depth tour and then a personal information session. Jamie offered to sit on the bench in the waiting area but she wanted him with her. He was introduced as James Palmieri, intensely pleased hearing Missy give his proper name to the registrar.

"John Healy," the man said. "I'm filling in today."

He wore a tweed blazer and knitted tie and eased them into his office, motioning to a pair of tufted club chairs. Missy sat stiff-backed and attentive, her palms pressed into the seat cushion.

To Jamie's surprise, the Culinary Institute wasn't a place for some weekend cooking classes. This was a full twenty months of study. Courses on food management, sanitation, and labor. Specialized kitchens and bakeshops. Chefs from Europe as teachers. Rolling admission brought in a new class every three weeks. Cordon Bleu medals around their necks at graduation. State loans and federal loans to cover the tuition. The campus was technically in Hyde Park, directly north of Poughkeepsie. The larger town was where most of the students found housing.

Though Missy remained quiet, Jamie sensed more of an undercurrent that day, as if the school was setting off an electricity within her.

"Do you have any questions for me?" Mr. Healy asked. "Anything?"

"No," Missy answered. "I think it's all here in the brochures."

"Well call if you do. Call anytime," he said, making eye contact with Jamie. Missy softly thanked Mr. Healy for helping her understand the process. Then she passed through admissions' frosted glass doors armed with her store of reading material.

Once outside, a fierce wind rose from the river and whipped against them. Jamie wrapped Missy into his side protecting her from the cold. Most of him was covered in his coat and scarf but his hands were exposed. He slipped one into her jacket and felt her soft sweater, pressing her closer still and folding her into him so it was awkward for her to walk. With her face buried, she couldn't see his steeled look. He knew how much she wanted this. He'd stayed by her the entire day, watching every step of the tour nick into her a little deeper, her longing cresting as the registrar described the graduation dinner and ribboned medals.

Back at the house, he didn't ask Missy if the school was something she wanted.

"You may need some help with this," he told her.

"I don't like needing help."

"It won't always be this way."

There'd be the visit soon to First National Bank where Mr. Gentile was a vice president. He'd known Aunt Ro since their days in high school and given her the mortgage for the house when still at Gentile and Segreto, the Italian credit union. Peter Gentile had done that although she was simply Rosemary Palmieri. Single and female, without a brother or father to co-sign her loan. When the family credit union folded, Mr. Gentile moved to First National. A bank would involve more formalities and Jamie had to make sure those formalities wouldn't become obstacles. He couldn't sit by and watch Missy save her nickels the way he knew his aunt had for years. He would get her the loans.

Debra had lacked something. He didn't know what when they'd broken up. He just knew it was vital and essential and it was missing. It grew on him in time, that she didn't have imagination. Missy was different. She was frightened, yet she dared to have dreams. Jamie knew to deny Missy would be to sit by and let her wither. What he flat out couldn't ignore, even with his growing want for her.

FIFTY-ONE

LUNCH HAD TAKEN MOST OF THE DAY. BETWEEN DIN-
ing, the tour, and meeting with the registrar. Not that long after they
got home, it was already dinnertime. Missy wanted to make omelets.
It was the only thing she could think of that wouldn't be too heavy.

"You have to eat," she said.

"We finished lunch at two o'clock. I'm not sure I'm even hungry."

"Don't you want a little something? You have to have dinner."

Jamie stretched his legs over the arm of the couch, scrolling
through channels before finding Edward G. Robinson. A few minutes
in, he realized the movie wasn't *Little Caesar*. It was a confusing one
he'd never seen about an oil geologist and an heiress and striking it rich
in Oklahoma and dark premonitions. A deep, meandering plot Jamie
wasn't following. He was sleepy from lunch and sure he'd pass out once
he'd had an omelet.

"Don't put anything in it," he yelled. "No cheese or peppers. I just
want a plain omelet."

"Okay."

"Please."

Nugget liked eggs. He was going to whisper his plan to the dog,
but Nugget was suddenly pacing near the front window. Then his
loud barking.

"Is something wrong?" Missy appeared from the kitchen, still
holding her mixing bowl.

"I don't know. Maybe there's a cat or a raccoon outside," Jamie said.

"I've never heard him growl like that. He seems really upset."

Nugget was nosing the front door, circling, his bark low and menacing, and sounding more like a Doberman and less like the small dog that he was. Jamie was about to get his gun from the bedroom when the barking began to subside, the growls intermittent, then stopping.

Jamie hovered at the foot of the stairs with Missy staring at Nugget.

"He seems okay now," Jamie said.

"I feel so nervous," Missy said. "That scared me."

"You're okay, aren't you," Jamie said to the dog. "What'd you smell out there?"

To Missy he said, "It was probably a raccoon or a cat. Let's hope it wasn't a skunk."

Throughout everything, Edward G. Robinson had remained undisturbed, the television giving off his powerful, snarling vocals. A staticky vision of Los Angeles in black and white. In the next yard, the rough growl and barking of the Cosgroves' dog was just beginning. Feral sounds rolling across the neighborhood like a low thunder.

FIFTY-TWO

JAMIE KNEW SANDY WAS NO LONGER IN PATERSON. HE'D heard complaints from Gary that she'd disappeared on them. Jamie reviewed what he could of the West Milford file and drove to her last known address anyway. The minute he had some time off, he went straight to 59 Adams Street to gaze at the corner apartment. Only one shade was up, the rest drawn. He went to the exposed window and saw the still-life of four rooms no one was living in. He imagined the refrigerator never having been emptied and the smell of garbage throughout the kitchen. Dresser drawers left open and clothes scattered. The sad and hurried decision for Sandy, running out and leaving everything including Drew's never-to-be-worn again clothes. Sandy wasting no time as soon as she heard that Drew had been shot, grabbing as much as she could and then gone. He hoped she'd been smart enough to leave that quickly.

Jamie settled back into the driver's seat, staying laser focused on the apartment. Mounting a stakeout that would yield nothing was the downtime he needed to collect his thoughts about Sandy, though he'd have to push back on his thoughts about Missy to do that. He was trying hard to put her and the story she'd told him into another part of his brain. They'd been sitting in Jamie's car when she'd shared it, the Datsun idling near one of the upper trailheads on Ramapo Mountain. Off-road parking was where Jamie took girls in the days when he had a driver's license and an old Cutlass and nowhere else to be alone. That night he'd taken Missy to Quick Check and meandered to the overlook above the valley, where Jamie pointed out some of the particularly bright spots. Ramapo College. Trinity Church. Brightly lit traffic snaking below.

Normally, she liked to talk about food. Over dinner, she'd spent ten minutes describing sugar flowers. Delicate roses and violets that she once made from a paste and colored with vegetable dyes with Jules guiding her. Jamie noticed that cooking for her was a way to make beautiful things. He noticed that talking about cooking was a way for her to not talk about much else. He'd all but stopped expecting her to bring up the night she'd come asking to sleep on his couch.

Then her hand tightened on his knee. The extra pressure of her fingers was far from the soft caresses he was used to, flagging their warning.

"I did something stupid," she said. "I didn't go through with it. But I agreed to do this thing."

The cassette eased into the next song, an intro he recognized. "Morning Final."

"What thing?" he asked.

"Pick up drugs in New York."

It was a tingling. The apprehension brought back the man in his pressed slacks slumped over the wheel of his Ford LTD. Someone driving to work and then a slick of black ice and life takes a bad turn. The helplessness Jamie recognized. Helplessness and dread. No one, not a single person, could stop that stuff from coming at them.

"Okay. Tell me what happened."

"I lost all the money I had saved up in Jacksonville. I gave it to my mother for her accident. And when I got back here, it was different. I'd been lucky at the bistro, but that was Jules taking me in, under his wing. I wasn't really a waitress there. He hired me to be a pantry girl. My job was preparing salads and relish trays and things like that. That's why I was always around the kitchen. They were training me to be a waitress, but I wasn't there long enough to get any real experience. I couldn't get hired up here at a good restaurant except as a hostess and I needed tuition money. I didn't know about Poughkeepsie, but I thought I'd take classes somewhere. I always wanted to do more. Get a real job."

Missy released the grip she'd had on Jamie's leg and began picking at her coat. Below them, rows of red taillights streamed on one lane of the highway while headlights backed up on the other side.

"Anyway, my roommates, they knew I needed money. They're the ones who helped me get some work at hospitality, where I met you, and I guess they thought I'd go along with their brilliant idea. You know, it wasn't a secret they dealt drugs. I'm sure Kenny warned you to be careful backstage. So, I was the perfect person. They said I had the girl next door look so no one would suspect me. I needed money so I agreed to do the pickup."

And? And then what happened? Jamie couldn't voice that obvious next question. His thoughts already bounced so far ahead. What would he do with the knowledge that Missy was involved with drugs? Would he have to break up with her? Just go along and pray that it never came out?

What Missy? What did you do? Jamie didn't dare ask.

"I had the address for a place on Fourteenth Street. The drive through the tunnel felt like I was driving through lead, but when I got to New York, it all went fast. Real fast. I found the building pretty quick."

"New York," Jamie said. "Fourteenth Street in New York."

"It wasn't a nice place. I knew right away I didn't want to go into the building. It looked terrible. Trash bags on the fire escape. I double-parked for a while, watching the kinds of people who went in and out, ripped army jackets and chain wallets. With the weather getting bad as it was that night, a few stayed sitting on the stoop."

She turned to face him.

"They sent me there because I looked the part, and I didn't even know what that meant. If cops were watching, I mean, if that was you,

you'd figure anyone going in there was up to trouble. Especially someone like me, really standing out."

Jamie actually didn't know what he'd do on a stakeout if he saw something so unexpected as Missy.

"I started to look for a parking spot and ended up driving around the block, going around and around until I was a half an hour late. And then thirty-five minutes late. And then forty. I never parked. I drove back to Haledon, but I was afraid to go to the apartment, get to my room. You can imagine."

"Who are these people, the ones that sent you there?"

"They're just from around. People I was living with and their friends. I had a nice place in Jacksonville, a real nice job. But, you know, I had to come back."

"How much trouble are you in? Is anyone looking for you?"

Her face was streaked with tears but Missy laughed with that.

"These aren't like guys that are dangerous. They're mostly users. Occasional dealers. They were angry at me for sure, but they found someone else for their pickup. It was just all the drama when I didn't show up in New York. I told you I wasn't a drama girl, but really, there was drama. I couldn't go back to my apartment. I didn't have my clothes or my own money. I was stuck in my Vega, driving around. Running low on gas, the rain getting harder. And I thought of you. I knew I'd be okay if I could stay with you that night."

He'd pulled her into him, feeling a bottomless sense of relief. He'd feared her story was about a boyfriend or ex-boyfriend being the dark thing that had driven her to his house. Missy found her way there because she wanted to feel safe, but it was Jamie who felt safe when he was with Missy. He always felt safe with her. Hearing the whole story, he'd been able to relax into that, even with Missy getting herself close to real trouble. In the end, she'd known how to get the bad friends and their drugs out of her way. She had that bone of strength inside her.

"You're smart," he'd said to her. "You did a smart thing, not a stupid thing. Taking care of yourself."

He'd been sitting for almost twenty minutes filling up time, alone on Adams Street, lost in his thoughts about Missy and coming up with an insight he hadn't foreseen. The unmistakably truth on what Sandy and Cindy and Missy had in common. All three, girls trying to become young women, had been funneled into lives that were fraught and where they had to be careful. Falling in with the wrong people dragged the vulnerable down quickly. It was too easy for them to be washed over and erased.

Sandy, should he ever find her, would no doubt give him a story just like Missy's. Staring at her empty apartment was the closest he'd come to getting it. The time he'd spent watching gave him little else. All he'd confirmed was that Sandy hadn't left a trail of clues for him to follow.

The case was consuming him, to the point where he barely had the concentration to deal with the simple things in his life like reading his psychology textbooks and otherwise preparing for the spring semester courses. But that was what he owed Cindy. She hadn't been as fortunate as Missy and she'd met up with the wrong guy. Jamie had to let his mind say it; she'd met up with the wrong cop, the person who ought to have been safe for her to trust. Jamie knew he wasn't going to let that be the end of it. He didn't know when he'd become Cindy's voice, but it'd slowly evolved and that worked on him.

He took a final look at the apartment's wooden door. The round peephole in the center, the pushbutton bell beneath it. Not at all different than every other door in the complex.

FIFTY-THREE

THE DRIVE TO ROUTE 80 TOOK JAMIE THE LENGTH OF Market Street to its intersection at Mill, a route that was getting familiar. Before he realized where he was going, he'd reached the stretch of rural roads winding away from the highway without really paying attention. He didn't need directions to the high school this time. The gravel kicked up on the sides of his car, although no truck came barreling towards him. He hadn't announced the visit. He hoped that he wasn't rude and in the same moment didn't care.

Mrs. De Carlo was alone in her classroom. She wasn't surprised to see him back.

"Glad that you usually stay late," he said. The clock noted it was almost five.

"Not so late. Not typically. You're lucky there was a poetry reading last period that ran over."

Jamie nodded. He was lucky.

"Tell me about Sandy. Why wouldn't you give me her address?"

"I never knew her address."

"But you said you wouldn't give it to me, even if you did know. Why not?"

Mrs. De Carlo looked at her nubby, rust-colored sweater. An answer resting in her lap.

"A feeling more than knowing anything. She was always trouble from what Cindy said. I didn't want to know."

"About what?"

"About Cindy. The man she was involved with. I never liked the way that he sounded. Cindy didn't say anything, but the last time we spoke, her voice was worried. I asked her what was wrong and she said she had gotten someone angry. She'd listened to her friends, followed their advice, and had angered the man she'd been seeing."

"What advice?"

"She didn't say. I assumed, like me, they had told her to end things. That she'd broken off from him and he was unhappy."

"That was it? The whole conversation?"

"I didn't press her. It was a reasonable assumption, that they'd given her the advice I'd given her. She said advice. They'd *advised* her. She said it just like that."

And then it came to her. She brought her hand to her open mouth. The seemingly insignificant piece of the puzzle she'd been told and almost forgotten.

"There was a plan to put a real end to the relationship. She didn't want to give me the details."

Mrs. De Carlo seemed pained. For the first time, the poised demeanor was unraveling.

"I had no idea these things would happen. No idea," she said. "I could have pressed her for more information, but I didn't."

Jamie had heard of cops feeling like they were caught in a vice when tough cases really got to them. What he saw was a blender. The double homicide. A witness who said the guy was in the military, based on absolutely nothing. Cindy's side fling with a cop. She'd gotten him angry. But if it was jealousy, why was Drew dead? And then in front of him, Mrs. De Carlo, suddenly losing her composure and revealing her heartbreak at losing Cindy. It began with her shoulders and then her whole body was shaking.

The set jaw of his field training officer whenever they'd taken a call involving a child had given the message. Emotion meant weakness. Jamie found himself standing at Mrs. De Carlo's side, an awkward hand on her forearm.

"No one could have expected the outcome," he said. "Not you, not anyone."

A single follow up question would have made all the difference, but Mrs. De Carlo had let the opportunity slip by, and now the plan would never be known.

FIFTY-FOUR

JUST LIKE THE LAST TIME, HE HAD NO TROUBLE FOL-lowing the red Datsun along the streets of Paterson. The car wasn't so fast going around the city. Too many lights. Too many blocks with cars parked on both sides. Very easy to trail his mark on the drive from Adams all the way to Mill Street before reaching Route 80. But on the freeway, the sports car whipped through traffic. He couldn't keep up.

He did gain some good information from staking out the apartment to see if Steinle's girlfriend showed up, although what he'd got was information he really hadn't wanted to know. There was that one cop who kept coming up with little scraps of this and that. In spite of the odds, that cop had turned up on Adams Street.

That meant the puzzle pieces against him were coming together. It was only a matter of time. When, not if, the whole thing was put into place. He figured it was days, maybe a week at most, for him to stop it.

What to do?

Following the blonde would be easy. She drove a cheap Vega, not a 280 ZX. Anyway, it wouldn't be about following her to a destination. It would be about pulling her over while she was still in Paterson.

That was one option. There were, of course, others.

What to do?

He'd need to find out who had what he was looking for, before settling on his next move.

What to do?

FIFTY-FIVE

GIL INVITED JAMIE TO A CLOSING PARTY THE LAW FIRM was hosting. The partners had put together a large deal for an office complex in Roseland and to celebrate, they'd taken over a private dining area at The Establishment, a relatively new steakhouse, for a cocktail hour followed by dinner. Gil, having some understanding of Missy, specified he was asking Jamie and his date. Missy was working late and told Jamie to go have fun.

"You love steak."

"I don't like you coming home to a dark, empty house."

"You've had other late nights."

"I don't know."

"Nugget is here."

"I don't know."

"I think you should go. I don't feel right having you miss this."

She didn't like that he worried over her. He was beginning to suspect he might be hovering. To please her, he agreed. It was the first time Jamie met the other Christians. Not just Gil's father and brother, but his mother, June. A poised, discreetly dressed woman who looked at home in her designer suit and brooch, her diamond starburst the size of a healthy musk turtle. She gave warm, crinkly smiles whenever introduced to someone new.

"Jamie." She took the hand he extended and grasped it in both of hers. "Gil tells me you've been to the club for sporting clays. He says you do quite well."

"I'm at a real advantage with that," he said.

"Well, we'd love to have you back when the weather's better. It's lovely in late April, early May."

If Gil was the son who'd dropped out of college and lived a life that was probably unsettling for his parents, he'd cleaned up well for the party. There was Gil in a blue cashmere blazer, gamely accepting his mother's adjustment to the knot on his tie. A well-trained host, he rescued Jamie the minute he'd been wedged into a conversation with elderly real estate agents.

"Jamie," Gil said, taking his elbow and extracting him from a discussion on rising interest rates. "C'mon. Let's find you a fresh Jack and Coke."

Jamie left before the celebratory cake, blaming the shift he was working the following day. He made his goodbyes to Gil and his family. The Establishment's automatic doors opened to the valet station, and a teen in a matching forest green jacket went to fetch his car.

The night air felt like glass. Cold and bracing and pure enough to purge the mash up of names and half-descriptions and bits of information asking to be put together, letting him think only of home.

Jamie turned off Union Ave. towards Maitland, anxious to find Missy unharmed. She'd argued convincingly that she and Nugget would keep each other safe, and he'd been fighting off a rotting feeling since leaving the party, rehashing what he saw as a bad decision. As he crept closer to the house, he was struck by the glare ahead of him. Everyone's holiday decorations were long pulled down and in storage and it wasn't that. It seemed all the porch lights were on and a few of his neighbors had repositioned cars in their driveways with motors running and high beams facing out. The whole block was crisscrossing each other's snow-covered lawns with flashlights. Even the Pistellis, who lived directly behind Jamie.

He caught a blonde ponytail shining beneath the streetlamp. Blocked by a swarm of woolen hats and scarves, he maneuvered his car to the curb and ran to Missy.

"It's Diesel," she said. "It was just like the other night. Nugget started barking. Then he stopped, and I heard Diesel barking. And then that stopped, too."

"What? What about Diesel?"

"He's missing."

All three of the Cosgrove children in pajamas beneath hastily-buttoned coats stomped in their winter boots and called for their dog. Too icy to be on their banana bikes, they wandered by foot inspecting hedges and the underside of porches. Jamie caught Bill heading back from the field that ended their small street. Red-faced from running. Drained.

"I think I saw him in the brush. It's so dark out there." Bill rubbed his arms absently. "Dog likes to run and get himself a good stretch. That's what he does whenever he gets loose. Goes as far as he can. He'll come home when he's tired."

He said the last part overly loud. A statement meant to soothe his family.

"I can look with you," Jamie said, surveying the Cosgroves' rear yard. The gate had been left wide open and allowed the dog to escape. What Missy had said played like a soundtrack. *It was just like the other night. Nugget started barking. Then he stopped, and I heard Diesel barking. And then that stopped, too.*

Bill shook his head, wheezing a little. "He needs to get his running out." By then, Amy, the Cosgrove daughter who had Aunt Ro's old bedroom set, was at her father's side.

What Jamie wanted was to believe his neighbor. Believe that Diesel was fine and would be home once he was exhausted and covered in burrs and missing his dog food. Jamie wanted to bathe in that belief. But he was the one attracting the eyes of his neighbors, especially the little ones, overheated from chasing after any movement and unfastening their coats. Even in the pressed slacks and sports jacket he'd worn to Gil's party and not in uniform, even if he was at least a decade younger than Bill, he was the police officer. The block was turning to him for answers.

Jamie reached for the words he'd heard so often by then, the special ones for families holding out hope. Bending down to get eye level with Bill's six-year-old, what he wanted was the cadence from Miucci whose formal statements were both assured and genuine.

"Right here." Jamie pressed his finger into the boy's left side. "Right here is where you keep all of your hope. You don't want to let go of that, do you?"

The boy's face, sweaty and scared looked back at him. A first grader's voice answered, "No."

"Good," Jamie said, clapping the boy's shoulder. "Good job. That's the best plan for tonight. Diesel's a tough dog. We all know that. If anyone can take care of himself, it's Diesel. We have to hold on to that."

Jamie found Missy's hand and held it tightly as they made their way back to the house, his heart still pounding even when they were inside hanging their coats in the hall closet, Nugget accounted for. He feared for the missing dog. It wasn't just the streets around Maitland and nearby highways that were busy and dangerous. Diesel was loud. A black-tongued mix, part chow and part something even bigger. In his early years, he'd lived at a gas station owned by Teri Cosgrove's father. Never quite a family pet, he stayed outside and served as a trusted guard dog for the neighborhood, immediately sensing strangers and warding off the kinds of people who might be looking to cause trouble. That had clearly made him an irritant to the person who'd been lurking past the Cosgroves' house, back and forth from Jamie's.

"Did you know that Diesel sleeps in a doghouse?" Missy asked. "I thought that was just an old shed in their yard."

"What?"

"They insulate it with straw. Mrs. Cosgrove told me that."

"I don't know. Maybe it is a shed."

"Are you even listening to me?"

Jamie went to the sink and opened the faucet, letting the water run hard, warming his hands and breaking the conversation. He wanted to ask if she'd seen anything odd or heard anything other than Nugget and Diesel barking. Missy turned on the light at the side door, then turned it off.

"How was the party?"

"The steak was good," he said. "We should go there some time."

She raised her fingers to his cheek. A trickle of cold on his skin. Jamie rolled her hands into fists and squeezed them in his palms.

The next morning, as Jamie was leaving for work, Bill flagged him before he'd finished backing the Datsun onto the street.

"Keep this to yourself," Bill said. "I don't want the kids upset."

"What happened?" Jamie asked, fearing he'd gotten news about Diesel overnight.

"I went out this morning, checking the gate."

"Anything wrong?"

"Blood," Bill said. "On the ground, near the side of the house."

Jamie pulled his car to the curb and flung the door open.

"I'll take a look."

Jamie made his way towards the path leading to the rear yard. The back of his neck stiffened from the cold. Stiffened just because. It was plain from a few feet away. On an icy patch off the driveway, a red discoloration had frozen into the ground. As he got closer, he noticed a larger splash of red high on a pile of shoveled snow.

"There's no other blood. Not in the pen. Not near the gate. If he gashed himself on some metal, there'd be more," Bill said.

Jamie nodded.

"Damnedest thing."

"He could have caught his side or his rear on something sharp. Not a lot of blood. It doesn't look like he's real hurt. There isn't a trail or bloody paw prints," Jamie said.

"I don't want to make a big deal."

"No? We could write it up," Jamie said, certain that was the last thing that would be helpful. There wasn't much to examine. More than that, a sense was solidifying. Jamie knew Diesel's escape was part of a growing imbalance and wrong in a way that could not be reported to the police.

"Nah," Bill said. "That'd have Terese and the kids all crazy."

"I get that."

Jamie returned to his car. To the blur that surrounded and haunted him. RJ's investigation wasn't any clearer than it had been the first day he'd been assigned his mid-level interviews. He didn't have the slightest proof of any crime other than a botched robbery. He wasn't sure he had an alternate motive. He wasn't sure of so much.

FIFTY-SIX

JAMIE COULDN'T UNDERSTAND THE PRESENCE OF THE seagulls in the wide parking lot beside the courthouse. Usually around three or four, they hovered near the tops of the telephone lines. Often in the winter. It was bewildering. He considered the odd birds as he walked towards his car and said his hello to Sam. He'd logged off his shift on the hour, leaving the station directly, not in the mood to be anywhere but driving for a while where he could scrutinize the single phone call that was causing him so much trouble. Not telling his superiors about Sandy meant it was information he'd withheld too long. It was well past the time when disclosing that brief conversation could be done without some real blowback. He didn't know what to do about her and Mrs. De Carlo and the nagging thoughts he'd been having over Eileen Brandsher's statement. Was she right the man she'd seen running was in the military? Was she someone lonely and bored with a story she'd made up? It was eerily close in timing to Tomasz's story and checked Mrs. De Carlo's description of Cindy spending time with a cop.

But where was that going? What was the reason to shoot Cindy and Drew? And where did Randall fit into it?

Jamie was turning all of that over on his drive out of Paterson, thinking it would be good to get to Steele's and burn some energy as he approached Stop the World. The headshop had opened a few years earlier on a stretch of Main Street he passed almost daily. The name popped up only once in the RJ's file, apparently where Sage was currently working.

In John Greene's report, the minimal details she provided covered three typed paragraphs. She and Cindy had overlapped a few months. It hadn't been that long, and she hadn't known Cindy, not really. She'd said the shooting had been intense for her and she was taking a break from dancing. Her contact information listed her new employer. Jamie had read the files so often, he knew even the most worthless minutiae. Yet a sense there might be more began gathering in his mind as he passed Stop the World, making him circle back and park near a hydrant. The file said she was nineteen. Her real name was Michelle Carbone.

Filled with bongs and rolling papers but usually not drugs, not openly, Stop the World sold mostly paraphernalia but also a certain style of clothing. The front window displayed a pair of red velvet pants and rayon shirt, a typical outfit seen at Aldo's, worn by guys with coke spoons around their necks. Clothes like that went hand in hand with the guys Jamie stayed clear of on his nights off.

He walked inside as the shopkeeper's bell announced him. The owner seemed to know he was a cop. Jamie caught a movement beneath the counter, fairly certain something had been shoved into a drawer.

"Can I help you?"

"Sage," Jamie said. "I hear she works here."

The man, full-bearded, with combed over hair and broad shoulders, faked a weak smile.

"Not anymore."

"As of when?"

"As of last week."

"Can you give me her phone number?"

"Don't have it."

Jamie walked the store's compact aisle slowly. Rows of hanging clothes were on his right, the glass counter to his left. In the very back, he stopped at an arrangement of water pipes and picked up one that seemed recently used. He smelled the bowl, turned to the owner, then inhaled again. Definitely resin. Not enough for a big bust, but there was resin.

"She worked for you and you never got a contact number? What if she didn't show up?"

"Look, what do you want?"

"I told you. I want Sage's phone number."

"The thing is, I don't give out personal information. Kind of a rule I have. My word is my bond, you know? How about I give you her current employment? That's not a secret."

Jamie put the pipe back on its shelf.

"Go on."

"She works at the Frontier Room. Sage likes to keep her weekends free. You can probably catch her tonight, tomorrow night. I'd try that."

Jamie eyed the shelves of drug paraphernalia behind the counter, wondering what arrest he could make. Saving that for another day, he left the world of Day-Glo posters and burning incense, figuring he could get to the bar on the earlier side.

He went to Steele's first. Lifting and feeling healthy and sticking to as much of a routine as he could was important. To balance his world. Still, he kept his workout short, specifically noting the time as he was leaving so he could spare an hour to make a stop. Missy was due home around eight that night and Jamie was increasingly nervous. The neighborhood disruptions made him edgy but also told him it was time to move faster, work even harder.

The Frontier Room was more familiar to Jamie than he'd have cared to admit. It'd been a favorite for a year or two after he and his friends turned eighteen. He still felt that rush of the forbidden as he passed through the barn-like front doors.

It was pushing dinner time and he easily found a place at the bar. The man who served him was the same bartender who'd been there for years. Lincoln wore a shirt with a jagged print, much like the ones sold in Stop the World. As he poured beer into an angled pilsner, Jamie motioned with his thumb to the dancer who'd been on since he got there.

"Sage?"

"That's Denise. Sage's up next," Lincoln said.

Jamie checked his watch and sipped his beer and listened to top forty music as Denise moved her hips in time with the repeating chorus of "fever" and "dancing." Her body circling, a strip of gold fabric flashing, she was briefly incandescent.

Eventually, a new girl appeared. Southern Italian olive skin and platinum streaks through her hair. Jamie let her pass him twice before he tipped her a twenty rolled inside a dollar bill. After four or five songs, Denise came back and Sage took the seat next to Jamie. He kept his gaze on the oval riser behind the bar.

"You're new."

He turned to find two dark eyes framed by thick mascara fixed on him. Beads of sweat dotted her temples.

"I am," he said. "Kind of. I haven't been here for a while."

"Welcome back."

Lincoln set a frothy mixed drink in front of her that Jamie understood he would pay for.

"So, you look fun," she said. "Fun to party with."

"I can be fun," he said. "But not tonight."

Sage registered that. Confused.

"I have a few questions to ask you. Just a few."

Jamie hadn't even needed to show his badge.

"I told them, the cops . . . I told them everything. I wasn't in the bar when it happened. I didn't see anything."

He let her grab her Tequila Sunrise, bite down on the straw, then empty most of it.

"Sage, that's your name in the clubs, right? The file says your first name is Michelle."

Her frosted hair moved slowly along her shoulders as she nodded.

"Shelly. That's what they usually call you."

Again, she nodded.

"I'm looking for Sandy. Cindy's friend. Someone told me you know her. Could put me in touch with her."

In an instant, her face betrayed her. Jamie had never seen anyone go pale like that so suddenly. Ashen. Like in a dime-store novel. She didn't have time to think of a good lie. No time for a simple response that sounded believable.

"I wish I knew where to find her. I'd tell you. Honest, I would tell you. I really don't know."

It had been slow to bubble forward. Sage was a few months older than Cindy and they'd likely been friends. Michelle and Shelly, the names she was trying to cast off, were the only connection within the two files. One tiny piece of light. Like all the others, it was nothing but it was something.

"Do you want the twenty back?"

"I want to know what you know." About Cindy, about Drew, about anything. There was a limitless amount unanswered.

Sage shook her head. "I knew Cindy a little from RJ's. We hung out, for sure. I met Sandy through her. We partied a little on a Saturday night in the fall. I didn't really hang with her, other than with Cindy that one time. That's all."

"Did you know who Cindy was seeing?"

"You mean Brad?"

"I mean anyone."

"She was just seeing Brad, I mean as far as I knew, and I don't know. I think that they spent a lot of time together because we didn't, like we didn't go clubbing on our nights off or really ever. I mean not much. I don't know what to tell you."

The explanation was garbled and what he'd expected. The look on her face, the fear told Jamie she knew more than the choppy sentences she'd come up with. She probably knew a decent amount about everything, even Drew. Jamie took Sage's fingers and folded them over the bill in her palm. He pulled a card from his jacket and wedged it in between her knuckles.

"Call me if anything changes."

FIFTY-SEVEN

IN THE DUSK, THE SKYWARD TURRET OF THE OLD POST office, the dome of the courthouse and the spires of St. John's peeked out, giving Jamie a brief view of the city's core from a spur off the main highway. It was the skyline he saw in various forms and from various angles every day. All he wanted then was comfort like that piled on him. Wanting. Needing. He was hungry and tired and finding Missy home would be the start.

When he got there, she had the canister of Morton's open, pouring salt carefully into a shaker. He bent to pet Nugget as they both watched her movements. He waited for her to fit the tiny cork into the bottom of the ceramic hen and set it next to the rooster filled with black pepper.

Jamie's fingers pressed into her slight upper arms.

"Did you do your curls yet?"

"I always do them in the morning."

There were women in the academy. Not many, but they had to do all the same things as the men. Chin-ups, push-ups, wall jumps, free weights. He recalled those women, an awareness forming. He'd have to get Missy on a better routine and there wasn't much time. It was a hard thought to maintain, wanting her prepared while trying to forget her school in Hyde Park. How far away she would be. How soon that would happen.

After dinner, Jamie walked Nugget keeping his eyes keyed to the street. The dog zigzagged along stopping at the same spots and not anywhere special that signaled to Jamie. Still, it was out there. The darkness falling and then the barking. He had to keep watching. Once he was back inside, Jamie began opening and closing the deadbolt he'd added two years ago, pulling hard on the door to make sure the strike plate was stationary.

Missy was shaking Nugget's damp towel.

"Did you ever go to those beefsteak dinners?" she asked, following Jamie as he moved to inspect the front window.

"You mean the ones at Donahue's?"

"Out on Route 23."

"Donahue's. I've been to a few."

Once finished securing the house, he spread himself fully across the couch as he used to when it was just him and Nugget, then adjusted his position so that all three of them fit under a throw blanket. There wasn't much space and Nugget moved to the backs of Missy's legs.

"It wasn't real waitressing. Just setting out platters. I worked those a few times."

"You did? You never said."

"The police there were a real crowd."

"You thought they were loud, huh?"

"Loud and flirty. Not acting bad, but real flirty."

"How flirty?"

"Teasing, good natured. They were polite but you could tell when all the waitresses walked away, there were jokes. Men's jokes and laughing."

"They like to let off steam."

"I'll say. I've never seen that side of you."

"They're the older cops who need to get away from the job and their families and pretty much everything."

She put a hand beneath his untucked shirt, her fingertips cool on his stomach. He pulled her towards him. He couldn't get over how easy it was to have her there, going deep into a kiss, his breathing shallow, until she drew back. Her face was flushed, and her mouth open.

"I forgot," she said. "I forgot to tell you."

Jamie had to reorient himself.

"Diesel came back."

"Diesel?"

"I saw Mrs. Cosgrove and she was with Amy, and they were both so happy."

Missy was flashing a wide smile. She was so happy too. Happy and unworried. Jamie didn't want to upset her by racing to their neighbors to ask all the details about Diesel's return. He hadn't stopped wondering why there was blood high on a snow pile, but he needed to keep that unease to himself.

"He came back?"

"Actually, someone found him and they'd been taking care of him, letting him sleep in their garage. The lady that does Teri, you know, Mrs. Cosgrove's hair saw the sign posted in Shop Rite and called to tell her right away. All she had to read was 'dog with black tongue' and she knew it was Diesel."

Jamie wanted more, thinking fast for a way to get to Bill Cosgrove without scaring Missy or leaving her alone and realizing there was none. He didn't like Missy by herself. Nugget continued to bark at night. His agitation was erratic and hard to predict. The only constant being that after the first week—whenever it happened—it was in the hours past sundown, when evenings were ending and the entire neighborhood was getting itself ready for bed. So far, there'd been no disruption, but that hour was nearing.

Jamie got up and went to his room. What concerned him was his dresser. His holster, his badge and a shoehorn were arranged neatly on top. Both his guns were kept in the top drawer that he unlocked. Finding them exactly as he'd left them allayed a pressure that'd been steadily rising until he remembered the double barrel. He'd rubbed it with a lint-free cloth the night before and placed it back in the attic and was suddenly desperate to check that it was still there. He wasn't sure what the point was. What it was that might happen in the far corners of the house if he dropped his constant vigilance.

"Is everything okay?" Missy called up.

"I'm good. I just needed to find a paper."

"For school?"

"Yes."

Her voice was getting closer and then she was floating beside him. Stroking her back, everything felt calm and stable. Pulling off her shirt, he crept into the small universe where he let her distract him, losing himself in her. For a brief time, there was only that. Holding Missy while she fell into a half-sleep, the dog next to the bed, curled atop a worn cotton sheet, Jamie returned to the world outside and the task of listening. He had to keep them both safe.

FIFTY-EIGHT

SAGE DIDN'T KNOW ANYTHING, THAT'S THE STORY SHE'D stuck with, but the timing was uncanny. On his way into work the next day, he stopped at Parisi's, then walked out with his lunch in a white paper bag and found a note on his windshield. "The Capitol Diner. Tonight at 9." It wasn't a place he knew and he'd had to look it up in the yellow pages. The Capitol bordered Passaic County in Lyndhurst. The note said to meet at 9:00 p.m. He wasn't sure what to do with Missy. He couldn't leave her alone. He couldn't bring her to the diner. He called Gil.

"I need you to take Missy to dinner."

Gil was a person who would do that without asking a single question.

Jamie got to the Capitol early, allowing enough time to hang back in his car and watch the parking lot. When it was five after nine and he hadn't seen anyone, he went into the vestibule, hesitating for another half-minute. An off hour on a weeknight, there weren't many people inside and none of them had the dark hair he was looking for. Taking the menu handed to him at the register, he walked to the back, wanting the very last booth to study the front door and wait on what he hoped wasn't a fool's errand or a scheme, but saw it was taken. A young woman sat there alone. She was wearing a knit hat. A strand of black hair had escaped, marking a thin line across her forehead. Her head didn't move as he approached. Only her eyelids.

Jamie slid into the opposite side of the booth and started to introduce himself, but she seemed to know who he was.

"I went to see Mrs. Sutter. Probably wasn't the safest thing to do, but I've been thinking of Cindy so much. It was when I was home for a short visit with my parents. I've been bouncing around. Trying not to be found. It's been hard on me."

Jamie didn't ask for any specifics about her invite, namely why she chose to leave a note instead of calling again. Maybe Missy answering the last time had thrown her off. Maybe she'd become worried that he could trace a call. He imagined the intrigue, starting with Sage watching as he left the bar, looking to see what he was driving. You didn't need to be razor sharp to find him near the police station or the deli all the cops went to. His red Datsun stood out.

"I knew the police were looking for people to talk to. Lorraine had said you seemed like a good person. I heard that early on. Cindy's mom said the same thing."

Jamie screwed his mouth, taking it in. Not ready to stop her from talking and begin with his questions.

"At this point, if you are, you are. If you're not, you're not. I don't care that much anymore. I'm kind of done."

She still hadn't mentioned Sage, who was probably the link between Lorraine's view that he was a good person and Sandy's first call, and who'd probably phoned Sandy the minute Jamie stepped out of the Frontier Room. As Bachman would have said, it was a side issue that really didn't matter.

He didn't know Sandy at all, other than seeing her in the photos he'd been shown by Marlene Sutter, but he knew from her skin tone she hadn't been sleeping well. She didn't know who to trust. She'd been able to dodge talking formally about what'd happened to Drew, avoiding an interview with the detectives assigned to his case. That much was clear.

"Coming here, meeting me. It won't be bad for you. I'm not going to do anything except listen and make sure whatever you tell me won't get you in trouble or make you unsafe."

It was all he could give her. His promise that he wouldn't betray her.

"All right," Sandy said.

Their booth, being the last, ensured no one was behind them. The diner stayed fairly empty. A few customers had taken seats close to the front and at the counter and a single green parka hung on the freestanding rack. Sandy scanned the room and gave a little shrug.

"My grandparents live a few blocks away from here. We used to come here on Sundays after church."

A waitress appeared and Sandy asked for the soup specials.

"Vegetable and chicken barley."

"I'll have the chicken."

"Cup or a bowl?"

"Oh . . . um. A cup, please."

The woman toyed with the sleeve of her cardigan, waiting for Jamie. He wasn't hungry but ordered a plate of fries.

"You can tell me whatever you want. Whenever you want to get started."

"So, I'm not going to get arrested?"

"No. I'm just asking you questions about what you know. You're a witness. You're not a suspect in any of this."

He wanted to add that she would be safe and fix how tired and worn she looked. Her eyes were hooded and sleepy, and Sandy as resigned as Jamie had ever seen anyone. She pulled her pocketbook into her lap and flipped the top open, baring a small envelope. She slid it across the table as the white border of a Polaroid jutted out. There was another beneath it. The photos were not at all what he'd expected to get from Sandy. He'd seen pictures like that in the grimy magazines his friends managed to get hold of in high school.

It wasn't the best angle, but he could tell by the side of her face it was the girl he'd seen in other photos. The girl who'd been wearing a theatrical wig. Miss Adelaide in her high school play.

"It's not a nice picture. It was his idea. Take sleazy pictures of her doing stuff."

The next picture was almost the same. Cindy, on her knees, a clear view of her profile as she's half looking up. A man's legs, one of them streaked, but the photo was too cloudy to tell what that was.

"So?" Jamie asked. "The man. Do you know who he is?"

"No. She didn't tell us a lot. Me. She didn't tell me. I only knew about the pictures because Cindy had me take them from her. She didn't want Brad to see them. She didn't know what to do. The guy wanted them, his trophy thing. He couldn't bring them to his house. Like, he was older. A married guy. So, Cindy was stuck holding on to them. And then I had them in my apartment which meant Drew came across them. Had his big idea."

The waitress had slipped her chicken soup next to Jamie's plate of fries. Sandy reached for the packet of Saltine's in the saucer, pressing her nail into the crackers. Jamie wanted to know every detail of what happened but didn't want Sandy to cry. Time to be patient, he thought, wishing he had that talent from Gil, where people opened up to him. Maybe the trick was to tap them a little, though he didn't think Sandy needed that. She wanted to tell him. He could feel it.

"She wasn't eighteen yet. Not when they took that picture. Not when he was messing with her," Sandy said. "That's what started all the trouble."

"How would the picture prove that?"

"Her shoulder. There's no tattoo. See? The one she got the day she turned eighteen, it's a lily with a stem and leaves. It sort of goes up by her neck. Everyone knew. She had the party at RJ's. All those guys, it was like a joke. They knew she was seventeen before, and they sure knew what she looked like, every inch of her. Every one of them knew there was no tattoo before she turned eighteen."

"So, Drew called that guy?"

"No, he talked Cindy into saying something. I think she'd broken off with the guy, but he kept on calling her. Drew was pretty convincing. He told her the guy had been using her and that's why he was still chasing her. He wasn't gonna ever help her like he said he would. She could get some real money. Get away from Brad. Drew made it sound easy. Like it wasn't a bad thing to do, and it would solve all her problems."

Mrs. De Carlo. Cindy. *She went with the wind. Whichever way it was blowing.*

Sandy was clutching herself. The only one left of the three. A small idea that went so wrong. He wanted to calm her down, but he had to make her go further. There was no other way.

"What happened when Cindy had the call? Were you there?"

Sandy shook her head. "I wasn't there, but man. Cindy was scared. Real scared. I saw it on her face when she came to the apartment. She wanted the pictures back, but Drew wasn't home and I didn't have them. She had to go to work and that guy was going to meet her. All I know is that she wasn't going to go through with any of it. She wanted to give him the pictures, forget the money. Forget the whole thing. She was terrified."

He let Sandy pause so he could catch up with his notes. Jamie wrote deliberately, not thinking of Cindy and how frightened she'd been when Sandy saw her and later when the night ended at RJ's. Keeping his focus would be his guardrail. He couldn't get off course with how sorry he was for Cindy. How very sorry he was for her and Drew and Randall.

"So, she had no choice. She was going to meet him and she didn't have the pictures," Jamie said.

"She tried to push it back, get him to meet her the next day but he was mad. She was too frightened to tell him where the pictures really were. She thought she could reason with him when he got there. She said the owner was nice. She thought he'd help her."

Jamie remembered Eileen Brandsher. She'd seen Randall drive off with Cindy once before. Maybe they were friendlier than anyone knew. Cindy's secret plan could have been Randall as her backup when the other guy showed up. The one with the military posture. The cop.

"The idea was to meet once the bar closed?"

"I'm guessing. I didn't ask about when. I only knew where."

"Why didn't Drew go to RJ's once he got home. Just meet her there and give her the pictures so she'd have them?"

This time, when Sandy pressed her nail into the cellophane, the Saltine package popped open. The sound prompted Jamie to scour the diner for eavesdroppers or possibly worse. The man at the register was bent over the *Daily News*. The waitress must have been in the kitchen. It was down to a spike-haired couple at the counter. He turned back to Sandy.

"Look, Drew was Drew. He didn't come home that night. It wasn't unusual for him. Sometimes he'd be hanging with his friends. I don't know. Maybe sometimes it was another girl. He didn't rub that in my face, so I don't know. But there were nights he stayed out. That was his deal."

Jamie wanted to take his hands and rub his own face. Rub it all off him, then drive Sandy into New York and leave her at the Port Authority so she could get a bus and never worry about being the only one of the three still left. But he was the cop.

"What happened next?"

"Once we knew what happened to Cindy, I mean, it was awful. We saw the paper. I called her mom. Next thing I thought is I need to burn the photos, but Drew said no. That if someone wanted them that bad, we'd need to keep them. In case."

"In case what?"

"He didn't say. I mean, like honest, we were real scared. We knew whoever was in the photo with Cindy was the guy in RJ's, we felt that and we didn't know what to do."

"You didn't want to go to the police?"

"We were part of it. Drew started the whole thing."

Sandy pushed the cup of soup she'd been staring at to the side of the table.

"What happened next?" Jamie asked again. The night's burning question.

It was coming. Her eyes glistened. Biting her lip. Trying so hard to keep it together.

"I don't know how. But he found us. Drew got a call."

"When?"

"There'd been some hang ups for a week or so. Weird stuff. We didn't feel safe. Almost like we were stalked. Then the phone call for real."

"Were you there?"

"When he called? I wasn't there but boy, when I walked in the door. Drew's face. That awful look, like with Cindy. Shit scared. Totally shit scared. The guy told him nothing would happen. He only wanted the pictures. They were going to meet up by Garret Mountain, but Drew said no, it had to be a public place. He picked Gilly's. A big sports bar. Bright, tons of people. No one could start trouble there."

"Any name? Any description?"

"The guy said he knew what Drew looked like. He'd find him inside Gilly's and get the photos. That was all. No questions. Clean deal."

"Why did Drew hold back two?"

"He had a feeling that something might go wrong. He didn't have much else. Like, what choice did he have? Go to the police and get arrested. He was the one who got Cindy killed. It was his idea, so the photos were going to be an insurance, in case, I don't know. In case the guy was going to shoot him too, he could say there's still two more photos."

Botched insurance. Jamie figured Drew got cornered in the parking lot, probably got shot before he even handed over the photos. He was hearing that same thing, where life veers off. Another version of that story. The black ice and the old man who couldn't control his car. If only the temperature had been a few degrees higher. If only Drew had given Cindy her pictures. If only Randall hadn't kept the gun in his pocket a beat too long. If things had been different by seconds. He pressed his pen hard on the paper. His hands might have been shaking.

Sandy lowered her voice. With all she'd told him, this was the confession getting caught in her throat. The crime she and Drew and Cindy were guilty of, setting off their descent.

"Blackmail," she said. "It was blackmail. That's what we were involved in."

"Look," Jamie said. "There is an ongoing investigation and this will be taken care of. And I want you to understand that you are not at fault." He sounded like the rookie he felt like. What it seemed he'd always be.

Sandy looked drained. She'd let go of the burden of holding all their stories inside. Who could say if she was better off having passed on what she knew. Jamie considered what he might do with the information if it were tangible and he could sand it down or solder it or hammer it and make it useful. A physical object he would know how to handle instead of something vaporous. RJ's became more and more unwieldy with each new piece of evidence. That seemed to be the lone solid rule.

It was time. The confession from Sandy pushed the search as far as he could take it. He'd have to go to someone with the investigating he'd done and explain how it took a turn and grew beyond what he'd expected. Jamie had no one but Gianelli and Andres to trust, even if the man in the photographs was a cop. Gianelli would probably be easier to approach. He'd have to speak with him tomorrow and get his ideas on how to navigate the department.

Jamie took the check and with his wallet out, gave a few bills to Sandy to buy herself a bus ticket and get away for a while. For the time, she just needed to get home.

"Let me drive you."

"I'm okay. I know this neighborhood. It's safe for me."

"I just want you to get there."

"I'll get there."

"You still don't trust me one hundred percent," Jamie said.

She turned away from him, checking herself in the diner window and smoothing the strands that were loose from her hat.

"What makes you think that he's still interested in you?" Jamie asked.

"Maybe he knows how many pictures there were and realized Drew didn't have all of them. Maybe that's why Drew got shot."

Jamie doubted that's why Drew got shot, but there was no comfort in telling her. Amazing, really, that Sandy survived this long, enough to hand Jamie the last photos.

"You said you don't know him. You never knew his name, and no one can really tell anything from these pictures."

He'd set them aside by then. The lighting in the diner was harsh, the Polaroids were overexposed, and examining them with Sandy on the other side of the booth hadn't felt right.

"I never knew his name. That doesn't mean someone else couldn't tell who he is from the pictures. Especially if *they* know his name . . . "

Sandy trailed off. A million theories had to have worked their way through her. The aftershocks of the murders would have her days and nights combining into one long sleepless rehash of everything that happened and how it all could have been different.

"Anyway, he may not know what was in all the pictures. His face was in some of them, the ones that Drew gave back. But who knows what he knows and thinks."

"You saw those? You saw his face?"

"I did," Sandy answered, seemingly surprised this was useful.

"Can you describe him?"

She took her time, harnessing her energy and trying to remember. Names and dates for a history test. The address she'd forgot to write down. That searching look.

"He was like my dad's age. My dad's forty-seven. The guy had light brown hair, maybe blond."

"Anything else? The color of his eyes? Did he have a beard or a moustache?"

Sandy's face colored. The most animation she'd had the entire time they'd been sitting together.

"They were like, having sex. I mean, they probably had a stand for the Polaroid, you know one of those timers, and it took a few pictures. I'm sorry. I didn't get a real good look at his face."

"It would have been better if Drew kept those pictures," Jamie said, maybe to himself.

"It would've," she said. "But he was in a real panic. He wasn't thinking the right way."

She lowered her voice again, noticeably. "He shot three people. He's paranoid, don't you think? Having even two pictures out there is going to keep him paranoid."

"Why don't you let me drive you where you're going?"

Sandy smiled. "Maybe I'm a little paranoid, too."

Jamie walked with her down the diner steps. Sandy steadied herself on the railing's bitter cold metal. He wondered how much the night had taken out of her. Telling her story, bringing up Cindy and Drew and everything she'd been through because of some dirty Polaroids. Who'd have ever seen all that raining down on her?

"Okay," she said.

She patted her jacket near her heart and where she'd placed the money from Jamie inside her shirt's front pocket. He half-waved as he turned away, giving her the privacy to disappear into the night. Jamie kept his head down, avoiding Sandy for the minute or two she'd need to round a corner. Facing the windows, he saw a clear view of the booth where they'd been sitting. A shivering sense of being watched passed through him. She said there'd been hang ups before the actual phone call. That she'd felt unsafe. Stalked.

Whoever shot Drew had been smart using a different gun. Jamie needed to anticipate what someone that clever might do to close the circle. Bathed in the diner's outside lighting, he walked slowly, listening for the crash. A car speeding down the road and into Sandy. The long hollow inside of him waiting for the next thing to happen.

FIFTY-NINE

HE WAS GIVING HIMSELF TWO DAYS. TWO DAYS TO GET IT done. He checked his forearm, the wound from the dog healing. He should have brought something bigger. Killed it with the first strike instead of getting its side, losing the momentum so it was able to lunge at him. Bite him hard. It was a setback, but the pain was manageable. A reminder there'd be no more mistakes.

He was giving himself two days to get it done and over with.

SIXTY

IT WAS THE FIRST TIME SINCE THE DOG WAS BACK THAT Jamie saw Bill. They met on the Cosgroves' front walk, Bill chipping at some ice, runoff that had melted and then froze, and Jamie catching him for a casual minute or two to ask about Diesel. What neighbors do. Bill kept it short and terse. Jamie learned Diesel had a few broken ribs.

"Damn dog," Bill said. "Cost me a fortune at the vet. They think he got hit by a car. Something big and heavy."

"He's a real tough dog. I bet he had a few cuts and bruises to go with those cracked ribs."

Jamie wanted to know why there'd been blood. Bill said it might have been a paw that healed quickly or a cut inside his mouth. The vet wasn't worried.

His paw. His mouth. The blood was high on a snow pile.

"Can't tell you how happy Teri and the kids are. The ribs are mending pretty good and the time he was missing he was living in a garage and getting food," Bill said. "I think they fed him raw liver." He shook his head. "Cost a shit load of money for the vet but the dog's fine."

Bill zipped his work jacket heading for his driveway, letting Jamie know he didn't want to worry about Diesel or whatever happened. For Bill, it could have been worse, a lot worse, and in the end, nothing bad had happened to Diesel. Just like nothing bad could ever happen to his family. Jamie knew that need to believe.

Jamie remembered what Gianelli had said. Something wasn't sitting right. Before Bill backed his Buick Skylark into the road, Jamie trotted to the driver's side and knocked on the window, which Bill impatiently let down.

"Quick question. Which side got hit?"

"Left side. The ribs on the left. Why?"

"Just curious," Jamie said. It was reason enough for Bill. Jamie's neighbor didn't care why he asked or whether there was meaning in the answer. All he wanted was to forget the blood and vet bills and leave for work.

Jamie drove from Hillcrest into downtown, picturing a man standing and a dog jumping on him. If the man was holding a baseball bat or a stick, he'd have to be right-handed to get the dog's left side.

SIXTY-ONE

HIS MEETING WITH BACHMAN WOULD BE A RECAP OF THE warehouse information they'd been given, mostly from an informant the FBI was working with. Jamie was charged with tracking down the basic background on the cooperative inventory clerk. He'd been told specifically by Bachman there wouldn't be interviews or interrogations.

"You have one role in this. Find out who their guy deals with. We need to know before the defense attorney does and tears him apart on the stand. That's the instruction from the DA's office. You get what you can from the area around Straight Street. Has he done some fencing of his own in the past? Names, you hear me. That's what you get."

He was testy and the last thing Jamie needed was to addle him with details about RJ's and possible theories involving dogs being attacked and his thoughts on Drew's killing being connected and accusations against another officer. What Jamie had to do, what he'd known for some time, was to place his trust in one particular person. But that day, Gianelli wasn't in his office and no one could tell Jamie when he'd be back.

"He's got a new case. Girl got dragged into a van on her way home from school. Just sickening. Sickening. He's checking the neighborhood with Andres and if he gets back this afternoon it'll be a shock, I'll say that. Those guys will be combing the area, that's for sure."

That was Elizabeth's answer to him. She closed herself to further discussion by going back to her *Ladies' Home Journal*, a world where fifteen-year-old girls weren't abducted on the familiar routes they walked every day. A world of knitting patterns and post-holiday recipes and advice for disciplining teenagers. Jamie had occupied himself scanning the cover once it became clear he wasn't going to get more from Elizabeth on Gianelli's likely whereabouts. He could have told her the best way to discipline teenagers was with a wooden spoon. At least for boys. At least according to his aunt.

Back at his desk, he thought to call Steve, who'd phoned on Tuesday when he'd been in a bar having too much fun.

"Come down here. Come down here now," Steve had said. It was actually more of a demand.

There'd been fierce music in the background and Jamie didn't hear much beyond Steve's occasional shout, "Get down here." They hadn't really talked in a while. Jamie had never been so busy. He'd never had so much going on in his life, with no one to sort it all out with. Work was an off-limits conversation. Missy was a handful. He didn't have time to understand what he felt for her or the words to explain her to another person.

When things ended with Debra, all Jamie told Steve was that she'd wanted a ring. That's all he'd needed to say. One sentence about his breakup with the young woman he'd dated for two years. There was quite a lot more to say about Missy. What presently concerned Jamie was her move to Poughkeepsie. It had come together quickly. Her loans. The rental they'd found when he'd brought her to complete paperwork at the school. He ran the many paragraphs it would take to describe their relationship over in his mind and no matter how he arranged them, it would all be inexplicable to anyone else. Steve didn't even know who Missy was. Jamie had only told his friend that he'd met someone he thought might be special.

He punched Steve's number into the dial pad.

"Sports bar. Friday night," Steve said.

"Sure," Jamie answered.

The phone wasn't back in the cradle with Jamie immediately reflecting on the conversation and the plans he'd just made. The worry he had leaving Missy alone, even with Nugget. He tried calculating the hours he'd be away until he heard Fred Gerritsen's Brooklyn-tinged accent interrupting everyone within close range.

"Hey, what happened to the candy?"

Gerritsen was poking around all the empty desks in the squad room, dramatically rustling papers and pawing through inboxes as if turning over a crime scene.

"Hey, Palmieri! You seen any chocolate?"

"No idea what you're talking about," Jamie answered.

"John bought Sheila a nice box of Russell Stover's for her birthday or anniversary or I don't friggin' know, and she made him take it back. Diet she's on. She's been dieting."

"I didn't see it but if he brought it here, it wouldn't have lasted too long."

"Yeah, no, it wouldn't have."

A few more desks picked over, then Gerritsen headed towards Wayne, looming above the trainee but not saying a word. What Jamie did hear was Wayne's chair sliding across the floor, and the scratching noise of his arms pushing against the liner of his jacket sleeves.

"What do you want with your coffee?" Wayne asked.

"I feel like some pastry," Gerritsen answered.

Jamie could be a touch bossy with Wayne, but Gerritsen had a distinctly ex-marine bearing. His demeanor itself an implied threat, reminding Jamie of what he didn't want to know. The person he was looking for might be a cop, possibly with a military background or the trappings of one. He gauged that against what he knew to be true. Officers, high ranking and low, were the last line of defense. They were out there. They showed up. If one of them was at the root of a blackmail scheme leading to three murders, that behavior was an outlier. It wasn't who the rest of the officers were. Jamie's accusations would shake up the department. Possibly disgrace it. With all he'd been stitching together, there wasn't enough yet to go that far, certainly not on his own. Since the academy, Jamie had been told his work as a cop meant he was part of a team. A brotherhood. He was also in a department trying to earn back the trust of a community that'd been tested with a high-profile case and charges of police abuse. There was zero room for even the small est misstep.

Jamie flattened his hands on his desk, positioning himself as if to stand. It'd been less than half an hour since he'd last checked with Elizabeth. There was no point peppering her with more questions. He had to change direction until Gianelli got back. His time was better spent concentrating on the rote work available to him, falling into a rhythm for the rest of the day. Routine matters. The head prosecutor for juvenile wanted to go over testimony on a current case that Jamie really didn't have any information on, beyond what was in the report. He placed the call and was told the lawyer would be on trial until the following week anyway.

"Just leave a message that Officer Palmieri returned his call."

It wasn't until his shift ended that he let his thoughts drift, his worries pulling him further and further from a world that was predictable. When he reached into the glove compartment for his cinnamon gum, his fingers brushed against the envelope from Sandy.

It was dark and biting cold when he stepped from the car, a winter that wouldn't end. Jamie jostled the side door, anxious for the needed rush of heat. Missy and Nugget were both waiting in the kitchen. He got washed and changed.

"They made up new menus at Casa Romano."

Jamie stared at a bowl of roast potatoes shiny with oil, salt, and rosemary. He gripped the serving spoon as if it were a weapon.

"It's still Italian. There's an archway that's like a window with open shutters and then blue water. That's the new cover," she said. "They didn't add any fancy appetizers or entrées."

She let a little space linger, not expecting an answer from Jamie, not moving quickly to her next thought. With the tips of her fingers, she pushed the serving bowl closer to his side of the table.

"I think the new menus are how they raise the prices. Maybe, I don't know. I wonder if the regulars will notice."

Jamie let Missy talk about her job. He had no desire to discuss his.

The idea of a Friday night with Steve nagged even more while they watched an update on the weather. The close of the evening news as daylight faded. Like clockwork, Nugget became agitated. Diesel eventually joined in. It was early enough that Jamie was still dressed. He wasn't going to let someone muzzle the dog's barking with a baseball bat or worse. Missy trailed Jamie as he ran. He didn't have the time to stop her. His only goal was reaching Diesel and whoever was near him before any of the Cosgroves. The dog was growling and snapping. Missy was planted on the sidewalk, her fearful cries followed Jamie.

"What's the matter? Is it a cat?"

As her voice grew smaller, there was only his breath and the crunch of hardened snow breaking as he made his way through the Cosgroves' front yard and over a trail of near perfect footprints running in both directions, to and from the end of the block. The Cosgroves' rear light flicked on. Then it all began winding down, with the last of the barking. The side of their house dark again and a short silence. The frigid void filled when a car accelerated on the other side of the scant woods framing the dead end. The screeching of tires.

After the car's loud exit, Jamie retreated quickly. Like most people, the Cosgroves probably didn't think as much about the barking as he did, and Jamie didn't want a long conversation in their yard. The threat had passed but he was still wired. Instead of returning to his house, he jogged towards the dead end of Maitland using the newly formed tracks to direct him. It didn't take Jamie a minute to find the two by four covered with a recent frost and tinged with blood. It confirmed what he already knew about Diesel's escape but got him no closer to what he needed. He dropped it by the cord of wood he kept stacked against his property line with the Pistellis.

When he was back in the house, sweating and agitated and suddenly cold with the adrenaline wearing off, he sank into his chair and surveyed what was supposed to be his haven. Nugget was alert and crossing the floor, like on a full-on sugar high. Missy was hugging herself, having stayed outside for much of the time Jamie had been chasing after shadows. He'd stopped someone from permanently silencing Diesel's warning. This time. It should have felt crazy. He was investigating three murders and worrying over the neighbor's dog.

"The yard," he said. "It was probably nothing. Car thieves sometimes, you know, they come to a neighborhood, checking for keys on the seat."

"Stolen cars?"

Missy clutched her stomach, the threat of that possibility panicking her. Trying to make light of the barking and his bolt to check Diesel, Jamie hadn't done well. Her car was the only thing she owned. The only thing that was hers.

"Don't worry. They won't steal your Vega."

"Really? How do you know?"

"Because I live here and I have a gun."

It was the stupidest, most full of swagger thing he could have said, but it satisfied Missy.

SIXTY-TWO

THE REST OF THE NIGHT, MISSY WAS HAPPY. FOR HER, everything was in place. She sat with her back propped against the couch and did the *TV Guide* crossword. Jamie went to the fireplace and removed a chunk of burnt wood. He let it rest in his palm and examined it like it was a scrimshaw. The house was noiseless and unsettled enough for her to stop writing.

"You're awfully quiet."

When Jamie didn't answer, she tried wheedling him into doing the puzzle with her.

"What was the last name of Ralph Kramden's best friend?"

"You never watched *The Honeymooners*?"

Missy shook her head.

By midnight, Jamie was still awake. He lay on his back, straining to hear a rustling in the yard he knew wasn't really there. Missy was breathing steadily. She turned to her side. Jamie thought she was talking before she exhaled with a light snore. Her face relaxed and untroubled in sleep.

When Jamie wasn't thinking about heavy footsteps and the shreds of details he had to sort through and put together, he gave himself the narrowest slot to think about Missy. What Jamie wanted was for it to never be the Sunday she'd be leaving. Not like the Sunday mornings he'd become used to so quickly. In ten days, it would all be different. For the day he was dreading, Jamie had everything planned.

He'd move her in, make sure she was settled, and then they'd have dinner at the restaurant on the water he'd seen on their last drive. The

River Dock, with its floor-to-ceiling windows facing the Hudson. He'd hold her hand and say everything right to her. He knew a part of her was anxious and unsure of herself.

A few days earlier, she'd cut herself slicing an apple. Though it wasn't deep at all, she began crying. He'd taken a napkin to her, then raised her arm, telling her to keep it above her heart until the bleeding stopped. He'd tried tending to her and still, she'd fallen apart. She needed good knife skills. She wouldn't be as good as any of the other students. She didn't belong there.

He'd wanted to tell her that everyone was learning and fighting hard not to be a fraud, but he hadn't known how to admit that to her in all the commotion of her cutting herself. He thought he'd be better at the restaurant when he'd convince her she'd be a success at school. He'd encourage her, then drive back to Paterson knowing she was off to the start of her life and hope that he wasn't losing her.

Saying the right things meant swallowing the words he'd found surfacing more and more. *We were meant to be together.*

Missy was what Jamie fell asleep thinking on. He slept for less than an hour. The clock radio read 1:42 a.m. and Jamie's thoughts were back with the intruder. Nugget was nestled on his sheet. That wasn't enough. The thought of Nugget agitated, as he'd been earlier and so many times over the past weeks, tapping his nails across the wood floors and nervously pacing turned into Connie De Carlo letting out Cindy's secret that she'd been involved with a cop. Drew had been shot with a .44. Cops collected guns. The exact person to have a host of guns and to know it was better to use different ones. The file that might name the cop he was looking for conveniently missing. The pieces turning in the tumbler of the combination lock, never lining up.

That's how it worked. The middle of the night when everything took on a sharper focus. Every insignificant detail came out fuller. There was one in particular he'd tried to ignore. Missy had asked a day or two earlier if she was a bad driver. She thought a police car had been following her. Starting near Lafayette Street, then with each and every one of her shortcuts and all the way to the Straight Street Bridge. She described coming to full stops and making sure she used her blinkers.

"It felt like he was right on my bumper the whole time."

"It happens sometimes. A car gets behind you, going in your direction for a while. It always makes you nervous when the car's got lights on top. Even if they're not on."

Jamie had reassured her. He'd even reassured himself. Now he was less sure.

Whoever was watching the house knew who Missy was and that she was living with Jamie. Easy enough to stop her on a side street or vacant lot and plant pot on her. Her arrest a straight line to his immediate suspension and that would just be the start. All that trouble avoided when she'd crossed the river and left Paterson. The modest luck her job was in Haledon. The *reprieve*.

Another thought passed over him. It could go even darker for Missy. The same execution-style bullet to her that Drew got. A warning for Jamie. Going after Jamie directly, shooting a cop and the attention that would get, was a line the killer might not cross if he didn't have to. Missy was different, as disposable as Cindy. The thought sickened him.

Jamie didn't know what he knew, but he was close to something. Close enough that he was in danger and that meant all of them were. The cop following Missy, whatever he'd aimed to do, wasn't going to lay off. It wasn't as if Jamie could either, even if he'd been willing to. Whoever he was circling around seemed to know Jamie's progress and was turning the tables. On him. On Missy. If he was going to get her somewhere safe, it needed to be when no one would be following them. It was the best plan he had.

She was half asleep. He'd been shaking her, and she awakened enough to move her hand, drowsy and dreamy like the rest of her, to where she thought he wanted her to put it.

"No, Missy."

"Mm."

"C'mon. You have to get dressed."

He gently moved her hand away and let it rest on his stomach. She was so warm. So agreeable. He hoped he knew what he was doing. He got out of bed and stood over her in the still darkened room.

"C'mon Missy. Get up."

"Mm. It's not morning." Her eyes blinked. "Is it?"

"Not really. But we need to get out. You have to get dressed."

"Dressed?" Missy propped herself on an elbow.

"It's not safe. It's not safe for you."

"What? What's not safe?"

"It's just this feeling. I have to get you to Gil's house."

"Gil's house?"

"Close your eyes, I'm turning the lights on."

With the sudden brightness, she flinched and brought her hand to her face.

"Missy, where are your clothes? Where are all your clothes?"

In the car, they stayed silent. The heat wouldn't kick in for another few minutes and they were rigid with cold and fear. Nugget sat vigilant on her lap.

"If it's not safe for me, how is it safe for you?"

"It's safe. I'm safe. I'll be fine."

"But how? How is it safe for you but not for me?"

"I can handle myself."

"Really? You can. Without any help."

"I'm okay, Missy. I really am. Don't worry. We just need to get you to Gil's."

"Does Gil know I'm coming?"

"Gil?"

"Yes, Gil. It's the middle of the night. Does he know I'm on my way there?"

Jamie chewed on his lip. "No, he doesn't. But it'll be fine."

Jamie thought some more on the drive to West Paterson. Someone was looking at the house. The only thing he had were the photographs and he mulled over how anyone could know that. Either someone got to Sandy or had been following him. He remembered the Capitol Diner's windows. Drew was dead because of those Polaroids. He changed his mind as he drove in the near dark to the secluded apartment complex. He wanted Missy even further away, but he still needed to stop at Gil's and leave the dog. Someone tried to take on Diesel to quiet his bark. Diesel was a big dog. Nugget wouldn't have a chance.

Jamie had Missy get out of the car and walk to the front door with him. He didn't trust anything or anywhere. Maybe he could let up when they were far away and he was sure they hadn't been followed. Gil was tired but not surprised to see them.

"I need you to take Nugget," Jamie said. "He can't stay with Missy. They don't allow pets."

He handed Gil the keys to Missy's car. "Hold on to these for now. It's at my house. We'll need to get it at some point."

Gil was silent, the little dog in his arms.

"I forgot to bring his food."

Gil nodded.

They drove over the Bear Mountain Bridge once more and stopped at the Starlight, a single-story motor court coated in slick white paint with a dozen blue doors. Jamie found a space for his car behind the building, then rented a room for six hours. He had to wait until at least 8:30 to bring Missy to the house she was due to move into. A Victorian at 228 Miller Street.

They'd picked up a copy of the *Poughkeepsie Journal* and found a furnished room with bath, kitchen and laundry privileges that would cost $85 per month with the $10 student discount she'd been given. Described in the paper as "well furnished, home atmosphere, convenient to shopping and buses." Jamie had met with Adelle, the landlady. Eyeing the place too much, in Missy's opinion. Asking too many questions. Missy wanted to know what exactly he'd been looking for and Jamie answered her. "The creepy guy."

After barely sleeping on the Starlight's thin mattress, they ate a silent breakfast in the coffee shop across the road. Jamie surveilled the parking lot, the adjacent property, and the length of Route 9 in both directions until he was satisfied, then shepherded Missy back to the Datsun.

"I can't just show up. She'll think I'm undesirable. Erratic. I could lose the spot."

"It'll be fine."

Jamie explained to Adelle that Missy was out of her current apartment earlier than expected. She'd given notice and the landlord changed the locks, needing to paint the place to get a new tenant. Jamie didn't care what that sounded like. He handed Adelle twenty dollars and she didn't care what it sounded like either. He'd been throwing bills around lately, like a vice cop in New York.

He walked back to his car, Missy behind him.

"You're leaving without kissing me goodbye?"

He opened his arms and she stepped into them. He kissed the top of her head, scrunching the wavy hair she'd tried to comb with her fingers on their way to Adelle's. He was so scared. So frightened. He couldn't bear to kiss her lips and have his begin to tremble. He didn't want to go back to his empty house and be without either of them.

Jamie let a minute pass, then bent to kiss her cheek.

"I'll be okay. We'll be okay."

As he began to move back, she grabbed at his jacket. Her small, fierce, determined fists.

"Jamie."

He kept his gaze on the tan house behind her. The dried-out flower beds. The holly bushes framing the doorway. Missy's window was somewhere in the back.

"Gil will get your car to you so make sure you have a number where he can call you. You get in touch with him first. Then you'll need to get yourself set up for school. It's going to be fine. You're going to be great. Really, I can't wait to try all the new things you'll be making."

SIXTY-THREE

HE DIDN'T HAVE MUCH TIME LEFT AND WAS MAKING HIS
runs later. He had no choice. He'd been giving his wife half-assed excuses for leaving
the house at odd hours. This time he hadn't bothered giving her any excuse at all.

He had a pretty good view inside the apartment. Like the other nights, the
TV had been left on, a few glasses and one empty bottle on the table in front of the
sofa. Hard to tell where the guy was in the apartment. He never found out much
looking there. But he'd seen the guy, first at the funeral parlor, then hanging around
the cop with all the questions. And covering bases meant covering bases.

Suddenly the dog ran from the back, straight to the window, jumping up
and growling. Dachshunds were good that way, recognizing his smell immediately.
The deep bark was a surprise and he stumbled backward, barely catching himself.
Wondering as he picked pine needles off his sleeve, what else had been left at the
apartment? Just the dog?

The guy inside was frozen in between the kitchen and the back hallway,
pivoting when he saw the dog beneath the living room window. Barking, then
growling, then barking again. He watched the guy dial the phone quickly, tugging
at the top of his pajama pants with his free hand.

He'd have to leave soon. Gil wasn't Jamie, someone who couldn't call the cops
because he was a cop.

It was a good reminder. He really didn't have much more time to wrap this
thing up.

SIXTY-FOUR

ONCE HOME, JAMIE WENT TO THE BATHROOM AND BE-
gan with a faceful of cold water. He was greasy from a night of not
sleeping and unbuttoned his shirt like a mulish ten-year-old while
the shower filled with steam and a faint mix of mildew and Missy's
peppermint. She hadn't had time to pack her bath soaps, her Clairol
shampoo, or her manicure kit. He wondered what he and Missy would
figure out. There'd have to be strategies for busy schedules and long
drives. He gave himself a few minutes to think about her, then put that
away. His shift began at three.

Teri Cosgrove answered on the first knock. Smiling. Curious.
Normally, she was a plain woman, her brow usually furrowed. At two
in the afternoon, she seemed entirely different. Serene with her kids at
school and not due back for another hour.

"Can you have Bill call me at the station when he gets in?"

Teri's hand rose to the top of her blouse. The fact that he'd never
had Bill at the house for anything and that their dog had recently gone
missing wouldn't have been lost to her. He lightened her fear with a laugh.

"I need a hand with a few boxes in the basement. Heavy stuff, even
for me to lift."

"Okay."

"He can call the main number and they'll transfer him."

On the way to the station, he stopped for gas and remembered Missy's Vega, a thought he pushed aside. What he needed was
pure concentration.

Before the Market Street exit, taking in the view of downtown, he began to wonder if he was overthinking the case. Sandy's story. The Polaroids. Paterson wasn't a wild place. It was a sleepy old city with drug addicts and warehouses that needed to be watched and kids who got into trouble with knives and were given Snickers bars.

Blackmail. A cop at the root of what started as a double homicide and was now three deaths. What did he really have to base any of that on? He tried to piece together what he would say to Gianelli. That Sandy had handed him two photos with an unidentifiable man. That there'd been other pictures but those were gone. No proof of the guy around her father's age with light brown hair. Or maybe he was blond. Nothing about him was particularly clear in the Polaroids. What Jamie did have was a motive to give Gianelli and hopefully tie in all the other scraps he'd collected.

He took a last look onto the skyline. City Hall loomed ahead, still a crown jewel from a distance. The previous century's nod to the silk industry, it had been designed by New York architects and modeled after the historic *Hôtel de Ville* in Lyon, France. Not that Jamie knew any of that history. What he knew was that the building was regal in its way and also a quick walk to the outdoor lot where cops left their own cars.

About a half hour into his shift, he got a call from Bill. Gary was typing and Wayne was on patrol with his field officer. Henry was at the courthouse, scheduled to testify in another juvenile case. Everyone else was in the back working out assignments and finishing reports, not really near Jamie. Still, he kept his voice low.

"Listen, can I call you back?"

The line was silent for a few beats.

"I'll be home."

"Great. I'm in the middle of a last-minute thing here. Give you a call in a few."

Jamie went down the stairs and through the lobby with his head down, avoiding hellos and opportunities for small talk, then to a phonebooth on the corner. He told Bill it looked like there were some car thieves in the area. His favorite new ploy.

"They're going around to different neighborhoods. I know you can keep this quiet."

"Thieves? What make of cars they going after?"

"It's probably kids. No one is especially worried. Thing is, I'd keep Diesel inside for a few nights. Daytime is okay, but, you know what I'm saying."

"Sure do."

"You'll think of something to tell Teri?"

"I'll say the vet recommended it."

"There you go."

He grabbed two coffees from the deli and went back to his desk. Gary turned in surprise when the paper cup was set in front of him. Apparently, he never noticed Jamie had been gone. For the rest of his shift, Jamie was kept busy. Driving the Fourth Ward in an unmarked car for a few hours. Then, back at his desk, fielding the phones. The odd people that called into the station at night with complaints and demands. An elderly man who needed aspirin and thought there ought to be an all-night pharmacy downtown. Jamie had agreed with him.

It was almost eleven thirty when Jamie returned to Maitland. He found his street the quietest it had been in all his memory. Nugget was tucked safely away with Gil. Diesel was sleeping indoors in what was likely a first for the black-tongued dog. Jamie pulled into the driveway and let the Datsun's engine grow silent before he got out of the car. The freestanding garage looked exactly as it had all winter with a hardened crust of snow along the edge and only his footprints. The light he'd left on brightened the path to the stairs. It was hard to reconcile the gnawing fear overtaking him with everything so much unchanged.

What Jamie knew, what he couldn't escape, was how the simple act of entering his home was both terrifying and real. His pursuer existed and he'd left three people dead. He climbed the four steps, alert to every groan behind him, every stirring in the brush that circled the yard, pausing at the rattle of a nearby garage door being raised. The kitchen's curtained window and the outer door's glass insert both revealed shadows he'd never noticed. He forced his key inside the deadbolt but didn't quite feel a release, as if it hadn't been set when he'd left for work and yet the bottom lock was in place. Trying to remember the details of that morning's routine didn't matter. Jamie had no choice but to turn the knob and ease the door open. Whatever was waiting for him, whoever was waiting, he wasn't going to hide.

Jamie pushed back his jacket, exposing his hip, yet staying short of ready position. Somehow, entering his own home with the gun fully drawn was a line. What his aunt would call a bridge too far. This was where he'd grown up and he fought himself, refusing to be reduced to the imaginary fears of a nine-year-old. Someone in the basement. The closet. Beneath a bed.

Still, everything the house had ever been, the place where he'd had birthdays and Christmases and where he'd held Missy, all the changes of his life, all of that was gone. It was pine floorboards and penny tiles in the bathroom, icy cold and hard. Sheetrocked walls and nails and hinges and glass, empty of feeling and not the refuge that had taken him in long ago.

As he stepped into the kitchen, his right hand reached for the switch, a movement of muscle memory that was both deliberate and full of dread and followed by a wave of relief, finding no one in his immediate view. He did it all. The slow walk to the basement, the front closet. Once in the bathroom, he moved towards the tub and raked the shower rings over the rod as the rustle of plastic screamed his location. Then he waited. The stalked feeling that Sandy and Drew had known, he knew that too. Nothing was keeping him inside except the sense that he was the one now. This wasn't pretending to know what to do, fighting hard not to be a fraud. He was doing what needed to be done.

Jamie felt for the thumb break on his holster. Only the upstairs rooms were left. The regular house sounds hoisted him forward. Heat turning on without warning. The Westinghouse's compressor. Humming. Gurgling. Crackling. But also, there was silence and that was worse, following him as he swept through the bedrooms and alcoves, until he was back in the hallway.

The attic rope hung before him. That would be last. The very last. The braided cord was perfectly still. There was no way to enter the attic noiselessly. Jamie drew his Python.

The opened hatch released the folding steps, their familiar creak magnified. Using only his left hand for support as he readied for the darkness, afraid of what might be waiting for him but needing it known, his boot pressed on the first wood slat. He climbed into the attic until he was standing on the cross beams. Faint light rose from the landing beneath him, ghostlike and ethereal. It was the only room where Jamie couldn't keep his back to a wall and he turned slowly in the blanket of dust until his dread began ebbing back to where it was manageable. He'd swept through the house and done what he needed to do. Only then did he see the wisp of a figure on the unfinished wall and the unmistakable contours of a revolver.

Jamie, alone in his attic, confronting his own shadow and what fear really looked like.

Someone had turned Jamie's life around. Even if he wanted to stop pursuing the killer, that wasn't a choice any longer. He was also the pursued. The best he'd done was taking enough control and refusing to stay a mere target. He prayed if anyone was looking down on him, in the smallest way, they'd be pleased. He'd never openly called for his aunt's presence, but in that moment, he silently plead for the chalky mist feel of her to return.

As he lay in sweatpants and a T-shirt on top of the blankets, embracing the cold, Jamie went over all of it and tried putting together what he knew for the millionth time. How someone on the force had committed three homicides and all he had for solid proof were two photographs of basically nothing. A partial view of the suspect's leg. He needed more, like a way to start sifting through files for the department of four hundred officers, as if he could do that on his own. He didn't have a wide expanse of time. He didn't have any time. None at all. And even if he had, finding the right cop, that wouldn't uncover enough. He still had to put him at the scene of both crimes.

It was tatters of information, but he'd take them to Gianelli and things would begin to settle. That was all he cared about. He'd loosened the hold of his pride and ambition somewhere around the time he'd learned Drew Steinle had been killed.

SIXTY-FIVE

THE WORKING THEORY WENT FROM A GUY HIDING UP-
stairs to possibly a crime of opportunity. Maybe someone Randall trusted too much
stayed a while longer at the bar. Maybe a guy that said he was driving Cindy
showed up. Someone into drugs. Instead of giving her a ride, he made her take the
money from the register. Then grabbed her purse. Things got heated the way they
always do when there's a gun and a nervous guy behind it.

The working theory was that Cindy was shot by accident, then I'd had to shoot
Randall. But that wasn't exactly what happened. More like Cindy got hysterical
when she saw me and ran to Randall. He had no idea what was going on. Pulled
a gun from his pocket. Cindy got in the way and she got shot first. Pretty easy to
make the scene look like a robbery.

Not everything was perfect. Rookie mistakes.

That's what happens when you don't plan two steps ahead. Not like now.

SIXTY-SIX

JAMIE SLEPT FITFULLY, IF AT ALL, AND FORCED HIMSELF out of bed around six. He tried to take a shower with his gun in the bathroom, which meant leaving the door cracked open, allowing no steam at all. The spray was cold and sharp and came nowhere close to reviving him. As bleary as when he'd gone in and dripping water on the floor, he fumbled for a towel. If not for the threat of his desk sergeant, Jamie wouldn't have bothered to shave. It was a relief to get in his car and head to Addie's. There, nothing was required of him. All he had to do was order eggs and toast. Jamie blended in with the long-distance truckers at the counter sporting end-of-the day, worn out looks. He hoped whatever ward he was assigned to that morning would be quiet but not too quiet. He feared he might drift off in the squad car.

Jamie was way ahead of his schedule when he got to the precinct with a couple of hours until he had to punch in. Setting off to find the detective was the first thing he did. Not going to his desk or checking his daily sheet.

"Where's Gianelli?"

Elizabeth didn't answer the first time he asked.

"Elizabeth?"

"I am feeling such a headache," she said and reached for a water glass. Jamie waited for her to finish taking a series of pills. It looked like three or four in her palm and she was swallowing them one at a time.

"Gianelli," he said. "Do you know when he'll be in?"

"He's either at the courthouse or over at the juvenile holding center."

"Juvenile?"

"Seventeen-year-olds commit violent crimes."

"But you don't know exactly where?"

Elizabeth, pasty and sweaty, gave Jamie an I'm-not-answering-any-more-questions look and he retreated to his desk. He thought he'd catch up on some paperwork, typing slowly and with little interest. Then he heard Bachman's voice.

"Hey there!" It was a booming, cheery shout.

Bachman was approaching his desk, wearing his outercoat.

"You didn't check the schedule yet, did you?"

Jamie shook his head. He knew he should probably stand but he'd missed the opportunity and now it would just be awkward.

"We're doing target practice," Bachman said.

"Oh, yeah? Which unit?"

"A few of you young guys. I like that. Makes me feel good, having one thing I can do better than you. All that time in Korea wasn't a waste."

What would have been better? Falling asleep with Henry driving or getting low target scores? Jamie was untwisting his jacket, pushing an arm into the sleeve as he passed Elizabeth, wanting to give her a message for Gianelli, but Bachman was hurrying ahead of him. Unusually brisk with his steps.

Jamie was technically still off-duty.

SIXTY-SEVEN

WHEN THEY GOT TO THE GARAGE, BACHMAN FLIPPED THE keys to Jamie without comment. Jamie maneuvered the Dodge onto Washington Street, inching along behind traffic, then headed north, weaving through a web-like path towards Haledon. When they reached the border, Bachman cleared his throat.

"You know the indoor range is closed, don't you?"

"Passaic County Target?"

"Passaic County Target. Closed it on Monday."

"I didn't know that."

"They closed it for cleanup. The walls have too many bullets imbedded. A live round ricocheted and almost hit Miucci's old partner."

"That's something."

"That is something."

"So, where to?"

"I think we can head up to the mountain."

"Outdoors?"

"It's early in the season, but not too early. Noise won't be much of a bother to the locals."

The morning sun was strong that day. Deceiving the way it often was in late winter, concealing a bitter cold.

"Heard you were outdoors a few weeks ago," Bachman said.

"That's right, I was."

"Sporting clays?"

"I was at the Windsor Club."

Jamie wasn't sure how that would have gotten back to Bachman. He wasn't sure he'd even mentioned it to Gary or anyone else and cued up his past conversations, hoping any comments he'd made about the club or his shooting hadn't sounded like bragging.

"That's a plan. Practice on a moving target. I'll have to give that a try."

Jamie found the highway and they made their way to West Paterson, towards the apartment complex at the top of the mountain where he'd left Nugget. Feeling suddenly foolish, all the bright daylight having changed his perspective, Jamie pictured himself going through his own house, inspecting the basement, sliding back the shower curtain, shuddering as he pulled down the attic stairs. Waiting for a monster to come into view.

The roads climbing up the mountain had a thick snow piled on the side. Maybe the cold would be good for him and help clear his thoughts. He anticipated the chilling air as they neared the gravel lot.

They were the first to arrive. Jamie hadn't asked who the other young guys were. John Greene and Fred Gerritsen were pushing five years in. Possibly Gary or Wayne. He hadn't seen either in the squad room, but he didn't always keep track of their shifts. Jamie slid out of the car and soon the two were stretching, then Bachman walking around to the driver's side. Jamie had meant to go to the trunk and get the rifle, but Bachman blocked him.

"What're you shooting these days?"

"Python. I got a Python about a year ago."

"Great gun."

"Are we doing rifle practice?"

"Not today. I'm thinking we'll keep it to handguns."

"Right."

"You have the Python today? Not your Detective Special?"

"Yes, the Python. That's what I've been carrying. I . . . uh, I hadn't checked. I mean, I didn't even know we'd be doing practice today."

"Not a problem at all."

It would just be the one gun. No rifles. Easier to concentrate, Jamie thought. He felt a heavy fatigue from the past few days and an even heavier one from the past few months. The basics of practice shooting might be a relief from his constant search for puzzle pieces and the secrets to Cindy and Randall's last moments in the bar and Drew's outside of Gilly's. But the same voice that had sent him to look for Sage was speaking again. There was a worm of unease within Jamie. Something clicking. Whoever was meeting them ought to have been there already. He scanned the parking lot for another car, turning to the entrance and listening closely for tires or brakes, anything familiar, when metal pressed into his neck. The cold nose of the sergeant's pistol.

"Slowly," Bachman said. "Turn slowly and keep your hands up."

Jamie raised his arms as Bachman bent and lifted the Python from his holster.

"Now, very slowly, take out your car keys and throw them on the ground."

The seconds it took for that simple task, then hearing Bachman bending to retrieve them, Jamie understood the distortion of time. It felt like an hour. Two hours.

"We're going to walk up towards the trails. Don't do anything you'll regret. Keep your pace steady and I'll be behind you going the same. Do that and we won't have a problem."

Jamie was silent. His mouth dry. Almost dizzy.

"You got that?" Bachman asked.

"Right," Jamie said.

The unease he'd been feeling turned to a bewilderment. He moved into the line of pine trees, the scrubby trail, with no idea where they'd be going. The target range was south of Lambert Castle and following a path along the side of the mountain, all Jamie knew was that they were going higher.

They continued walking away from the parking lot and the castle. Nothing but the sound of rocks beneath their boots and an occasional cough from Bachman. Jamie had been right. The cold air was clearing his head. He began to focus on where the trail led and if he had any options. The shooting range was notorious for the sounds of gunshots. They had to be going far, where a gun could go off without being heard. Jamie knew the layout of the mountain. The overlook at the top. Then Bachman began to talk.

"It's all fun and games until it's not fun and games," Bachman said. "Your mother ever give you that one?"

Actually, his Aunt Ro had said it quite often. But Jamie didn't answer. It wasn't time to engage. It was time to drill into the things that were important. Whatever was going to happen, he had to prepare himself. He listened more to the inflections of Bachman's voice, trying to figure out if the man was nervous.

"Photos still in the glove compartment? Or did you move them into the house or give them to your friend? You know, the friend who's watching your dog."

"They're in the car."

"You're not lying? Lying could get someone else hurt. The pretty little blonde you spend time with. The one with the Vega, she works at Casa Romano. Someone like that."

"I'm not lying."

Jamie had left them in his car since the plan was to hand them to Gianelli, once he was back at the station.

"For the record. Just for the record. I didn't start this. Those shits were blackmailing me. Those pieces of shit. What the hell did they ever do for anyone? Smoke pot all day and go out at night, dancing around in a G-string. They ever go to Korea? They ever street fight in Paterson?"

Jamie didn't care much for Bachman's explanations. He'd put the last of the pieces together right when Bachman pressed a gun to his neck. Hearing Bachman go on, telling him that Cindy smacked him first, hit him with her purse when Bachman went for Randall who was pulling a .38 from his pocket, that story didn't matter to Jamie. He wasn't going to disrespect Cindy or Randall or Drew and give Bachman the sympathetic ear he was looking for. That was Jamie's second decision. The first had been he wasn't going to beg. He'd decided that before they'd even left the parking lot. The promise he'd made to himself.

Bachman finger pointing and claiming he was the one who'd been maligned and arguing that he had every right to "take care of things," reminded Jamie of the three innocent people who had been murdered. Those were the people Jamie still felt a duty to. All he could do was ignore Bachman.

Even without a word from Jamie, the details hadn't stopped coming and he wondered whether all of that talking would get Bachman winded. If the older man was even considering that. He was rambling at that point, no longer going on about blackmail and the last two Polaroids he planned to burn so he could be done with the whole mess.

"Got called on a case, a little girl and her mother. Tall blonde, nice figure. She's all flirty and nice. Rubbing up on my arm. Nothing going on here she says. The neighbors, they're so nosy. Always looking for drama."

Bachman was angry, it was rising in his voice. But this wasn't the story about Cindy. This was a very different one. Bachman coughed. Jamie thought he might have stopped for a moment, he heard what sounded like faster footsteps, Bachman catching up with him.

"That's what happens. It's always the neighbors. Always the nosy neighbors. Got another call not a week later. Went into the apartment, the mother pointed to one of the bedrooms. She wasn't so flirty that time."

The trail was winding closer to the edge of the cliffs. Jamie didn't want to turn his head, aware that any movement would alert Bachman. In the corner of his eye, a wide vista opened. The trees thinned. The trail narrowed. The cliffs below were sharp. A straight drop.

"I thought it was a doll lying on the bed. Couldn't believe it was the same girl had been sitting in her mother's lap, smiling at me. Her hand was so cold. Of course . . . well of course, the mother and the boyfriend had separate trials. Appeals. Never let me get it out of my head. I'd gone to see that little girl. The mother said everything was fine."

Jamie listened to Bachman solely to make sure he was still talking. Listening, but not taking any of it in. Jamie didn't want to know the sergeant's story. He didn't have the space for distractions. He catalogued the pitch of the sergeant's voice, the terrain they were walking on, and the amount of time they'd been on the trail. He'd find out soon enough if his field officer had been right about Bachman's bad leg and, if so, how he could turn that to his benefit. That was all he was attuned to. Bachman's story stayed a white noise until Jamie heard the man whisper. "I live with that, I can pretty much live with anything."

Bachman sealed what Jamie knew. There was only one way through this. He was getting shot. That's how it would end. His earliest reaction was confusion and that had been replaced with fear. Onto the next step. Fear replaced with blind rage. A hot liquid ran through Jamie. It could throw a fighter off balance. That's how good fighters lose. He had to let it go and find his center. Jamie took slow, intentional breaths, telling himself to keep walking until what happens happens. Aware, he thought. Stay aware.

The cold weather helped. A snap of Arctic air late in the season. Jamie felt it, even with the intensity of everything else. Bachman had to be feeling it too. Jamie noticed the sergeant had stopped talking. Maybe his leg was stiffening from the steep elevation and temperatures in the low twenties. To test Bachman, Jamie quickened his pace, then heard the bitter voice.

"Watch yourself, Palmieri. You in some kind of hurry?"

Bachman shuffled closer as Jamie reconsidered the benefits of rushing. He raised his arms slowly so as not to alarm Bachman.

"I'm going to stop. Only for a second. I need to rub my calf. I've been running all week. Pushed the muscle too far, just now."

"Fuck you," Bachman said.

"Look, it hurts and it's slowing me down."

Bachman laughed, a kind of black empty noise. "Yeah, well, I don't know how to say this, but it's not going to matter much to you. I mean, you probably figured that out."

"Yeah, well we're not going to get anywhere fast if I can't lose the cramp. You don't want to sprint, but you don't want extra time in this cold, either."

"Keep moving." Bachman sounded harsh, but also a little tired.

"I'm bending. That's all I'm doing. Just bending over to rub my leg."

Bachman didn't say anything. Jamie took that as a sign. He listened once more to what he thought were short gulps. Then he tilted at the waist, enough to see behind him, his one hand poised to grab his left calf and the right arm straight out, a gesture of surrender. It was the arm he used to hit Bachman. With one quick turn, Jamie's right fist cracked Bachman's jaw and pushed him into the dirt. The gun fired. Jamie's shoulder was hit hard, thrusting him backward and into a pile of ground cover. The bracing shock of ice-coated leaves. In the time it took him to react, minutes, days, seconds, he was looking for Bachman. The older man had been thrown to his side, wincing, and cradling his forearm. He'd shot from an awkward position, not from a ready point, and there was some recoil, as Jamie hoped there'd be. Both of them scrambled to gain the physical advantage.

Jamie was up first. There was pain in his rotator, an unbelievable pain, but there was also adrenaline and the training he'd had at Costello's gym. His mind dialed to a single goal. Get balance. He'd never kickboxed before but knew he couldn't use his right arm. Surprised at how far he could push Bachman with his leg, Jamie sent him into the crusted snow at the ledge. Far, but not far enough from where the gun had landed. Jamie hadn't thrown decisive force into the kick, and even with that effort, his shoulder was pounding.

Bachman had been hit twice and labored, finding his way into the crouched start of a runner, his eyes on the metal grip. Jamie made the rapid calculations he knew Bachman was making, about who was closer to the gun and which of them was normally faster and stronger, adding in that Jamie was bleeding and in pain from a gunshot. Bachman had the headway, so near to getting that gun, his arms extended and the path clear for his outrunning Jamie, who was on his left and not moving to the gun at all. Letting go of the fighting stance burned into him, Jamie leaned back, not forward, with a full extension of his leg. One more kick. A solid, kinetic drive that pitched Bachman to the mouth of the gorge. And Jamie, unable to control the advance of his own body, followed. Tumbling headlong.

A brutal wind swept from the opening, stabbing Jamie's cheeks and scraping his throat. So close to the vertical drop, he lost his sense of space and staggered uneasily, managing one shaky step onto stone-hard dirt. Searching for a fixed landmark, all he saw were the branches of dead pines framing a slash of pale sky, and then a fleeting look at eyes that were wild and raw. Just beyond them, a thrashing movement. The sergeant had lost his footing. Flailing, as if he could right himself instead of falling into the inevitable pull of gravity. His heels sliding over loose rocks. Over the edge of the cliff.

Jamie bucked sideways, landing in the underbrush, dimly aware the ground was solid. Then he began to register sound. The scream was primal and haunting. He would hear that scream for months after. It was never satisfying in any way.

SIXTY-EIGHT

THE VIEW OUT OF THE HOSPITAL WINDOW WAS NO BET-
ter than what Jamie had seen for three years walking around the Eastside
section. Medical buildings and Curell's Pharmacy. The only relief, a
single storefront selling exotic fish wedged in next to HDI Radiology.
The exterior was black and foreboding, like the depths of an ocean.
Lettering across the plate window in the vibrant colors of a tropical reef
advertised saltwater aquariums and zebrafish and koi. Not the chaos of
a pet store like Krauser's.

The day before, he'd woken in recovery. Coming out of anesthesia,
there'd been the disorientation of lying on a hospital bed and not quite
knowing why he was there until he tried to roll to his side and felt the
piercing stab in his shoulder. Seeing Jamie's awkward movements, an
orderly had darted over explaining he had to stay prone. Later, Jamie
had been wheeled to his current room, greeted by a candy striper
who'd brought him an ice pitcher and offered to read to him from *Look*
magazine. Then he'd slept through the night.

Resting his eyes on the sign for tropical fish, he'd spent the day dozing
on and off. With his medication, all the movement and activity outside
his door was mostly a dull hum. As the afternoon quieted down, Miucci
came by for the rare personal visit reserved for officers who'd been shot.
He'd spoken with the doctors treating Jamie and seemed pleased with
the prognosis. Given the many crimes that led to Jamie's hospital stay—
blackmail and three murders resulting finally in the death of a high-level
police officer—it was unavoidable that Miucci had questions he needed to
ask. As the lieutenant explained, he was sewing up a few items since there

was confirmation for the story Jamie had shared in the emergency room before the trauma unit waved off the officers on scene. Those abridged statements made up the crux of a report Miucci had brought with him in a manila file folder that he checked occasionally. Jutting his chin and scratching at his pencil moustache, he'd mostly nodded in agreement with the specifics Jamie repeated. There'd only been half a day to gather the supporting evidence, but that had seemingly been enough time.

Sandy had never left town. She was afraid of New York and couldn't bring herself to take a bus to the Port Authority. Gary, of all people, had tracked her down through Sage and found her at her grandparents'. Other evidence came together in the aftermath. The medical examiner noted a large dog bite on Bachman's forearm and that was most curious for Miucci who'd wanted to know if Jamie had any idea how that happened.

Jamie had tried to explain Diesel and that it appeared Bachman began prowling Maitland Ave. soon after Steinle was shot. Jamie's best guess was that Bachman didn't know enough about the last two Polaroids and thought Jamie had access to whoever Steinle had given them to. Or it could have been that Bachman was increasingly frustrated and wanted to plant a few ounces of pot on Missy and get Jamie out of the way in the process. Maybe worse. So many maybes. After Steinle was killed, the game widened, the stakes that much higher. Jamie had given his rough thoughts to Miucci.

Not long after the lieutenant left, Jamie noticed there was someone new in the doorway.

"Look at you. Getting all this fancy medical treatment. All this R and R."

Jamie propped the thin pillow under his neck, wanting to appear alert.

"Andres says hello."

"He's in court?"

"At this hour? No, it's the flu. He's home getting Vicks rubbed all over him. Sends his best."

Gianelli came closer to Jamie's bedside. He must have noticed Missy curled up and sleeping on the guest chair and lowered his voice as best he could. He turned to the tray rolled near Jamie.

"These don't look like hospital food." He took one of Missy's cookies off the plate, lifting his brows and bobbing his head in approval as he chewed. "Very nice." He looked again at the sleeping Missy. "So," Gianelli said, "Good thing those kids found you."

"Hikers," Jamie said.

"Yeah, right. Gaines told me they were reeking of pot."

"They might've been high."

"Yeah, well. Why else were they hanging around Garett Mountain in the snow? Heh? Not too high to get you here, though. Decent hospital. Looks like a shithole, but those ER guys, they know their way around a gunshot wound. Took good care of you."

Jamie wasn't quick with an answer. Gianelli put out a hand, palm flat, letting Jamie know it was okay.

"You'd have made it down the mountain yourself. Blood loss but not like Bachman hit an artery. Would've sucked but you'd have made it. Bachman wasn't able to do much damage."

"I was lucky."

"Better to be lucky than smart. Andres always says that."

A nurse padded by, stuck her head in, then moved on to the next room.

"Of course, there's lucky and then there's doing your job. Being in the right place because you were doing your job. That's not luck. You came up with more than Bachman thought you would because you did the right things. That's for sure."

The detective crossed to the window and spent a minute taking in the view of Broadway's early evening traffic.

"Let me tell you," Gianelli said. "You had Bachman. You had him good. I know what closing in on a case is and you were closing in. You sure n'hell were."

Gianelli hesitated, then took another cookie. "Damn, these are good."

He handed one to Jamie who let it rest in his fingers. The medication they'd given Jamie was almost worn off. His shoulder sore. His whole body feeling unlucky.

"Give those guys, those *hikers*, a PBA card when you can. They'll need it the way they smoke their pot."

From the looks of the gun Bachman had with him, it had occurred to Jamie that those hikers, the kids who hung out at the top of Garret Mountain in all weather, were the likely foils for Bachman. The Saturday night special Jamie had been shot with would've killed him at close range and Bachman knew who to easily blame for it. That theory explained their destination. Bachman's setup was a failed drug raid. He'd have claimed Jamie climbed the mountain faster than he could, got ahead of him and found the group along with some hard evidence and got shot. A straightforward arrest for Bachman to have pulled off. The reason Bachman hadn't targeted Jamie with the Python.

That wasn't what Jamie wanted to talk about with Gianelli. He wanted to apologize for not being smart and needing luck instead. All the things he'd done wrong, starting with not turning over all the information he'd had on Sandy and Mrs. De Carlo and not fitting the pieces together and walking into Bachman's trap without a clue. He didn't have the energy to make a different face. There was no way to hide his embarrassment and resignation. Bachman wanted the case to go nowhere. Jamie wasn't the only patrol officer working it, but he'd been thrown extra responsibilities. Bachman letting him sit in on the interview with Lorraine. Handing him Gil. It had always felt like Bachman singled him out. Had Bachman considered him not too smart or easy to control? Both? Gianelli seemed to know his thoughts.

"You know you were the perfect choice for him. Inexperienced so he could look over your shoulder, steer you where he wanted. But smart enough that no one would give him shit for giving you some of the interviews you got. He wanted that cover. Making it look like someone was doing an actual investigation. Didn't really work out the way he thought it would."

That, more than anything, was what Jamie had been desperate to hear. Jamie regarded Gianelli before turning to the open door and the gurney waiting in the hall in full view. The ceaseless reality that he was in a hospital and that he was there because he'd been shot.

"I'll get going. Leave you to feel miserable and play it up for the nurses."

Gianelli worked a Russian-style hat over his ears. "Look for me, when you get back," he said. "Look for me."

Another swell of nausea hit Jamie. He'd been feeling that the entire day. He couldn't get past the picture of Bachman, the last image of him. His arms in that see-sawing wave, trying to gain balance. Jamie had caught his eyes in that moment, full of knowing there was no way for him but backwards over the cliff. If Jamie hadn't kicked as hard, Bachman might have been able to regain his footing. But unless Jamie had pivoted quickly and got to the gun first, they'd have ended up getting there at the same time. He'd only had that split second, making the choice to not hold back. Still, he saw it on a loop, repeating. Bachman's last look at him.

In time, Jamie would get another private talk, this one with the captain. A few words from him about the first suspect he'd ever shot and killed, a man who'd been running at him with a machete. The restless nights he'd spent wondering if it could have been different. Other officers would dribble in to share their own moments and how they got past them. Father Giordano, the police chaplain, would meet with him.

Jamie tried to bite Missy's cookie, the crumbs staying mostly on his chest. She was still a ball on the chair, asleep beneath the window as the sun faded from the room. When a nurse appeared carrying a metal tray with a white paper cup and a needle beside it, Jamie raised a finger and pressed it to his lips, then pointed to Missy. He dutifully accepted the medication, knowing he'd soon have the feeling, leaving him only vaguely aware that something had happened. Until that hit, he stayed awake, resting and watching her. Her left ear peeked out from the tufts of hair falling over her face.

She'd made her way back after Gil got in touch with her. The Culinary Institute had rolling admissions and she'd spoken to both the registrar and Adelle, then packed up her Vega and driven herself to Paterson, getting to the hospital that day an hour or so after lunch. Her Wind Song fanned into the room as Jamie slowly realized he smelled sandalwood.

If she'd been crying, she hid it, stroking his arm and cheerfully listing all the specialties she wanted to make for him. There'd be breakfast served on the rattan tray she'd unearthed in one of the cabinets. Sandwiches for lunch and she'd roast turkey breasts and fry pork chops and bake chicken pot pies for dinner. He knew what would follow. That he'd begin to recover and she would leave again. He would make sure that she did.

The smart choice would be telling Missy to return to school straight away. It would be better for both of them to accept Teri Cosgrove's offer to bring Jamie the hearty noodle casseroles she was known for. She and Mrs. McElroy and all the other women on Maitland and nearby would pitch in. Better for him to allow that arrangement and negotiate the sponge baths on his own and not have Missy changing the bandages that protected his shoulder and tending to the wound that still hurt a lot. After all that care, it was going to be harder for him when she'd eventually leave and go back to her school where she would wear her white toque and learn to be a chef.

But she was here for him now. Sleeping on the chair in his hospital room. He took it as a good sign. It spoke of hope. The kind of hope that allowed him to make the decision he was making, letting her stay for a while. Feeling good about everything even with his gunshot wound. The yellow pills working into his system, his eyes nodding. A last look at Missy's tiny ear before he fell asleep.

ACKNOWLEDGMENTS

To my husband, George, behind me at every step. My super fan. My partner and best friend for life.

To my children, Michael and Chrissie. You are my heart. You are my everything.

To Kimberly DeRosa. Decade after decade after decade. There's no world for me without you in it.

To Shanna McNair and Scott Wolven. You made this book come to life in every way possible. It's been a journey. It's been a joyride.

To Leigh Stein. More than you could ever know, I am so grateful to have you in my literary life.

To Jessie Glenn, Bryn Kristi and Emily Keogh. Rock solid and kind in just the right measure.

To Chris Miral, the best armorer I could have ever hoped for, and to Cathy Bartzos, so much humor and heart and there when I need it.

To all the writers I've met along the road, most especially at the Writer's Hotel and the Sarah Lawrence MFA program, with shoutouts to Patricia Dunn; to David Ryan, my mentor with the Gurfein Fellowship; and to David Hollander, my thesis adviser.

And to Cherry. You were with me every single day. There are no words that were written without you by my side. There are no words for the ache I feel every day without you. Forever in my heart.

ABOUT THE AUTHOR

Melanie Anagnos is a crime novelist and editor who was born in Paterson, New Jersey, the backdrop of her police procedurals. Melanie has been a waitress, an attorney, and a stay-at-home mom to her two now-adult children. She received her MFA from Sarah Lawrence College and currently publishes a Substack, *Cherchez La Femme*, drawing on media and pop culture from the 1970s.

www.ingramcontent.com/pod-product-compliance
Lightning Source LLC
Chambersburg PA
CBHW040720290625
28891CB00020B/1006